A SMALL NOISE PIERCED THE DARKNESS OF THE TENT. . . .

Ashlee clutched the sheet to her bare chest and sat up. "Vivian?"

"I've been mistaken for a lot of things in my life," Connor said quietly, "but never a female."

"What are you doing here," she hissed. "Where's Vivian?"

"In Nathaniel's tent . . . enjoying a private game of checkers."

Her nerve endings went crazy. "Why-y are you here?"

He leaned over, his mouth so close she could feel the moistness of his breath on her lips. "I think you know the answer to that, little witch—especially after that enticing display."

She leaned back, seeking to gain some distance from his tempting mouth and trying to grasp what he was talking about. "What display?"

"Let's just say your come-hither look, along with your naked silhouette on the wall of the tent, served its purpose. . . ."

Books by Sue Rich

The Scarlett Temptress
Shadowed Vows
Rawhide and Roses
Mistress of Sin
The Silver Witch

Published by POCKET BOOKS

THE SILVER WITCH

SUE RICH

POCKET BOOKS

New York   London   Toronto   Sydney   Tokyo   Singapore

This book is a work of fiction. Names, characters, places and incidents are products of the author's imagination or are used fictiously. Any resemblance to actual events or locales or persons, living or dead, is entirely coincidental.

An *Original* Publication of POCKET BOOKS

POCKET BOOKS, a division of Simon & Schuster Inc.
1230 Avenue of the Americas, New York, NY 10020

ISBN: 0-671-79409-4

First Pocket Books printing January 1995

10 9 8 7 6 5 4 3 2 1

POCKET and colophon are registered trademarks of Simon & Schuster Inc.

Cover art by Edwin Herder

Printed in the U.S.A.

To my grandchildren,
Ashlee Rich, Westly White,
and Brandon White, whose names
inspired those of my characters.

To Marion Schiffgen, Ronnie
Cernusak, Betty Campbell, and
Bonnie Campbell. My critique
partners. My friends.

And, as always, to my
husband, Jim Rich.

PROLOGUE

Her heart pounded at a vicious rate as she ran frantically out the door. The trees! She had to get to the trees! Vines tangled around her feet, dragging her down. She scrambled on her knees. "Help me. Oh, somebody, please." The cypress loomed closer—but not close enough. The man's footsteps pounded right behind her. She wasn't going to make it!

"Beau!" she screamed. "Oh, God, Beau. Where are you?"

Cruel fingers snagged her hair, jerking her backward. A hand closed around her throat.

"Beau!" she cried aloud, jarring herself awake. Gasping for breath, she glanced about her moonlit bedchamber, but there was no cypress . . . no man.

She clutched the quilt to her chest, trying to still her racing heart. The dream she'd been having since childhood had never been so vivid. So *real.* She'd always been running and frightened, but until this moment, she'd never known she was fleeing from a man. And the realization scared her more than the nightmare.

Pushing away the covers, she rose and struck a flint to the bedside candle, then sighed when a warm yellow glow filled her room, forcing remnants of the haunting visions back into the darkness. All except one.

Who was Beau?

Her trembling fingers rose, brushing the scar on her face as she laced them through her hair. Bewildered and anxious, she escaped out onto the balcony and gazed over the moonlit beach below. Silver foam rushed to join the shore in a pagan dance of swirling motion, then retreated in a sheet of lazy shimmering bubbles. Hills of seaweed darkened the sand, and the smell of brine and kelp drifted on the moist wind. But the tranquillity did nothing to sooth her yearning soul . . . and never would until she had the answer.

CHAPTER
1

Charleston, South Carolina, 1821

I can't believe you're going to duel your best friend."

Connor Westfield stared out the window of his motionless carriage, barely aware of the dawn mist hovering over Buckley Wentworth's east field, and trying to ignore the gnawing ache caused by the man's words. Connor hadn't believed it either—until Branden Delacorte, the friend he loved like a brother, had called him out in front of half of Charleston last evening at Edenbower's soiree.

"What's gotten into you?" Buckley continued, making him wish he'd never agreed to let this newest acquaintance act as his second. "And what's the matter with *him?* Bloody hell. Delacorte can't possibly think you bedded his wife!"

The cramp that hadn't left Connor's chest since he'd been accused of the deed grew. Even though he'd denied the ridiculous accusation, Branden hadn't believed him. *Hadn't believed him!* As if Connor had ever lied to him. Which he most certainly had not.

3

Not in all the years they'd lived next door to each other, taunted the same tutor, competed for the prettiest women or greatest fortune.

Disappointment and anger shook him. Had Branden changed so much since his marriage to Louise? And what lies had she told that could turn best friends into enemies?

He released the window curtain and sat back, fighting rolls of nausea when he thought of how Branden's wife would proposition him at every opportunity.

Louise had made it quite clear that she preferred his bed over her husband's, even though she'd never been in Connor's bedchamber, much less with him. And she never would be. Still, he couldn't help but goad Wentworth. "What makes you so sure I didn't bed her?"

That gave the younger man a moment's pause. Then he flicked his lace-encrusted hand. "Doesn't matter. If you did, deny it. If you didn't, say so. Anything's better than being maimed or killed."

"Your faith in my marksmanship is exemplary."

"That's not what I meant. I know you could aim—*and hit*—the bastard in the heart with your eyes closed. Your expert marksmanship is renowned throughout the colonies. But you won't. You'd rather die yourself than live with the guilt of having killed a friend."

After this latest row with Branden, he felt as if he already had. "Do you have a better solution?"

Wentworth tapped his skinny fingers on the bottom of the window frame. "Perhaps you could denounce—"

The rattle of carriage wheels echoed across the oak-studded field where they waited.

"Bloody hell," his parrot-nosed companion swore. "He's coming."

4

Wishing there were some way he could talk sense into Branden without publicly humiliating him or his wife, yet knowing he was beyond rational, Connor opened the door and stepped down. A spring breeze ruffled his cape as he strode through the dew-covered grass to meet the slowing team. The wet shine on his knee-high boots caught a glint of new sunlight.

Grim-faced, Wentworth walked beside him.

As Branden and his man alighted, Connor stared at his friend, hoping for a sign of vacillation. Any semblance of the mischievous rogue he grew up with. But not a hint of that rapscallion could be detected behind those hard features. His normally expressive mouth was drawn into a tight line, his square jaw set at a determined angle, his ocean green eyes narrowed, his broad shoulders stiff beneath his gray superfine coat. Connor sighed, knowing there was no hope. *Damn him.* With an irritated swipe of his hand, he removed his top hat, then tossed it to Buckley. The cape followed.

Branden's second, a stocky man Connor recognized as one of Louise's in-laws, opened a leather case and presented it with ceremony. "Choose your weapon."

Staring at the identical dueling flintlocks for a long moment, Connor met Branden's eyes. "Is this really what you want?"

"I thought I made that perfectly clear last night."

A muscle twitched in Connor's jaw. "So you did." He chose the pistol on the right, knowing he couldn't shoot Branden, no matter how foolish the man was.

A mockingbird trilled overhead as he and his friend took their back-to-back position and pointed their barrels skyward.

Delacorte's companion retreated and opened his mouth to call out the ten paces that would precede the blast of powder.

Connor took a breath and prepared his body for

pain, praying Branden's aim was true. If he was going to die, he wanted his death to be quick and clean.

"One . . . two . . . three—"

The thunder of advancing hoofbeats cut off the second's count.

Connor swung his gaze to see a young man riding at breakneck speed toward him.

"Mr. Westfield!" The youth waved a folded paper in the air. "I have an urgent message." He bounded off his mount and sprinted across the damp grass.

For a moment, Connor wondered how the lad knew how to find him, then, assuming one of his servants relayed information they'd overheard, he lowered the pistol.

"The missive can wait," Branden snapped.

Connor cocked an eyebrow. "You do plan to kill me, don't you?"

"Without a shred of remorse."

"Then I'd better read it now." His hand shook with fury as he read the scrawled message. The words almost buckled his knees. *No. Damn it, no!* In a careless motion, he tossed his pistol to Branden's second. *"This* will have to wait." He turned for the carriage.

Branden caught his arm. "Running away, Connor? I never thought you a coward as well as a bastard."

Jerking his arm free, he glared at the man he'd once called friend. "I don't give a damn what you think. My aunt may very well be on her deathbed, and I'm going to her. So either you shoot me in the back, or this nonsense will have to wait for another time."

In quick strides, he made for his carriage. "Cooper, take me to Aunt Vivian's. Immediately!"

The harried ride through Charleston was minimal compared to the chaos running around inside Connor's head. *Please, God. Don't do this. You've taken everyone else from me. Everyone I've ever loved. Isn't that enough? Please don't take the only mother I've ever known.* His throat tightened, and he felt moisture sting his eyes. *Ah, God, not her.*

The carriage hadn't fully come to a stop before he was out the door and racing up the steps to his aunt's cottage. Inside, Patty, the maid who'd been his aunt's constant companion, and his taskmaster, for a score of years, wrung her hands as she told him of Aunt Vivian's attack, and that Doctor Ramsey was still with her.

He started for the bedchamber.

"No, boy. Ramsey, he say keep ever'one out till he get finished. Don't you be causin' no fuss with da leech and grieve your aunt."

"What the hell am I supposed to do?"

Her chubby brown face softened. "Just wait, boy. Dat's all anyone can do. Now, sit," she commanded as if he were still a child. "I's gonna fix you a drink." Flicking the end of her bandanna over her shoulder, she waddled from the room. She'd barely disappeared into the kitchen when the front door swung open and Branden walked in.

Too distraught to be cordial, Connor glared. "What do you want? To finish the duel in my aunt's parlor?"

Pulling off his hat, he tossed it onto a low table. "The thought hadn't occurred to me, and if I didn't care as much for Vivian as you do, I might consider it. But, though she has a bastard for a nephew, she's always been like a mother to me. Our differences will wait awhile longer."

The concern in Branden's eyes was unmistakable, and Connor remembered how Aunt Vivian had stepped in to care for him after his mother had died when he was twelve. With Delacorte's father away so much with his political career, she had been the only stable influence in his life for many years. Connor felt some of the pressure in his chest ease. "I thank you for that much, anyway."

Taking a seat in a chintz-covered chair, Branden stared at the carpet. "What happened?"

"Her heart . . ." Connor's words trailed off beneath a rush of pain.

Branden nodded in understanding, but he didn't speak.

Nor could Connor find words that didn't hurt.

The silence stretched into minutes.

When Patty returned with a goblet of brandy and saw Branden slumped in the chair, she shook her curly head and quickly retreated to fetch another glass.

Connor downed the contents of his in one gulp, then paced before the glowing fireplace, making short work of the confining distance across the parlor. Unfortunately, neither his friend's presence, the alcohol, nor the persistent prowling eased the worry clawing through his gut.

He glared at the door that led to Vivian's bedchamber and was reminded of all the horrors he'd fought to suppress since childhood. Ones he thought he'd overcome.

"For God's sake, Connor, would you sit down? Your incessant treading is wearing on my nerves, if not your aunt's carpet."

He flung himself into a chair.

"Much better."

Patty returned with a bottle in one hand and Branden's goblet in the other. She filled both their glasses, then tossed a log into the fireplace. "I's gonna set on a pot of soup ta calm your bellies." Her dark eyes drifted from one to the other, and Connor saw a hint of sadness. "See if you youngins can't put your differences aside for Vivian's sake."

Having never been able to hide anything from the

overly perceptive woman, Connor gave a slight nod, then returned his gaze to the bedchamber door.

When she left, Branden shifted in his chair. "It's the doctor, isn't it?" he remarked with his usual, if uncanny, insight. "You know, I'll never understand this aversion you have to practitioners. Not that it matters. Your aunt has complete faith in the man. That should be enough for you."

It would never be enough. He'd seen those charlatans work before. That nightmare was the one horrifying secret he'd never been able to share with anyone, not even his best friend—nor would he do it now. "My aunt would trust a highwayman, if he smiled winningly enough," he said bitterly. "That's how she judges people—by their damned smiles."

Branden's mouth twitched, and Connor recalled how his capricious aunt had preached to them often about the extent of a man's worth being determined by the sincerity of his smile. Their eyes met in understanding for a brief instant, then Branden looked away.

"How did she ever measure your worth, I wonder?" Branden mocked. "You so rarely smile, and when you do, it's usually directed at some ninnyhammer out to snare an influential husband—and the Westfield fortune, of course." He lowered his glass. "Or at a woman you wish to warm your bed—regardless of her marital status."

Connor slammed his goblet down and came to his feet, cut deeply by the innuendo, but he'd be damned if he'd respond. "Vivian doesn't need theatrics to know my worth *or* my faults."

"You mean you have faults? I wasn't aware. . . ."

Rage skipped through Connor's blood, and he opened his mouth to give his *former* friend a long-deserved setdown. But the bedroom door opened, stilling his words.

Dr. Ramsey stepped into the parlor, rubbing his tired eyes behind gold-rimmed spectacles.

"Is she all right?" Connor and Branden asked in unison. Connor fought down a surge of panic as he awaited the man's reply.

"No. But she is better. And she will recover—this time."

The breath slid out between Connor's teeth, and his knotted fists uncurled. "Is there anything I can do?"

"Only if you can perform miracles," the physician remarked, then drew himself up. "Forgive my insolence, lad; that was uncalled-for. But 'tis so near the truth, 'tis frightening. The malaria she contracted on that bloody trip to Panama last year is putting a strain on her heart. With each recurrence, her heart grows weaker."

"Damn Bedworth," Branden hissed.

Filled with impotent fury, Connor silently agreed. Wilber Bedworth, the director of the orphanage, had informed Aunt Vivian of unfortunate foundlings who'd lost their parents in a plague, and had asked for her help. The task had nearly cost her life . . . and may yet.

"Unless something is done soon to stop the attacks of fever," the physician continued, "there is no hope for recovery."

Connor gripped the mantel to steady himself. God couldn't be that cruel to him—not after all the pain he'd suffered in the past. Unable to remain still, he paced to the window.

The wind slammed a shutter against the side of the cottage. Tossed by a sudden spring downpour, leafy branches slapped the water-streaked windowpane.

"Damn it!" he bellowed. "She's all I have. There has to be *something* that can be done."

"Connor, take it easy," Branden murmured.

The physician retreated a pace, placing some distance between himself and Connor's temper. "All we can do is pray."

Connor had been doing that since he got the message. What good had it done? He strode toward the bedroom, desperately needing to see his aunt, to absorb some of her steadying presence.

"If you plan to speak to her," the doctor called out, "'tis best you improve your expression. Her heart will not withstand upset."

Swallowing the tightness in his throat, he nodded, then continued on.

The heavy mauve drapes had been pulled, leaving the crowded room, crammed with bulky furniture, in darkness except for a low fire burning in the grate. Lavender and spice mingled with woodsmoke, filling the stuffy room with scents that were Aunt Vivian's alone. But the smell of quinine intruded. *That* wasn't an odor he associated with his spirited aunt.

A floorboard creaked as he stepped toward the bed. She looked so small and fragile against the mound of satin bed pillows.

"What was all that grumbling about out there?" Vivian asked tiredly. Her pale, nearly translucent skin still glistened with perspiration. Strands of limp white hair clung to her moist cheeks.

Connor eased onto the edge of the huge four-poster and lifted one of her veined hands, then kissed it with affection. *She shouldn't be like this.* She'd always been so vivacious. So damned invincible. "Nothing to concern yourself over, Nanna." He tried to force a smile but knew she wouldn't be fooled, so he settled for a shrug. "I fear I'm still not of the same opinion as your beloved physician."

A narrow gray brow arched in rebuke. "Your opinion isn't worth a fig. It's my life at stake, and I *do* embrace Phillip Ramsey's judgment."

He wasn't going to argue—no matter how badly

he wanted to. That was the one thing she'd never understood—his hatred of doctors. Because he'd never told her. He ran his thumb over the back of her hand. "Ramsey says the malaria must be cured very soon. Or . . . well, recovery might take considerable time."

"Is that all? I thought it was my heart."

He cleared his throat. "It is. But the malaria is causing the problem."

She considered his words, then, with eerie understanding, she met his eyes. "How long do I have?"

Only his deep, abiding respect kept him from lying to her. "I don't know, but Ramsey says something has to be done about the disease soon or . . ." His fingers tightened around her thin hand.

She lowered her lashes, suddenly looking very old, and very tired. "Has Phillip conferred with Nathaniel?"

"Who?"

Her voice regained some of its former strength. "Connor, don't be obtuse. Nathaniel Walker, of course."

Completely at a loss, he stared.

She released a frustrated sigh. "Never mind. Just send for him at once."

"I beg your pardon?" His brain wasn't working fast enough to keep up with her.

"Con-nor." She drew his name out. "You're usually not this slow, and the peculiarity is beginning to grate. Nathaniel is a friend of mine, and a brilliant practitioner, even if he doesn't tend common ailments any longer. If anyone can cure this wretched illness, he can."

"Another physician? Am I to be plagued my entire life by the incompetent blackguards?" Although he meant the words from the heart, he said them gently.

"Nathaniel is not incompetent. And don't scowl so.

It isn't becoming. Now, go, and do as I bid. We'll talk later."

From long experience, he'd learned not to argue when Vivian used that tone of voice. "As you wish." He kissed her withered cheek, and knowing her penchant for disregarding orders to stay abed, he added, "And behave yourself while I'm gone." With an affectionate wink, he slipped from the room.

When he returned to the parlor, Dr. Ramsey stood by the fireplace, nursing a glass of port. Branden was pacing by the window. "She says I'm to summon another physician. Some fellow named Nathaniel Walker."

"I had thought of that myself," Ramsey confided. "But 'twill do no good. Nathaniel has terminated his research."

"On malaria?"

The doctor nodded and readjusted his spectacles. "He ceased after an accident last year. The explosion destroyed his laboratory and killed two people. Maimed others. Even his daughter was injured. Badly scarred, from what I hear. Anyway, he retired immediately afterwards, claiming that coal—the ingredient needed for the malaria drug—was too dangerous. "'Tis a sad thing, too. Nathaniel seemed so close to success."

Connor remembered reading about the mishap in the *Courier.* Though the accident occurred elsewhere, the event was newsworthy because the man had resided in Charleston for many years. "Where does he live now?"

"In the Florida territories. St. Augustine, actually."

Familiar with the small costal town, Connor wondered why Walker had removed himself so far from his previous home.

Branden turned from the window. "Perhaps if we spoke to the chap, there's a chance—"

Ramsey shook his head. "'Twill serve no purpose. Nathaniel is as stubborn as, well . . ." He glanced at Connor. "Once he makes a decision, 'tis the end of it. I have never known him to change his position for anyone except his daughter, Ashlee—and she would not spare one the time of day."

"How old is the girl?" Branden asked in a casual tone, giving Ramsey the impression he was quite relaxed, but Connor knew better. The calculating gleam in his eyes gave away his true purpose—to gain information that might be of use.

"She should be nineteen or twenty by now."

His friend sent a satisfied sneer. "There's your answer, Connor. Just bed the wench—*like you have so many others*—and get her to talk her papa into resuming his research."

Branden's remark stung to the bone, but he'd be damned if he'd let him know. "You may be right, Bran. That does sound like a promising solution." Though the words were said in mockery, he knew they weren't far from the truth. He *would* do anything necessary to save his aunt. Even court the scarred daughter of a charlatan.

The doctor gave a delicate cough. "Well, whatever you decide to do, lad, 'tis vital you act soon. With these recurring attacks, Vivian hasn't much time. If the disease is not arrested within the next six months . . ." He gave a helpless shrug.

Cold chills swept him. Six months. That was no time at all. "I'll post a note to Walker today." With a quick nod to the others, he peeked in on his aunt and found her sleeping, then started for the front door.

Branden stopped him out of Ramsey's earshot. "Because of my affection for Vivian, the end to our differences will be delayed until she's out of danger. I won't cause her upset in her condition." His eyes narrowed. "But make no mistake, *friend,* your treachery is not forgotten."

"Damn you," Connor rasped in frustration. He would not defend himself again. He shouldn't have to. With a resentful glare, he stalked out.

When he reached his mansion on South Battery, he slammed the front door, tossed his damp cape and hat to Hector, the valet, then immediately retired to his study to write the hasty message—summoning Nathaniel Walker. Just to entice the man, he added a small inducement by implying that money was no object.

After sending his stableboy to the post, he headed for the parlor, desperately needing a drink to soothe his own ragged nerves. But what he found in the room only added to his irritation.

Louise Delacorte, draped in yards of lavender, reclined gracefully in one of his wine-colored settees as if she were mistress of his home.

"What the hell are you doing here?" he snapped, astounded by her insolence.

Her sultry perfume drifted through the humid air as she stood and walked toward him. Her full lips parted. "Darling Connor. Everyone knows that *to the victor go the spoils.*" She trailed a long, manicured nail down the buttons on his waistcoat. "And I, Mr. Westfield, *am* those spoils." She laughed throatily. "Assuming, of course, that my husband is dead rather than merely wounded." She tugged a button free. "If he isn't, I'll never forgive you for not seeing the deed properly done."

Holding on to his rage, he stared at the sleek, dark-haired woman. She made him ill. "I'm sorry to disappoint you. But your husband is very much alive, and, I assume, awaiting your return."

The hand at his chest curled into a fist, and her cat

gold eyes flashed. "Why isn't he dead? Curse you, Connor, I *know* you're an excellent marksman. You couldn't have missed."

"Do you really think you're worth killing or dying over?" He brushed her hand away. "Not hardly. Now, if you'll excuse me, I've more important matters to attend to."

Her features tight, she whirled around and grabbed her reticule from the settee, then faced him again. "You and I were meant to be together, Connor. You'll see that one of these days." Her eyes narrowed. "And I intend to have you. By fair means or foul." In a cloud of lavender lace, she glided from the room.

Connor muttered an oath and poured himself a drink, wishing he'd never set eyes on Louise Delacorte. What Branden saw in her, he'd never understand. And Connor sure didn't like her implied threat.

Still cursing, he downed his whiskey, then, in a burst of helpless anger, he threw the goblet against the hearth, shattering the crystal into a thousand tiny pieces.

CHAPTER
2

The bastard refused." Connor glared at the reply he'd just received from Nathaniel Walker. He took a breath to still the rising panic and glanced at Branden, who had just removed his cape at the front door.

Branden paused, surprised. "What?" He snatched the parchment and scanned the page. "The accident," he mocked. "Of course." Crumbling the paper, he tossed it on a nearby table and stalked into the parlor, where he immediately headed for the sideboard. "What the hell do we do now?"

"I'll find the blasted cure myself," Connor vowed in helpless frustration.

"I wasn't aware that research was among your studies at the College of Charleston."

"You know damned well it wasn't. But what alternative do I have? Watch her die?"

"Don't be absurd. But where the hell will you start? How—"

"There's only one place to start. The Library Company of Philadelphia. Somewhere among their store of volumes there must be information on malaria and the research toward its cure."

"And if there isn't?"

Connor didn't want to consider that possibility. "There has to be, Bran. There just has to be."

God, help me. I don't know where to turn, Connor fretted as he made for his study. Having just left his ship after a sennight in Philadelphia, he was no closer to a solution than he'd been the day of Aunt Vivian's attack.

"Well?" Branden demanded as Connor opened the study door.

Not surprised to see his friend sitting at the desk with his feet propped up and a glass in hand, Connor laced his fingers through his hair and sank into the nearest chair. "How did you know I was back?"

"I've had a man watching for your sloop. Now, what did you learn?"

"The only known treatment is quinine, the very thing Ramsey's been giving her." Connor paused and met an uncompromising stare. "How is she?"

"Better. But, then, she usually is between fevers."

Connor nodded in relief, then leaned his head back and rubbed his irritated eyes. He didn't dare close them. Every time he did, he saw a thousand jumbled words racing across parchment. He'd never read so much in his entire life.

And all for nothing.

"What now?" Branden asked, rising to stare out the window.

Exploring the carved border lining the ceiling, Connor tried to discern an answer. Only one course was open to him. "I'm going to Florida and see Walker. I don't have any other choice, and this time, I've got to make the man understand."

"And if he still won't listen to reason?"

Connor sat up, feeling helpless . . . and repulsed by his own thoughts. "Then I only have one option left. I'll do as you suggested and woo the man's daughter to my cause . . . using any means necessary."

Branden set down his glass and walked to the door, his eyes dark with disappointment. "I should have expected no less from you." With that, he strode from the room, leaving Connor feeling sick and disgusted with himself.

Hurt by his friend's snub, yet unable to do anything about it, he summoned his household staff to ready his trunks for another journey—this time to St. Augustine. He would deal with Delacorte when he returned. Once and for all.

A week later, the sloop sidled up to the wooden dock on the Matanzas River. Salty wind fluttered the sleeve of his shirt as he scanned the busy harbor. Seamen scurried to do the bidding of their bellowing captains. Winches creaked as nets of cargo were dispatched to and from various vessels, while scantily dressed women openly plied their wares to incoming sailors.

Seeing Fort Matanzas, he knew his journey was nearly at an end. His step lightened as he strode across the plank docks and hailed a carriage to deliver him to a suitable inn.

The bumpy motion of the conveyance was a welcome change from the rolling ocean, and he relaxed against the leather cushions to admire the towering coquina gates that announced entrance into St. Augustine. They were an incredible work of art made of soft limestone, broken shells, and coral that had been cemented together to form majestic twin pillars.

The delicious odors of baked bread, woodsmoke,

and cinnamon wafted on the damp breeze, and his stomach gave a welcoming growl.

He asked the driver to wait while he procured a room at the Cypress Inn, then quickly changed and set off to Nathaniel Walker's residence. Though the hour was late, he wanted to see the man immediately.

They traveled a road that paralleled the coast for a few miles, then, unexpectedly, the driver slowed the carriage before an impressive two-story redbrick mansion overlooking the ocean. Connor felt the first stirrings of unease. By the appearance of the man's elegant home, the money he'd mentioned in his letter to Walker hadn't inspired him at all.

A little uncertain, Connor climbed several wide stone steps to a covered porch.

An aging, black-garbed butler answered on the first rap, his pale features narrow and pinched. "Yes?"

Connor handed him his card. "I've come to speak to Nathaniel Walker."

The servant stared at the name on the card, then a pointed brow peaked and he gave a disdainful sniff. "Dr. Walker is not here." Turning, he started to close the door.

"I'll wait," Connor informed—and boldly placed his foot on the threshold.

"My good fellow. I have no idea when the master will return. You will simply have to come back at another time." He stared pointedly at Connor's boot. "Now, kindly remove your foot so I may close the door."

"Now, listen . . . ?"

"Charles," the butler supplied stiffly.

"Charles." Connor nodded. "I've come all the way from the Carolinas, and I must see Dr. Walker on a matter of extreme urgency. So either I wait indoors or on your step. It's your choice. But I'm not leaving."

A disgusted snort escaped, then the man whirled around and stomped off. "We will just see about that."

Wondering where the butler had disappeared to, Connor placed a finger against the door and gave a light shove. The panel opened to reveal a large, circular entry done in pale blue marble. A massive crystal chandelier hung from the center of a high, dome ceiling. A curving staircase wound its way up one wall, while gold-framed mirrors covered the spaces between several doorways lining either side of the foyer. One of them stood open.

He had just decided to investigate and taken a step when Charles's rigid form appeared in the opening. The man looked as if he'd break if he tried to bend, and his mouth was no more than a line across his skeletal face. "I have been instructed to allow you inside," he said, not bothering to hide his distaste at the command. "If you will follow me." He gestured toward the open door.

Irritated, Connor pulled off his hat and cape and shoved them into the butler's hands. "I'll find my way. You take care of these."

Trying not to smirk at Charles's astonished expression, he strolled across the entry and into the room, assuming he would await Walker in comfort. What he didn't expect to see was a small, exquisitely beautiful woman standing in front of a window, dressed in a high-waisted gown of soft peach. Her silvery hair rippled down her back in lazy waves, the ends brushing the gently rounded curves of her shapely behind. In profile, her spine was held straight, her breast full, uplifted, and her porcelain features delicately carved, from the tiny upswept nose to her lush pink mouth.

She turned as he entered, and across the elegant, candlelit room, her thickly fringed, blue-green eyes met his.

For a heartbeat, neither of them moved.

Time seemed suspended, then, out of nowhere, haunting images ensnared him. . . .

"Oh, Beau. I thought you'd never get here." She *threw herself into his arms, showering him with kisses.*

Love and warmth infused him. Her presence was as vital to him as the air he breathed. Dear God, how he'd missed her. He drew her tiny shape into his much larger one, yet somehow they fit together perfectly. Her hair smelled of sunshine and jasmine and was so downy soft, he wanted to bury himself in the thick strands. He wanted to kiss her until they were both breathless.

Hungrily he captured her lips, vowing to do just that as he savored the long-denied taste, the honeyed warmth that promised heaven. Thank providence he'd gotten the balance of the supplies and wouldn't have to leave her ever again. From this moment on, they would grow their own food and live in a world of splendid isolation. Just the two of them.

He deepened the kiss, then, in a burst of savage need, tore at the silky fabric that concealed her sweet flesh from his urgent hands. He needed to touch her—

"Mr. Westfield?"

Connor started and glanced around in bewilderment. Heat surged up his neck. Christ. What was happening? Never in his life had he been prone to fantasizing—and over a woman he hadn't even met, one he assumed to be Walker's daughter. Uncomfortable, he cleared his throat. "Miss Walker, I presume?"

She didn't smile in greeting . . . or meet his eyes again. She merely gave a slight nod that caused her shimmering hair to sway. "Won't you sit down?" She motioned with a slender hand to a settee.

He was too unstrung to sit. "No, thank you. I prefer to stand."

"As you wish." She walked to a teakwood sideboard

that had been carved in an intricate seashell pattern. Several crystal decanters and glasses sparkled against its richly polished surface. "Would you care for some port? Sherry?"

Noticing the slight quiver to her voice, he wondered at her uneasiness. "Port." As she filled a glass, he watched the sweep of her dark lashes, which were in such contrast to her pale hair. Then he was awarded another glimpse of those incredible eyes. Aquamarine was the only color that aptly described them. Feeling as if he was again losing his grip, he pulled his gaze away. "I understand your father isn't home at present."

She didn't respond as she continued to fill a goblet.

"I hate to impose upon you," he went on, "but I have urgent business I must discuss with him and wish to await his return."

With a poise that bordered on forced, she handed him his drink, being very careful not to touch him.

Irrationally, he was relieved.

She turned away from him. "I believe Father made himself quite clear when he responded to your request."

So she knew exactly who he was and why he'd come. He drew in a breath and was taunted by the scent of jasmine. A warmth moved through him, and he forced himself to focus on the conversation. "Yes. But I'm certain he doesn't comprehend the gravity of the situation. That's why I need to speak with him personally. I *must* have the cure for malaria. It's vital."

"He doesn't have one."

"But he was close to finding one," Connor countered in a quiet tone. "And his continued research is our only hope of saving my aunt's life."

She wasn't fooled by the soft entreaty—her haunting eyes relayed that message. She knew he was strung as tight as a forty-pound bow and ready to snap. "I'm so sorry. And I know Father would like to help you. But he can't."

Connor felt sick. What was the matter with these heartless people? He should have known better than to place his hopes in another physician. Still, for his aunt's sake, he had to try. "I'll pay whatever he asks. Just name the amount. I'll sign over every damn thing I own if that's what it takes."

Compassion filled her eyes as she placed her delicate hand on his arm, sending shock waves through every cell in his body. "It's not the money. It's—"

"The accident," he finished for her, stepping out of her reach. He couldn't think when she touched him. "I'm well aware of that, Miss Walker. But surely one setback hasn't completely discouraged him."

"Two close friends died in that setback."

"Again, I understand his reluctance, but unless he reconsiders, he may very well lose another friend." He met her eyes, unable to conceal his anguish. "Ask him to at least hear me out."

She lowered her lashes, but didn't reply.

Damning himself for groveling, he lifted his chin. "He can find me at the Cypress Inn . . . should he agree to speak to me." Having suffered enough humiliation for one day, he set his glass down, then set his shoulders stiffly and walked out.

But the minute he climbed back into the carriage and ordered the driver to return him to the inn, his whole body slumped in defeat. Panic and desperation turned his insides to gravel, and he cursed himself for not waiting to talk to Walker personally. But he'd never imagined he'd have such a passionate reaction to the man's daughter. The instant he'd entered that room and seen Ashlee Walker, he'd lost control of a vital part of himself. Aunt Vivian's situation had faded into the background as the girl's beauty, her heady scent, and those breathtaking blue-green eyes all came together to arrest his purpose.

For the first time in his life, he'd wavered from his intent. And the strangest sensation of all was that he felt as if he already knew her . . . intimately.

He searched his memory. Perhaps he'd known her when she was much younger and didn't recognize her now. No, he decided. He would not forget a woman who looked like her. No man could. Too, at the very least, he'd recall her name—or her father's. So what caused this gut-wrenching familiarity?

Almost afraid to know the answer, he shoved his fingers through his hair and fought the urge to swear. He had to get hold of himself. He could not allow the woman to speak for her father. *Would not.* He'd return tomorrow, and the next day, and the next, until he met with Nathaniel Walker face-to-face. No matter what his response to the girl, he would not ignore his purpose again. He couldn't. And he was certain of another fact, too. Playing on her affections must be avoided at all cost. The way she jolted his control, he might very well lose the game.

Ashlee slipped a hand beneath the fall of hair covering her left cheek and fingered the scar in front of her ear—the disfigurement she took great pains to conceal. With mixed emotions, she pushed aside the window curtain and watched Connor Westfield's carriage pull away. Never in her life had she been so attracted to a man—and the appeal had been based on more than just his dark good looks and lean body.

When he'd first walked into the room, she had been assailed by an urge so profound, it defied explanation. The urge to burrow into his arms. To taste that firm mouth, feel the warmth in that powerful body. Her skin tingled at the outrageous thought.

What a surprise that would have been to a gentleman she'd never met. And she still couldn't find a reason for the mysterious occurrence. It was as if something unearthly had taken hold of her senses for a few brief moments.

Dropping the curtain back into place, she sat down, suddenly anxious. Had she chosen the right course of action by duping Mr. Westfield?

Her father had never seen the gentleman's urgent request for assistance. She had taken it upon herself to deny his query without her father's knowledge. But what else could she have done? Watch her father destroy himself in an attempt to help the man?

No. As uncharitable as the act had been, she knew her choice had been the right one. The only one.

Still, the weight of betrayal lay heavy on her chest.

CHAPTER
3

Connor roused a groggy stable liveryman before dawn the next morning and had him saddle a gelding. He didn't want to miss Nathaniel Walker if the physician decided to depart early.

Swinging up into the saddle, he turned the horse toward the beach, knowing he could get to Walker's home by following the shoreline. Too, he wanted to race off some of his frustrations before he reached his destination.

Salty spray and flying sand stung his cheeks as he hurtled through the dawn mist at a hell-bent pace. Moist air dampened his shirt, sending wakening chills through his veins. Gulls cried overhead, and a stream of hot Florida sunshine warmed the legs of his buff breeches.

The pounding of other hoofbeats caught his attention, and he looked up. A jolt skittered through his midsection. His beautiful blond tormentor raced over the sand just ahead of him, her white horse kicking up sand, her silver hair whipping out behind her, and the skirt of her blue riding habit rising with the wind, offering brief glimpses of her shapely legs.

Though he tried to suppress the heat that shot through him, it was no use. His body reacted savagely to the spellbinding sight, and the impulse to join her was so strong, he shook with the need. Knowing he must be the lord of idiots, he nudged his horse into a gallop and raced after her.

He reared his mount to a halt just feet from the woman and sent her a glare that would have cracked stone. "Who the hell *are* you?"

She seemed surprised by his angry demand, but not frightened as he would have expected. "Mr. Westfield, are you well?"

"No, madam. I am not. Now, answer my damned question."

Those beautiful eyes narrowed ever so slightly. "I believe we met last evening."

We did more than that, woman. We made the earth shiver. "What is your Christian name?"

"Why?"

"I was under the impression you were Ashlee Walker."

"Then your impression is correct."

Stunned speechless for a moment, he explored the flawless lines of her face, then exhaled. "Forgive my obtuseness *and* my forwardness, Miss Walker. I thought you might have been another of Nathaniel's daughters. I was led to believe Ashlee Walker was disfigured."

Ashlee tightened her gloved hands on the reins to stop a tremor. How she hated that word—especially when it was so true. Though she'd once been the belle of society, she was now looked upon with pity and revulsion. The poor, poor *disfigured* daughter of Nathaniel Walker.

She took a breath to ease the pain, then met Connor Westfield's clear gray eyes, saddened to know that she would never again see him look at her with appreciation as he had last evening. Last evening . . . How she'd been affected by the mere sight of him.

With a silent sigh and deliberate slowness, she brushed the hair behind her left ear, exposing the jagged scar that trailed all the way down to the underside of her jawline. "You were not misinformed."

For a breathless moment, he didn't move a muscle in that powerful frame. He simply stared. Then his mouth twisted into a mischievous smile. "That's it? Absolutely ghastly."

No one had ever teased her about her scars, and she wasn't sure how to respond. *But then, she was the daughter of the man who could help him.* Raising her chin, she swallowed the hurt that clogged her throat. "No, sir, that is not all." Then she did something she'd done only once before—and had suffered the consequences. She pulled away the scarf at her neck, revealing the low cut of her riding habit and the deep, ugly red slash that marred her left breast.

His gaze rested on the exposed flesh and examined it with unnerving thoroughness. "I have one worse than that." He rolled up his shirtsleeve and showed her a tanned forearm, marred by a thick, purple scar. "A fencing accident."

Fighting down tingles from that solely masculine look and his offhanded acceptance of her disfigurement, she glanced away. His easy manner was a ruse to gain her favor in hopes of acquiring her father's. It had to be. She was under no misconception about her scars. "I have more."

A warm chuckle rumbled from his chest. "If the others are as bad as these, why, I'd recommend you join a freak's sideshow as soon as possible."

As much as she wanted to, she couldn't take offense to his jesting. In a backhanded way, he was complimenting her, and she couldn't resist a taunting rejoinder. "I've tried. They won't have me. They claim I'd chase off their customers."

"Mmm, yes. I can see that now." He moved the horse closer, until they were side by side, facing each other. "This"—he trailed a fingertip over the mark above her breast—"would definitely send a man screaming into the street."

Shock at his brazen behavior warred with the shivers racing to the center of her breast.

Sunlight glinted off his dark, overlong hair as he watched her with carnal interest, then he lifted those hypnotic eyes to meet hers. "Who are you, Ashlee Walker? Why do I feel as if I know you?"

The words were so quiet, they were nearly lost in the rumble of the surf. And, what could she say? That she felt the same sensation? "I'm just the daughter of the man whose help you seek. Nothing more." Yet, even as she spoke, she knew it was a lie. Though they'd never met before last eve, there was something mysterious that drew her to him. Something that defied description. Something that allowed him to take the most indecent liberties with her person without ever a mumble of protest on her part.

He pulled his gaze from hers as if to gather his thoughts, then drew the reins taut. "It's urgent I speak with your father." When she started to object, he held up his hand. "I know he's already refused, but I have to try. You must understand that. My aunt's life depends on it."

Although she ached for him and his relative, she couldn't weaken. "Please don't seek out my father. I implore you." Noting his look of determination, she glanced along the deserted beach. "Could we take a short stroll?" She didn't really want to walk with him.

His closeness unnerved her. But it was vital he didn't approach her father.

Mr. Westfield dismounted and helped her down, then looped her hand through his arm and started walking. "I'm listening."

The warmth of his skin seeped through the fine material of his sleeve, and she tried to still the tingles racing up her arm. Gathering her purpose, and not daring to meet his eyes, she clutched the scarf tightly in her free hand, feeling exposed and wishing she could replace the wretched thing without drawing his attention.

She stared at the sand as they moved over the shoreline. A damp, salty breeze fluttered the hair at her cheek. Since she didn't know where to begin, she blurted the first thing that came to mind. "I've deceived you."

His muscles tightened beneath her hand, but she couldn't face him, and she had to speak rapidly, before she lost her courage. "My father never saw the letter you sent."

"What?" He spun her around, his eyes dark with violence, his jaw tight and throbbing. "What the hell do you mean, *he never saw my letter?"*

She had to talk fast. "You're trying to save your aunt's life . . . and I'm trying to save my father's. I didn't mislead you for a prank, for pity sakes!"

His grip tightened on her upper arms. "Explain, and do it now—*before* I lose the thread of control that's keeping my hands from your beautiful throat."

A tremor of fear skipped through her. He looked quite capable of doing her tremendous harm. She took a shaky breath. "Since the accident, my father has gone into a severe depression. He's become so distant, it's frightening me to the point that I fear he might consider forfeiting his own life to ease his guilt over the death of his friends. He blames himself for the accident." She pulled free of his hold and rubbed her abused flesh. "I don't think he's capable of helping you."

"Son of a bitch."

"Cursing isn't necessary."

Staring at the horizon, his gaze remained fixed for a long time before he spoke. "Is there anyone else?"

"No."

"What about you? Surely you know something of his experiments."

"Not enough."

He shoved his hands into his pockets. "What about his assistants? Two survived, didn't they?"

"They did. And I'd already thought of them." She wound the scarf around her hands to steady them, recalling the guilt she'd suffered over his plight. "When I forged that note refusing Father's help, I didn't do it on a whim. I'd considered every option first. Believe me, I don't want your aunt's death on my conscience any more than you want to see her die."

"Forged?" His eyes narrowed.

Wishing she'd had the foresight to keep her mouth shut, she avoided his eyes. "I had to discourage you. Father's inner compassion wouldn't allow him to ignore Vivian's problem, regardless of the cost to himself. That's why I can't let you speak to him. To do so might very well cause his death." She regained her spirit and faced him, hands on hips. "And believe me, Mr. Westfield, dead men do not find cures for malaria."

"Damn it. What else can I do? She's all I have."

The urge to touch him was so strong, she trembled. She dug her nails into the scarf to keep from making a complete fool of herself. "Isn't there someone else with knowledge of malaria?"

"No."

"Then I don't know what to say. Believe me, I'm as

helpless as you are in this situation." She watched the pulse at the base of his throat pick up speed.

"You're wrong, woman. I'm not helpless. And as much as I hate to disregard your wishes, I *will* see your father. He's the only chance I have, and I'm going to do everything within my power to convince him." His tone softened. "But I swear to you, I'll take every precaution to avoid upsetting him."

She wanted to be angry with him, but she knew she wouldn't have done any different were she in his place. Still, she had to stop him, somehow. "Before you go to that extreme, would you give me a little time? Perhaps I can come up with a solution that won't involve him."

"Such as?"

"I don't know. But, like you, I must try."

Those silver eyes grew compassionate, but the stubborn set of his jaw didn't falter. "Time is a commodity of which I have precious little."

"A week. At least give me that."

He considered her request, then conceded. "All right. After that, I'll take matters into my own hands." With a last look, he strode to his horse and swung astride the animal's back, looking as sleek and powerful as the gelding. "You know where to reach me." With a solemn nod, he tapped his heels into his mount's gleaming brown flanks.

As Ashlee watched him ride away, she tried to rid herself of the heaviness in her chest. She took several deep breaths, but it didn't help. Nothing did. For the second time in the space of a month, she planned to dupe him. Before the end of the week, she'd see that her father left St. Augustine. It didn't matter where, as long as he remained out of Westfield's reach. "I'm so sorry," she whispered to his retreating form. "And I can only pray that someday you'll be able to forgive me."

Mounting her own horse, she turned toward the house, the animal's plodding gait resembling the dull beat of her heart.

When she reached the manor, she sneaked up the back stairs, not wanting to listen to another scolding from their cook, Tilly, about her indecorous behavior. Riding astride *and* unescorted in the wee hours of the morning was not at all proper for a young lady. And since that horrible scandal she'd caused three months ago, she'd tried very hard to not breed any more trouble. Unfortunately, discord usually plagued her as a hawk would a chicken. Waiting to swoop down and ensnare her. Just like that night.

Forcing the distasteful thought aside, she quickly changed, then made for the dining room, following the aroma of Tilly's delicious scones.

"Oh, sweet lass, donna ye look bonny," the aging Irish cook gurgled as she set a cup of tea and plate of steaming scones on the table. Either she hadn't been aware of Ashlee's ride, or was ignoring the fact, *until a more opportune time—like in front of Father.*

"Thank you," Ashlee replied, then took a seat and reached for the cup.

"Your mama, rest her soul, would have been proud of the way ye've turned out."

"I doubt she'd have noticed," Ashlee countered, not even trying to hide the bitterness in her voice.

"Oh, now, child. Ye shouldna think that way. I know your mama didna pay ye much mind and didna spend much time teachin' ye proper like. But she did love ye, lass. In her own way."

Yes. She loved me so much, she spent every waking hour attending social gatherings—or across the ocean touring Europe as if I didn't exist. Pain moved through her, and she directed her thoughts to safer ground. Her father. At least he'd realized she was alive on a few absentminded occasions—such as when she'd shown an interest in medicine. If it hadn't been for him . . .

"Would ye like some fresh plum jam?"

"Not this morning." She bit into a scone. "Isn't Father up yet?"

Tilly's lip curled in disgust. "He is. But he chose that devil drink over me scones."

Ashlee tried not to show her dismay. "I'm sure he didn't mean to offend you. He probably just has something on his mind."

"Too many things, if ye ask me," the cook grumbled as she stalked out.

Staring at her plate for a long moment, Ashlee at last shoved it aside and rose, wishing there were some way she could reach past her father's depression.

She found him in the parlor, nursing a sherry and gazing out the window. Morning sunlight seeped in through the red velvet drapes, casting a pinkish glow over his thick white hair. Even at fifty, he struck an imposing figure.

"Good morning," she said with warmth, kissing his lined cheek. "I saw Mistresses VanValken, Aberdeen, Beckman, and Whitehall at the dressmaker's yesterday. They all send you their regards." *Even if they did avoid contact with me as if I had the plague. Curse Stephen Frankenburg's treacherous lies, anyway.* She forced a continued lightness into her tone. "Personally, I think the quartet of widows are trying to gain your favor."

"They'd be better off with a snake oil salesman. At least his remedies don't destroy."

When was he going to stop torturing himself? Not wanting to meet his despair with her own, she continued her gay banter. "Oh, I don't know. Have you ever tasted that wretched stuff?"

A glimmer of amusement flickered in his eyes before they once again turned somber. "No, I haven't.

And speaking of food, Tilly announced breakfast a few minutes ago."

"What about you?" She looked pointedly at the glass in his hand.

"I'm not hungry."

"Father."

"Stop treating me like a senile old woman, Ashlee. I said I'm not hungry, so leave it at that."

Near tears, she wanted to shake him for hurting them both. "Of course," she mumbled, then hurried out the back and toward the beach, intending to walk the shores as she so often did to ease her unhappiness. But the threat of Connor Westfield reared its head. She didn't have time to feel sorry for herself. Not now.

Changing her direction, she made for the stables to have a carriage readied. While she waited with growing impatience as her driver, Henry, fastened the harness, her mind raced ahead. She would need help to spirit Father out of St. Augustine. Harry Milton and Joe Longtree, Father's former assistants, might be able to aid her—at least, she hoped so.

As she climbed into the open landau, thoughts of her friends brought back painful memories of Charlotte and Dave, who had died in the explosion. Dave Byron had been a young, enthusiastic practitioner who'd given up his patients to work with her father. Charlotte, Harry's wife and Joe's sister, had come from a family of devoted physicians who'd once tended King George himself.

All had been totally dedicated to their research . . . until the accident. Now Harry and Joe operated a small apothecary shop together . . . less than a mile from where the accident had happened in St. Augustine. Although the site had long since been cleared, she could still see the charred ruins of the small house they'd used for a laboratory.

The carriage slowed, and she glanced out the window to see a row of closely stacked buildings. The apothecary shop stood among them. It was a tiny store, crammed between two prominent buildings and set behind a single door, its interior long and narrow, and filled with the discordant odors of medicines and salves. Above the shop, the two men had taken up residence in an apartment Ashlee had seen once—and considered much too confining.

As she alighted from the carriage and opened the shop door, a small bell tinkled overhead.

"Ashlee," Joe greeted, weaving his thin frame around a bottle-clustered table. "It's good to see you again." He took her gloved fingers and bestowed a light kiss, his mustache brushing the soft kidskin. "What brings you here? Your father isn't ailing, is he?"

"No. But I've come on a matter concerning him." She wrinkled her nose at the stench of combined medicines and glanced around. "Where's Harry?"

Joe smoothed a hand over his slick brown hair. "He doesn't greet the customers, not with how he looks and all since the explosion. Leaves that task to me while he blends the elixirs upstairs." He motioned her to the back of the room. "Now, what's this about your father?"

"I'd like to speak to both of you—if you could get Harry to come down for a moment."

Joe shrugged a skeletal shoulder. "I can ask." He disappeared through a rear curtain, and she heard his light steps pad up the stairs.

Muffled voices filtered down from overhead, and for a second it sounded as if the two men were arguing, but a moment later, she heard both descend.

No matter how much she detested the emotion, she couldn't suppress a rush of pity when she saw Harry.

In the last year, his disfigurement had worsened. Purple scar tissue now covered three quarters of his once handsome face. His nose lay flat and spread to the right, blending with a wall of wrinkled flesh that replaced his eye.

Thin sprigs protruded grotesquely from his puckered scalp where once there'd been a full head of thick, shiny black hair. His lips curled up over jagged teeth, causing him to lisp when he spoke. Only his left eye and part of the same cheekbone had escaped injury.

Her heart ached for the attractive man he'd once been—the man who'd loved and cherished his wife beyond all else. She inhaled to ease the ache in her chest, then lifted a hand in greeting. "Hello, Harry."

"Ashlee." He nodded. "It's a pleasure to see you again."

"You may not think so after I tell you why I've come," she teased, falling into the camaraderie she'd shared with Harry for several years. "I want you to help me mislead my father."

Harry's hazel eye narrowed. "What?"

"Would you mind explaining?" Joe urged.

As clearly as possible, she told them of Connor Westfield, of her deception, and how she wanted to spirit her father out of St. Augustine before the man could approach him.

For the barest instant, she could have sworn she saw a flash of anger brighten Harry's eye, but it was gone before she could be sure. "Would Nathaniel truly consider resuming his research? Even after what happened?"

She touched Harry's gloved hand. "You know him, Harry. He couldn't refuse a cry for help."

He withdrew from her and edged closer to the curtain. "Of course." He thought for a moment—or was he trying to gain control of himself? At last he raised his head. "Doesn't your father have kin in London?"

"A sister," Joe confirmed.

"That's the answer, then. Send a message to him saying she's sick and needs him."

"The idea has merit, but Father knows his sister's handwriting. I'd never be able to forge it."

Joe grinned. "If she's sick, then the note would come from her physician, wouldn't it?" He winked at Harry. "The old ogre here, he could pen that for you. Your papa would recognize my writing, with me taking all those notes for him and such, but not Harry's."

"Yes," the older man agreed. "I'll send it round immediately. Just get rid of the envelope before you give it to him. Also, you need to find out when the next ship leaves." He sent her a hooded look. "And we can all pray this works."

"It *has* to work," she vowed, then, after spending a few moments to catch up on the latest news, she bid them both good day. Satisfied with the possible solution, she headed for her carriage, anxious to set the plan into motion. Still, she couldn't shake the feeling that Harry had been upset about something when she left, though he'd hidden it well.

Too, she was plagued with guilt over her plan to dupe Mr. Westfield. If only she could help him in some small way, maybe then her scheme wouldn't seem quite so brutal.

As the landau lurched forward, she searched for possible solutions to Connor's plight and at last settled on one that sounded promising. She couldn't allow her father to resume his research, but she *could* let another physician have his notes. Dr. Rhodes, she recalled, had retired last year. Since on a few occasions he'd shown an interest in the experiments, he might just be able to complete Father's work. She was grasping at the wind, she knew, but there just wasn't an alternative—nor was there any assurance the old doctor would agree.

Her only salvation was that, after pondering the reason for the accident for a year, she was fairly certain she knew what had caused the mishap, and she knew how to avoid letting it happen again. Maybe.

After reaching home, she made for her father's study to search for his notes. Yet she found nothing. Praying he hadn't destroyed them, she hurried to his bedchamber. But that, too, proved futile. Her only hope was to somehow worm the location out of him during supper, *at the same time she informed him of his sister's "illness"—and her physician's anxious request that he come to London at once.*

A disturbing thought hit her in that instant. She hadn't yet checked the availability of a ship to England. The week's time limit she'd asked Mr. Westfield for may not be long enough.

Overcome with urgency, she rushed back outside to find her driver. She had to get to the docks.

Within moments, she was on her way, her heart beating a rapid pace as she condemned herself again and again for not being more thorough. Her entire plan could go awry because of this thoughtless oversight.

Several merchant vessels rocked at anchor in the harbor, their longboats tied to the wooden docks, bumping into the jutting planks with the roll of each wave. The scent of salt and fish and rotting timber swirled through the damp air, unsettling her stomach.

Nervously, she glanced around at the crewmen and dockworkers in their baggy pants and soiled shirts. Nearly every leering eye was on her. She crossed her arms over her stomach. They wouldn't be so eager to gawk if they knew about her disfigurements.

"Miss Walker?" Henry asked as he turned on his

perch to glance down at her. "Are you sure this is the place?"

"Yes. I'm trying to find out when the next ship leaves for London."

He lifted a large hand and motioned her to remain seated. "Might be better if you stay here and let me talk to those fellows."

She wasn't about to argue. "Thank you, Henry. I'm forever indebted to you." Fixing her gaze on the wool carpeting beneath her feet, and ignoring the excited chatter of the sailors, she silently damned herself for being a coward. Still, she didn't attempt to correct the situation, and it seemed like hours before he finally returned. "Well? Did you find out?" she asked with nervous impatience.

"The *Northwind*'s heading for England a week from Friday, on the morning tide."

"A week from Friday?" Her heart sank. That was eight days away. How on earth could she stall Mr. Westfield for another whole day? "Thank you, Henry. I appreciate your help." She peeked anxiously at the men staring in her direction. "And I think it might be a good idea if we head for home now."

"Yes, mum. That does sound like a healthy suggestion."

As Henry set the team into motion, she struggled for a way to put Mr. Westfield off for the additional day. Suddenly a notion struck that just might work.

She tapped on the back of the driver's seat to gain his attention. "I've changed my mind. Take me to the Cypress Inn."

Going to a gentleman's room was a scandalous thing at best, and she could only pray no one of consequence saw her. She didn't want to risk another upset so soon. But it was vital. She needed to keep Connor busy while she secreted her father off to London.

She almost lost her nerve when she saw several people milling around on the boardwalk in front of the great double doors leading into the ordinary, but she took a stabling breath and rushed inside, grateful that none of those outside had looked familiar.

When she located Westfield's room and knocked, he answered the door immediately. "Have you brought my—" He stopped midsentence and stared.

"Supper? Drink?" she said lightly, trying to hide her discomfort.

"Clothes," he corrected with a slow smile.

CHAPTER
4

Connor knew he should be embarrassed, if not for himself, at least for her. But he wasn't. Admitting her into his bedchamber, wearing nothing but a towel draped low on his hips, seemed as natural as smiling.

A little undone by the sensation, he watched the play of emotions move over Ashlee's beautiful face. Those blue-green eyes widened in surprise; a shocked breath rushed in between her softly parted lips; smooth pink cheeks deepened to a rosy red. But somewhere in the midst he saw a small spark of feminine admiration.

Oh, Beau, do you know what it does to my insides to see you like that?

Shocked, he glanced around in confusion, then back to the girl. It took him a moment to realize Ashlee hadn't spoken the words that flashed through his thoughts. What on earth?

He met her eyes, and was surprised to see that she looked as stunned as he felt. Almost as if she'd heard them, too. Unsettled, he swung the panel wider and beckoned her inside. "This is quite a surprise." He explored the front of her lacy blue gown, which defined some very interesting curves—ones he could actually visualize beneath the linen bodice. Bewildered yet intrigued, he offered her a smile. "Dare I hope this isn't a business call?"

She regained her composure and sent him a quelling look. "Do be serious."

"I thought I was," he grumbled as he shut the door, wondering at the strange thoughts that kept popping into his brain while in her presence. Was he losing his senses?

When he turned to face her, she was standing in the middle of the room, her expression uneasy. "I've never been in a gentleman's bedchamber before, except my father's." She glanced at the tub of sudsy water he'd just left, then quickly looked away.

Feeling her anxiety, he tried to see the room through her eyes. His breeches and shirt lay in a pile next to the tub, forming a black pool on the cinnamon-colored carpet. The dressing screen he hadn't bothered to use was shoved against one of the pillars on the four-poster. Across its quilt lay the other towel he'd discarded after a few hasty swipes at his body.

Staving off a pinch of discomfort, he glanced to the corner of the chamber where his mug and straight razor lay at the edge of the washbasin, the soapy water dotted with his dark whiskers, while the brush he hadn't yet put to use sat on a bureau below a mirror.

Self-conscious, he laced his fingers through his damp hair. "Please excuse the mess. I wasn't expecting company."

She fixed her gaze on the drapes. "Mr. Westfield—"

"Connor."

"C-Connor. I want to speak with you, but it's

extremely difficult to do so while you aren't wearing any clothes."

He smiled at the rigid way she held her spine. "I don't have any clean ones. They're being brushed and pressed."

She folded her arms over her stomach. "A nightshirt or dressing robe, perhaps?"

His grin widened. "I don't use them. I find them too confining." He stepped up behind her, so close he could almost nuzzle her hair. Her intoxicating perfume sent pulsing waves of desire through his entire system. "I prefer to sleep *au naturel.*"

Her quick intake of breath caused heat to surge into his lower body. "Mr. Westfield, please . . ."

"Connor," he corrected, lifting a strand of hair and rubbing it between his fingers.

She stiffened. "I did not come here to be seduced, but to talk. If you're unable to manage conversation in your present state, then I'll leave and return at a more appropriate time."

The little shrew. He wanted to kiss her soundly. "If you insist, I imagine I could make myself a little more presentable." Not that he really wanted to.

"I do."

Smiling, he dropped the towel, then retrieved his discarded breeches from the floor and dragged them on. For a few seconds he didn't say anything. He simply admired her. At last he cleared his throat. "What's this all about?"

She looked over her shoulder in relief. "I think I've discovered a way to help your aunt without involving my father."

That got his interest. "How?"

Her gaze flitted away. "What if I told Father I wanted to go to visit my cousin, Beatrice, in London? The fabrication would give me the time away from him I would need without his becoming suspicious. I'll take his notes, and with the help of Dr. Rhodes, we can hopefully find the cure."

Connor experienced a flash of hope, but it was quickly overcome by wariness. "Another blasted physician?"

She looked a bit surprised at his remark, then shrugged. "Yes. With Father's notes, Dr. Rhodes, and your help, it might be possible. We were once so close to success." She tilted her head. "Unless, of course, you have a better solution."

"As a matter of fact, I have. Your father could do the deed much more efficiently."

"I said one that doesn't include him."

Damn, she was a stubborn wench. He shook his head.

"Then it's settled. I'll inform Father of my pending journey this evening—say, a week from Friday?"

"Woman, do you realize what you're asking? You want me to risk my aunt's life on a 'might be possible' decision."

"I know. But I've watched Father often enough, and with Dr. Rhodes's help . . ."

"I thought you didn't know enough."

"I have a pretty fair idea, or I wouldn't ask you to do this. I'm not a complete imbecile. Besides, his notes will tell us almost everything we need to know." She rubbed her upper arms. "Now, do we leave Friday or not?"

Something didn't seem quite right, but for the life of him, he couldn't grasp it. Too, though she hadn't actually said so, she was asking for another day. "Why not leave Thursday?"

Her lashes fluttered downward. "Because the next ship leaving for England departs on Friday. If Father's to believe my tale, I can't leave before then."

Connor was amazed by her thoroughness. "Won't he want to see you off?"

"I'm sure he will, but I'll see that he's otherwise occupied. Somehow." She nervously toyed with the gloves she held. "Actually, it will work out very well. We can set sail ourselves . . . shortly after the *Northwind*."

"Set sail? For where? Charleston?"

"No. I don't want anyone to discover what I'm doing. Word might get back to Father. There are tales of a huge swamp and lake a couple hundred miles southwest of here. It's not only uninhabited, it's damp, the two elements that are vital to this experiment. I won't risk another accident in a populated area, and I need the humidity to keep down the risk of sparks that could set off another explosion."

She gave him a weak smile. "We could take a ship down the coast, then travel inland to the swamp. Word has it the lake isn't far into the bayou." She stared anxiously at the carpet. "Or, better yet, you could go first, since we'll need coal for the experiments, and it's going to take some time to transport. The doctor and I could follow in a day or two. On a-another ship."

Again that unsettling feeling slid through him. "No. We'll leave together and stay that way." He wanted to keep her as close as possible, and he had the ungodly suspicion it wasn't just because of the experiment. Too, there was another problem. "I'm not so sure about the swamp area you referred to. I've read a little on the subject, and the fact that the bayou and lake are there has never been proven."

"I'm willing to risk it."

What made her so sure he would? "What about a guide? Do you know anyone who might be familiar with the terrain?"

"No."

He marveled at the way the sun turned her hair to liquid gold. "I'll ask around. Perhaps I can find one." He placed a hand on her shoulder and felt her slight tremor. "Can you meet me here tomorrow to compare our progress?"

"Mr. Westfield—"

"Connor."

She nodded. "Connor, I can't continue meeting you in your room. I've taken quite a risk with my reputation as it is." She glanced up. "Could we meet on the beach at dawn? My father would be devastated if I caused another scandal."

"Another?"

"Never mind," she countered a little too quickly. "Is the beach all right?"

He slid his palm down her arm and smiled. "Anything to protect your reputation, milady."

With a sigh of relief, she returned his grin. "Thank you." Though there was warmth in her expression, she stepped out of his reach.

Intrigued by the tiny dimple near the corner of her mouth, he lifted her fingers to his lips. "You're welcome."

Her delicate hand shook, and her cheeks grew bright. "Tomorrow morning, then," she said in a shaky voice. Withdrawing, she hurried from the room.

The instant the door closed behind her, Ashlee leaned against the wall to catch her breath. Her fingers still tingled. And the way he'd looked, leaving all that glorious bronze skin on display, still had her heart hammering like a woodpecker on tin.

Never in her life had she experienced the urge to trail her hands over a man's bare chest—*or actually felt as if she had done so many times.* But, oh, she certainly had moments ago. And she could have sworn she heard herself remark on his arousing state of undress. The sensation had been so real, she'd nearly reached out to him. What *was* it about this man?

And what about all the lies she'd told him? She felt like a criminal. And she hated that she'd have to confess the falsehoods to Connor when Father left, but she would. She owed him that. She only prayed Dr. Rhodes would help him.

As she climbed into the carriage, a surge of cowardice gripped her. Maybe she should consider going with her father to England. No. That would be foolish. She'd rather give *him* six weeks alone on his return voyage to come to terms with his anger at her when he learned of her ruse.

When the landau wrenched to a jarring halt in front of the house, she hurried inside. Thumbing through the post on the front table, she was reminded again of the lack of invitations due to her wretched behavior— and how devastated her father had been.

At last she found the letter she sought and carried it into the parlor. Thankful a small fire burned in the grate to ward off the spring chill, she removed the contents and tossed the envelope into the flames.

After scanning Harry's bold scrawl, she smiled. Perfect. And with the envelope *mistakenly* burned, Father would never know the parchment hadn't come from England.

"What do you mean Dr. Rhodes left for France a fortnight ago?" Ashlee exclaimed, her heart pounding as she stared at her manservant across the parlor. She tightened her fingers on the note she'd been about to give him to post to the physician. Although the hour was late, she'd wanted to schedule an appointment with the doctor early the next day. "He couldn't have left."

Charles's pinched expression didn't waver in the slightest at her outburst. "I assure you, madam, he could and did."

"Oh, Charles. What am I going to do?"

He elevated his chin another notch. "What have you gotten yourself into this time, missy? Why is it so important for you to see Dr. Rhodes?" His eyes darted to hers. "You are not in trouble, are you?"

After her knack for getting into *trouble* of one sort or another, she knew he was justified in his assumption, but it did strike her as funny. After all, according to rumor, she was incapable of *that* sort of activity. "No, Charles. I'm not in trouble, nor am I ailing. It's a matter concerning a friend of mine—who, I might add, is also not in trouble."

"I see."

She doubted it, but she didn't argue.

"See what?" Father asked from the parlor door behind her.

Not wanting the butler to recount their conversation, she lifted a hand. "That will be all, Charles."

When he departed, she turned back to her father. "Where have you been? I was getting worried."

Looking tired and drawn, he undid the cravat of his white shirt and released a button as he strode to the fireplace. "Don't nag me about missing supper again, daughter," he warned as he slumped into a chair.

"I wasn't going to. Like I said, I was merely worried about you. Charles said you received a message shortly after noon and left immediately—without telling anyone your destination. You've never done that before."

"There're a lot of things I've never done before. And there's no reason for concern. For God's sake, I'm fifty years old. Don't you think I'm capable of taking care of myself?"

"No," she muttered beneath her breath, then withdrew the forged letter from her pocket. "I was concerned because you received an urgent correspondence and I had no way to find you."

His head came up. "Urgent? From whom?"

She handed him the parchment. "Aunt Beatrice's physician."

A flash of anxiety widened his eyes, sending another stab of guilt straight through her heart.

His fingers trembled as he read the note. "Oh, God," he whispered, lowering the paper. "What am I going to do?"

Fighting her own demons, she touched his arm with an unsteady hand. "Go to London and be with your sister."

He shook his head. "I can't. Not now."

"What do you mean, you can't?" He *had* to go.

"I just can't, that's all," he snapped, pulling away from her.

"Father, please, you must—"

"I *can't,*" he repeated in a tortured voice. "Now, get out of here, and leave me alone."

"But—"

"Go!"

Whirling around, she darted from the parlor, her stomach twisting with panic. Once inside her room, she slammed the door and paced in nervous anger. Never had she given thought to what would happen if Father refused to go. And he shouldn't have. He adored his older sister and would kill to protect her. Yet there was now some unknown force that kept him from her side. What? Blast it all, *what?* And what was she to do about Connor?

She flung herself into a chair on the balcony, and cool, damp air moved over her skin, tightening the flesh into a million little bumps. Or was it a nervous reaction to the mess she'd gotten herself into?

Rubbing her arms briskly, she stared out over the

foamy silver waves pounding the shore. What was she going to do? How would she keep Connor from confronting her father? She leaned her head against the wicker frame and stared at the star-clustered sky. *Oh, God, I'm truly going to need your help to see me through this.*

CHAPTER
5

Connor stared up at the inn where he planned to meet a guide known as Santos, wishing he'd waited before summoning Ashlee to meet him in the common room. He didn't like the looks of the shabby Breakers Inn—and it was certainly no place for a woman of refinement. Damning himself for not inspecting the place before he sent her the note, he opened the door and strode inside.

Stale tobacco smoke and the odors of flat ale and unwashed bodies nearly robbed him of breath. He paused, trying to adjust his eyes to the dim, candlelit interior. He saw a long bar with several stools, and centering the dirt floor stood a pair of crudely built, scarred tables. Hay had been strewn over the bare ground and was littered with rusty spittoons and tobacco stains where the patrons had missed the receptacles.

Two men, seamen by the looks of them, lounged at the counter with their backs to him. A third man, dark and forbidding, sat at a lone table, his narrowed black eyes on Connor. With trepidation, he guessed it was Santos.

An unexplainable fear enveloped him. . . .

"Beau! Come quickly. That savage has led them to us. Oh, sweet Providence. What are we going to do?

He raced for the window and shoved the drapes aside. Panic clenched his chest. The bastard had, indeed, led Samuel and his cutthroats to their hideaway. Frantically he grabbed her hand and started running. "We've got to get out of here!"

Confused by the unexpected vision, Connor blinked and tried to clear the sudden terror from his throat. Reflexively his hand went to the side band of his breeches where tonight he carried a pistol. Reassured, he forced his feet into motion. "Mr. Santos?"

"Why do you want to go into the swamps?" the olive-skinned man asked without preamble, his attention on Connor's pistol.

If so many people hadn't declared their complete faith in this person, Connor would have listened to his better instincts and left right away. *Hell, he'd have run.* But, as it was, he tossed his own misgivings aside, pulled out a chair, and sat down.

The guide met Connor's gaze, and for a heartbeat, the man looked startled, then he relaxed and crossed his arms, leaning against the rungs of a ladder-back chair. "Well?"

As briefly as possible, Connor told Santos the whole story from the beginning.

"So you want to set up a laboratory in the swamps." The man shook his head, causing strands of straight onyx hair to sway on his forehead. "I won't comment on how absurd that notion is—but I will tell you only a fool would attempt such a journey."

Wondering where he'd learned such refined speech, and irritated by the abrupt comment, Connor fingered the cuff of his sleeve. "I've never considered myself a fool, but if wanting to prevent another accident and find a cure for my aunt makes me one, then I guess it's so." He directed a penetrating look at the man. "Now, will you guide us, or not?"

Again Santos shook his head and opened his mouth to refuse.

"I'm sorry I'm late," Ashlee huffed, rushing up to them, her chest heaving beneath the green brocade jacket of her riding habit, her silver hair unbound and tousled by the wind, her cheeks bright pink. "My horse picked up a stone." She flashed Connor a quick smile, then sent an uncertain glance at Santos. For the barest instant, she froze, then gave him a stilted nod. "Good evening."

Connor couldn't suppress a sudden quickening of his blood at the arousing picture she presented, but he regained control and followed her gaze to their potential guide. He was surprised to see Santos stiffen before making a conscious effort to appear calm. Did he know Ashlee?

The guide rose, but seemed to keep a healthy distance from her. "When do you want to leave?"

Ashlee remained silent.

Wondering at her unusual behavior—*and Santos*'s —Connor glared. "Friday. A couple hours after the morning tide—if that's acceptable." He knew he was being rude, but the man set his teeth on edge.

"It is."

The bastard wouldn't stop staring at her.

"And I know a place in the swamps where you can stay while you work." He sent Connor a dark look. "There's a deserted house near the big lake. But you'll need several sturdy horses to carry your supplies. A wagon wouldn't make it."

"You've seen this mysterious lake that no one else has been able to find?" Connor couldn't keep the suspicion from his voice.

"Yes."

"And just how did that come about?"

"I was born there. Now, will you be able to get the horses?"

"Yes."

"And three hundred pieces of silver for me to guide you?"

If Aunt Vivian's life hadn't been at stake, he would have told the swindler what he could do with his demand. But as it was, he had little choice. "Be ready Friday. I'll send a note around, indicating the time and place to meet." Gripping Ashlee's arm, he marched her toward the door. "Do you know that man?"

"I've never met him," she answered, trotting in an attempt to keep up with his brisk pace. "Where are we going?"

"I'm taking you to your horse."

"I had to leave him at the smithy's to get the stone removed."

He stopped. "How long did he say it would be?"

She brushed a dangling curl out of her eyes. "Just a few minutes."

"Damn."

"What?"

"If you're concerned about your reputation, we can't be seen coming out of the inn together." He glanced over his shoulder to see that Santos had disappeared. "And I'm not about to let you walk out of here unescorted. Especially since . . . it's nearly sunset."

She stepped away from him and placed her hands on her hips. "Why not? That's how I got here."

"And *that* wouldn't have happened if I'd known about this despicable place."

Her eyes flashed. "Mr. Westfield, I appreciate your

concern. But I am quite capable of looking after myself." She waved her hand. "You just go on about your business, and I'll make my way safely back to the smithy's."

For the life of him, he couldn't explain the fear he felt for her since their encounter with Santos. He reclaimed her arm, aware of how soft her skin felt against his palm. "Come on. Your reputation be damned. I'm escorting you."

"We could go the back way," she said, her voice now unsure. "Down the alley until we reach River Street."

The genuine worry in her tone cooled his anger, and he eased his hold. "It seems I'm forever destined to apologize to you for my high-handed behavior. And of course we'll take the alley." He tried to find the words to explain the ominous feeling Santos caused, but couldn't. "In my defense, I can only say that something about our guide sets me on edge."

"Then why did you hire him?"

"Because, according to the locals, he's the only man who knows the swamps." He stopped when they reached the alley and turned her toward him, searching her face in the dim light. "Maybe we should find another place. One that's closer and less dangerous. One we could reach without a guide."

"I would tend to agree if it weren't for the house he mentioned. But no matter where else we went, we'd be forced to sleep in tents, and at the risk of sounding soft, I do prefer the luxury of a warm fireplace and solid walls. The house sounds perfect to me—even if we do have to suffer the guide's presence." She urged him to start walking again. "He said you needed several packhorses by Friday. Will you be able to get them?"

"I'll manage."

She brushed her skirt aside to avoid a dark, suspicious-looking mound in the dirt. "What about a ship?"

"I came in my sloop, but it's too small to carry the supplies we'll need. I'll have to hire a larger one."

They reached River Street, and he could see the smithy's sign dangling over the covered boardwalk a few doors away. The shop sat on the corner of a merging street, a warm, yellow glow illuminating the doorway. A couple of blocks beyond, a group of men stood in front of a mercantile, in boisterous conversation. Fortunately, the men weren't close enough to recognize.

Relieved on her behalf, he placed his hand over hers on his arm and smiled down at her. His gaze touched her smooth features, lingering on the beautiful shape of her mouth. He wanted to taste her.

She must have sensed his thoughts. Her eyes shot to his, collided . . . held. The air grew thick. Heat radiated from her hand and spread through his body, its warmth settling low and heavy. Still, he couldn't retreat. Propriety be damned. He wanted to explore that sweet mouth until he drowned in its moist fire. Unable to stop himself, Connor lowered his head.

Female voices carried from around the corner, and Ashlee tensed.

He could have cursed out loud. With a frustrated sigh, he let her go and gave her a weak smile. "Well, milady. It seems as if your reputation will remain intact this day." *Not that he had anything to do with it.* "I'll watch you from here. But once you're inside, don't leave until you're on your horse, is that understood?"

"I have no idea what you're so worried about. And you're being high-handed again."

"It's a flaw in my otherwise perfect character. Now, do I have your word?"

She chuckled. "Oh, very well."

The sound of her musical laugh stroked his heart. He touched her cheek, loving the feel of her smooth skin and wishing for just one more moment of privacy. But it wasn't to be—at least not today. "I'll see you tomorrow. Now, go. And bring your father's notes, I want to take a look at them."

He thought he saw a flicker of panic, but it quickly vanished. "Of course. I'll meet you on the beach at dawn."

A group of women rounded the corner.

Hastily he stepped back and motioned her on her way. "Go."

She scampered a distance down the boardwalk before the women turned in their direction, then slowed her steps as if she were just out for a stroll.

He watched the sway of her skirts until she disappeared inside the smithy's door, then touched his brow in greeting to the trio of ladies and strode toward his lodgings, whistling a jaunty tune.

When he reached the Cypress Inn, he headed for his chamber. But as he started to press down the door latch, an ominous sensation slithered up his spine. He palmed his pistol, his senses alive and alert as he eased open the door.

Branden stood looking out the window, his back to the room. "Put that damned thing away," he grated without turning. "Vivian's not out of danger yet."

Staggered by his friend's eerie intuition—and presence—he replaced the weapon and shut the door. "What are you doing here?"

Branden faced him, the strain still between them. "Someone had to escort your willful aunt."

"What?"

"She learned of your journey here from your butler, and who you were going to see, then commandeered a ship. I tried to discourage her, but I'd have had better luck with a rogue elephant, so I accompanied her."

Connor sagged into a chair near the net-draped four-poster. "Where is the termagant?"

"In the room next door."

"How is she feeling?"

Snagging a spindle chair by the corner bureau, Branden straddled it. "Well enough to be a handful."

He shook his head. "I'd better go see her."

"She's already abed for the night. That's why I came in here to wait for you."

"Did she mention her reasons for coming."

"Yes." Branden crossed his arms on the chairback. "She said it's so she can be on hand when the cure is discovered." His mouth twitched with humor. "Besides, she didn't want to wait around until you got back. She was sure the uncertainty would do her more harm than the journey."

"That sounds just like her logic. And what the hell, she's probably right. I should have thought of that myself. By her being here if—*when*—the cure is found, it can be administered immediately instead of her having to wait weeks until I return with the drug. Her insight is almost frightening."

"So is her temper."

Connor laughed. "I know."

For a moment they shared a look that recalled several childhood memories, then Branden turned away to stare at the cold fireplace.

Another surge of weariness settled over Connor. "When will you leave for Charleston? If it's not soon, I'd like to make use of the ship for a few days. You did bring one of mine, I assume."

"Yes. And I'm not leaving yet. I told Vivian I'd stay until she was ready to return."

"Maybe it's just as well. We're going into the

swamps to conduct the research. She'll need someone to stay with her until we get back."

"Louise can stay. I'll go with you."

How Connor kept from swearing, he'd never know. "You brought Louise, too?"

"Although I might wish it otherwise, and have often mentioned the fact, she still *is* my wife, Connor. What did you expect me to do? Leave her home?" He snorted. "Of course, now that I think on it, with you away, I probably should have done so."

"Damn it, Branden—"

A loud knock startled them both.

Still stinging from his misguided friend's insult, Connor flung the door open and glared at a courier holding a folded parchment. The young fellow took a frightened step back. "Mr. Westfield?"

"What?"

He shoved the paper at Connor. "This just arrived for you."

Tossing the lad a coin, he took the note and closed the door, then quickly read the message.

"What is it?" Branden asked, crossing to his side.

"Ashlee Walker wants to see me right away."

"What's so disconcerting about that?"

Connor lowered the page. "We just parted not long ago and planned to meet tomorrow. I can't imagine why she'd want to see me now." He went on to explain the plan—and their meeting with Santos.

"Maybe something's gone wrong." Branden voiced the thought Connor had tried to dispel.

"That's what I'm afraid of." He crumpled the note and tossed it onto the counter, then nodded to his friend. "I'll see you later."

When Connor arrived at the cove below the Walker residence, he spotted Ashlee sitting on a large pile of driftwood near the water's edge, gazing out over the moonlit water. Her hair was tousled as if by a lover's hand, and she was clothed in a thin dressing robe, looking for all the world as if she'd been getting ready for bed. As he approached, she stood to face him, her expression wary.

He disregarded the look for a moment and greedily explored her sweet curves. A cool breeze molded the silky material to her full breasts, her slender thighs. It was becoming hard to breathe.

"You belong in the moonlight, duchess. You're as much a part of the night as you are my soul." He *wrapped his arms around her and drew her spine against his chest. Reverently he nuzzled her hair, wondering if any man had a right to love this much.*

"I'm sorry to summon you so late." Ashlee's voice cut into his thoughts.

He regained his senses, shoving aside the heart-warming vision. "What's this all about? Is something amiss?"

She lowered her lashes but didn't speak.

He was torn between wanting to hold her and wanting to shake her. "Well? Why did you send for me?"

She folded her arms over her waist. "I fear our plans have gone awry."

His stomach took a dive. "How?"

"I can't locate Father's notes." Her fingers wandered to her temples. "I've looked everywhere. They're not in the house. I'm going to need more time to find them. That's why I had to see you tonight. I know you have a lot of other pressing details you could take care of tomorrow, so I didn't want to waste your morning when you could be tending other matters." She sent him a nervous smile. "I'll notify you the minute I find them. It's just going to take a little more time."

"I don't have more time. If they're not found by tomorrow, then I'll see your father. Because without the notes, everything we've done today, everything we've planned, is for naught."

"Please don't," she countered, her voice shaky. "He can't bear any more stress."

The fear in her eyes cut into him, but he couldn't back down. His aunt's life depended on it. "I'm sorry, Ashlee. But I have to know my course of action. I've wasted enough time already. I don't want to hurt your father. But I'll do anything necessary to save my aunt." He touched her shoulder. He knew it was a mistake, but he was helpless to prevent it. With effort, he hung on to his thoughts. "Would you do any less to save the life of someone you loved?"

"No."

Her honest admission stirred something inside him. "Then don't expect it of me."

She hung her head, and he wanted to pull her into his arms and comfort her. His hand on her shoulder trembled. He cleared his throat, trying to hold his desire in check. "You say you've searched the house? Is it possible he placed them somewhere else? At his club, perhaps. A friend's . . . or his mistress's?"

"He doesn't have a mistress. At least, I don't think he does. Nor does he frequent clubs."

"What about a friend?"

"Other than his former assistants, I don't know of any. He keeps pretty much to himself."

Connor frowned. "Then where does he go? If you remember, he wasn't home when I called."

"He won't tell me. I've questioned him several times."

"There's the answer, then. Find the destination of his mysterious jaunts, and you may just locate the missing notes."

"I've thought of that. And I intend to follow him the next time he leaves the house." She sent him an uneasy glance. "I just wanted you to be aware that it may take more time than I first thought."

"I wish I could give you more," he said, his tone gentle yet firm, his fingers delving into her soft flesh. "But I have to know by tomorrow how we're going to continue with our plans. Either with you . . . or with your father." Seeing the stricken look on her face, he tried to comfort her. "Informing him may not be as bad as you think. I'll do it with care, I promise you that. I don't want his insanity or death on my hands."

He touched her cheek, and her woman's scent mingled with the salty air. "Besides, it may not come to that. You may still find the notes." He drew his thumb across her lower lip, wishing it were his tongue tracing that moist flesh. "At least I hope so."

She closed her eyes, her lovely face a soft glow in the moonlight. "Connor, please don't . . ." Her words trailed off when he touched the tip of her tongue with his finger. A shuddering breath left her, and she let her head fall back.

It was all the invitation he needed. He covered her mouth with his, took the gift with a longing that staggered him. Her mouth molded to his as if it were made just for his possession. Their breath mingled. Their bodies came together in a fierce, hungry embrace. Flesh against flesh. Heat against heat.

"Hold me, Beau. Hold me until they come for us." Her small body shook. *"Hold me until the end."*

The pain lancing through his chest jolted Connor back to awareness, and he released Ashlee. He stepped away, his pulse running rampant. The visions this woman stirred in him scared him to death. He had no business feeling the way he did about a woman he hardly knew. In confusion and self-anger, he lashed out. "Your attempt at seduction won't sway me from my purpose. I'll see the notes tomorrow . . . or speak to your father."

He walked away from her—more for self-preservation than anything else. Still, her startled gasp reverberated through every inch of his heart.

CHAPTER
6

Hurry, duchess," Beau urged, dragging her through the house.

Her side slammed into a chair, but she didn't falter. They had to get away. They had to!

He tightened his hold and wrenched open the back door.

A figure stood in their path. "No!" she screamed. "Oh, no!"

Beau shoved her behind him and dove for the man blocking their way to freedom.

They rolled off the porch amid the sounds of flesh meeting flesh, grunts and curses.

Another man joined the battle, then another.

"Run, duchess. Run!" Beau shouted, struggling between the powerful hands that held him down.

Her fear for Beau held her immobile for a split second, then she bolted into action. She couldn't help him if they caught her. Lifting her skirts, she raced out the doorway and off the porch. Her heart pounded at a vicious rate. The trees. She had to get to the trees! Vines tangled around her feet, dragging her down. Wildly she scrambled on her knees. "Help me. Oh, somebody, please." The cypress loomed closer—but not close enough. Footsteps pounded right behind her. She wasn't going to make it!

"Beau!" she screamed. "Oh, God, Beau. Where are you?"

Cruel fingers snagged her hair—

Ashlee woke with a start. Her hands trembled from remnants of the nightmare. Her temples pulsed with a vicious headache. Oh, why wouldn't the dream go away? Why had it plagued her since she was a child, only to grow stronger since the day she intercepted Connor's message? Did he have something to do with these visions?

She shook the absurd thought away. She was being foolish. Still, thoughts of Connor stirred memories of the kiss they shared at the cove. Her fingers rose to her lips as remembered tingles skittered over the sensitive flesh. She was both horrified by her actions and awed by the sensations she'd experienced with him.

"You're being a dolt," she scolded aloud. He had simply taken advantage of a secluded cove and a moonlit night. Nothing more. And she was sure it hadn't been an intentional act on his part. Why else would he have accused her of trying to seduce him?

Her resolve to follow her father strengthened. Although she didn't know Connor well, he didn't strike her as a man who made idle threats. He would confront her father tomorrow—if she didn't find the notes today.

Forgoing her dawn ride, she dressed in her forest green riding habit, then positioned herself in a shaded alcove at the end of the hall, near her father's door. She would follow him this morning if she had to stuff herself inside his saddlebags!

When more than an hour had passed, and he still

hadn't emerged, she became worried. Maybe he wasn't feeling well. Anxious now, she tapped on his door and shoved it open.

The room was empty.

Hurrying downstairs, she went in search of Tilly and found her in the dining room, placing a plate of steaming potatoes on the table. "Where's Father?"

The cook wiped her hands on a towel tucked into the waistband of her flour-streaked wool skirt. "I was just about to come lookin' for ye, love. Your breakfast is ready."

"Tilly! Where's Father?"

She lifted a hefty shoulder. "Left before dawn, he did. Wouldna even spare time for a cup of me tea."

Panic threatened. Ashlee had to find him. Whirling around, she strode briskly toward the back door. She'd find him if she had to search every street and house in St. Augustine.

The thud of horse's hooves out front stopped her cold. She raced into the parlor and brushed aside the curtain to peer out. Her heart exploded into excited beats when she saw her father leap from his mount and hurry up the front steps.

Not wanting to be seen, she darted to the archway that connected with the entry hall and peeked around the corner.

He raced past her and up the stairs, retrieved something from his room, and hurried back outside.

Terrified he'd escape her, she ran to the stables and leapt astride her horse's bare back, desperate to keep her father in her sights. The horse reared, unaccustomed to a saddleless rider, and for a few awful moments, she feared she'd lose her seat. Only years of scandalous practice when she was a child saved her from harm. She tightened her thighs, grabbed a handful of mane, and tapped her heels to the animal's sides.

The horse bolted out the stable door.

Ashlee held on, and winced at the jolting horseflesh bouncing beneath her. When she reached the road in front of the house, she saw her father farther down the lane, riding at a steady pace, then he turned and disappeared into the trees bordering the west side of the lane.

Curious, knowing there was only an old abandoned farmhouse and miles of orange groves in that direction, she followed, maintaining her distance yet keeping him in her sights.

They had gone what seemed like miles before he rode into the clearing where the old farmhouse sat. Only, to her amazement, it wasn't old . . . anymore. Someone had restored the building to its former dignity.

Thoroughly baffled, she watched him draw his mount to a halt and enter the dwelling without knocking. His bold behavior forced her to reconsider Connor's summation that her father might have a mistress.

But it was so unlike him.

She slid off her horse and crept toward one of the front windows, knowing she'd be embarrassed beyond redemption if she saw her father in the arms of a paid harlot.

Wary, she edged closer, then tilted her head forward to allow her a glimpse of the interior. What met her gaze sent a shock wave through her that was strong enough to shake her ancestors.

"What the hell are you doing here?" her father's voice boomed from behind her.

Startled, she whirled around, then regained her composure and placed her hands on her hips. "I might ask the same of you, Dr. Walker. Why are *you* here? *And what is going on inside that house?*"

* * *

"Is everything set?"

Sliding into a chair opposite Branden, Connor reached across the table for the teapot. "I think so. I was able to purchase nearly a dozen horses, and I've bought a hundredweight of coal. The freighter's crew will start loading the coal tomorrow."

"What about saddles?"

"Only six. A shipload of hides went down in a storm, so leather goods are hard to come by at the moment. But they'll have to do." He filled a cup and took a sip of the tepid brew. "Is Aunt Vivian up?"

"You haven't seen her yet?"

Connor nodded. "Last night. I slipped into her room, but she was sound asleep. And this morning . . ." He shrugged. "Well, you know how she hates to rise before noon."

Branden flashed a smile. "Yes, I do recall her penchant for sleeping late—and her temper if she's awakened early. But it's past noon. I imagine it's safe enough now."

Swallowing the last of his drink—and a chuckle—Connor set his cup aside and rose. "Care to join me?"

"No. I'm going to drown myself in lukewarm tea."

Noticing the shadows under his friend's eyes, Connor suspected he'd had very little sleep. Due to another heated altercation with Louise, no doubt. Although Branden hid his pain well, Connor knew him better than anyone, and he could see how Louise's actions—and her tales about Connor—were tearing him apart. If only he'd listen to reason . . . Resigned, Connor started for the stairs. "I'll join you later."

"Mr. Westfield?" the proprietor called out. "I've a message here for you."

Another one? he thought tiredly. Changing directions, he headed for the counter at the opposite side of the room, his knee-high boots clicking against the wooden floor planks. Taking the note from the man's outstretched hands, he scanned its contents.

"What is it this time?" Branden asked.

Too stunned to move for a moment, Connor stared at the page, then his confused gaze slid to Delacorte. "It's from Nathaniel Walker. He wants to see me."

"But I thought you said he didn't— Bloody hell."

"Exactly."

"I wouldn't miss this," Branden quipped, having miraculously recovered from his bout of depression.

When they arrived at the physician's residence, they were immediately shown into the parlor.

"Mr. Westfield?" a white-haired man asked as he rose from a chair, his glance flitting between Connor and Delacorte.

Connor extended his hand. "Dr. Walker." He motioned to his friend. "This is my companion, Branden Delacorte."

"Call me Nathaniel, please." He gestured to Ashlee. "I assume you already know my daughter."

Oh, yes, Connor thought with warmth, recalling the kiss they'd shared last night. He met her eyes and knew she was remembering, too. "I know her, but my friend here doesn't." Connor didn't take his eyes off the exquisite blonde. "Branden, this is Miss Ashlee Walker."

"My pleasure." Branden's voice dripped with masculine appreciation, raising the temperature of Connor's blood.

"It's a pleasure to meet you," she murmured, then looked away, her expression anxious.

Connor fought down a surge of jealousy and turned to the girl's father. "Mr.— Nathaniel, I understand you wanted to see me?"

"Please, sit first." He flung a hand toward a pair of red velvet chairs. "Would you care for tea?"

When they'd been served, Nathaniel leaned forward and stared at them both, his clear blue eyes intent and direct. "I am not sure where to start, so I imagine the beginning will be appropriate. As I am sure Ashlee has told you, I was quite distraught when the accident killed my dear friends and severely injured Ashlee and a cohort." He glanced in his daughter's direction, his eyes soft. "I almost lost them, too."

Connor's gaze flew to Ashlee. *She'd nearly died?*

"Anyway," Walker went on, "afterwards I swore I would never again endanger another's life with my experiments. So I gave them up. But, giving up my life's work was nearly as devastating as the loss I suffered in the explosion. I was miserable, and would probably have continued to be so if I had not received a missive from Vivian while Ashlee was out on an errand."

"Vivian?" Connor was pulled from the shock of Ashlee's life-threatening injury. "What missive?"

"The one your aunt, herself, sent when you left on some journey to Philadelphia last month." He smiled warmly. "Receiving that note changed my entire life. I have known Vivian for many years, and the thought of her condition—when I could help—deplored me. I had to assist her. I could not have lived with myself, otherwise."

Connor stared at the man, looking for signs of the depression Ashlee warned him about. When he saw no indication of despair, he went weak with relief.

Nathaniel leaned back and crossed his legs, then continued. "I bought an abandoned farm not far from here and restored it, then set up a new laboratory. But I did not tell my daughter. She would have wanted to assist, and I refuse to put her at risk again. So, rather than argue over the matter, I simply did not mention it."

A tidal wave of hope filled Connor, and he sent a

glance at Ashlee, who stood by the window. But it was apparent she wasn't as pleased. Her mouth was set in an angry line, her arms folded. *So the imp could practice secrecy but couldn't take it from another, hmm.* He tried not to smile.

"Anyway, you can imagine my surprise when I found that Ashlee had followed me this morning, saw my laboratory, then confronted me as if I were a child." He sent her a disgruntled look. "Then she told me of the scheme you two had cooked up."

Connor was the recipient of a reproachful glare. "Foolish children. My notes are not clear enough for me to read most of the time, much less someone else. I fear you would have been disappointed." He scowled at them both. "And if you would have succeeded in your attempt to snatch them, I could not have continued to work. Your doltish plan nearly cost Vivian her life. And for that, I am not likely to forgive you soon." His voice softened. "Though I do understand your noble motive."

Connor hadn't felt this chagrined since the last setdown he'd received from his aunt. And Branden, the grinning jackass, was enjoying the hell out of his discomfort.

"Too, you cannot imagine the tortures I suffered when I thought my sister was deathly ill, knowing I couldn't go to London to be with her until I'd taken care of Vivian's problem."

"Your sister?" Connor had no idea what he was talking about.

The older man arched a white brow at his daughter. "Yes. It seems that Ashlee thought to send me out of harm's way by forging a note from my sister's practitioner, asking me to come to London at once."

"She did what?" Connor glared at the little witch. She had set out to deceive him. *Again.* She hadn't intended to help him at all.

She turned pale, her eyes wide.

Her stricken expression didn't affect him in the least. The brat needed to be turned over someone's knee. *And he knew just the person who would enjoy it most.* Holding that thought for a later time, he returned his attention to Nathaniel. "You have my apology, sir, for my part in the subterfuge. But I would have done anything to save my aunt."

"I know that, son. She has told me of your remarkable loyalty, which I can attribute to the excellent job she did raising you. But, as she informed me earlier this morning, you do tend to be a bit single-minded at times."

This morning? It didn't make Connor feel any better to know the man was right—or that Walker had been welcomed in his aunt's room before noon, something *he'd* never been allowed. "So I've been told." Often, he added silently. "And since my plan has gone awry, I'd better track down the guide I hired yesterday and tell him his services won't be needed after all."

"What guide?"

Connor explained about their arrangements to travel into the swamps.

Frowning, Nathaniel glanced at his daughter. "I do not understand why you would want to go so far."

"Because I think I've determined the cause of the accident," she announced, regaining some of her former spirit.

Her father blinked. "What?"

"It's the vapors you force through water to create the coal tar. I don't think it's vapor at all, but a gas. I've thought through the day of the accident again and again. The last thing I recall before the explosion was Harry striking a flint. Evidently the spark ignited the fumes. That's why I wanted to go into the humid swamps. The damp air would lessen the chance of another ignition."

Her father surged to his feet. "My word! Why did *I* not think of that?" He paced to the door, then back again. With a joyous grin, he turned to Connor. "That changes everything. Young man, I think we should keep to your plans for the journey into the bayou. And I would very much like to bring my assistants, Harry and Joe, along. As dedicated as they were, I imagine they have been as miserable as I."

"Don't you fear for their safety?" Ashlee asked, her tone testy.

"Yes. Yet with this new development, we can take precautions—*and* the choice is theirs. But I know if they have been feeling as wretched as I have, there will be no choice to make." He glanced at Connor. "Well?"

Hell, at this point, Connor would have agreed to most anything. "We're scheduled to leave Friday."

Nathaniel nodded. "We will be ready."

Feeling as if the weight of the world had been lifted from his shoulders, Connor barely felt his feet touch the ground as he and Branden headed back to the inn. The one man who could possibly save his aunt's life was going to make every effort. He couldn't ask for more . . . unless it was that miracle Dr. Ramsey had mentioned.

Anxious to see his aunt, he took the stairs two at a time and knocked briskly.

A rush of perfume hit him in the face as Louise Delacorte opened the door. "Connor, darling. I wasn't expecting you"—her gaze traveled to Branden, who stood right behind him—"yet."

Connor felt his friend stiffen. Damn the woman. Why did she have to torment Branden at every turn? For the first time, Connor felt sorry for the man all the ladies of Charleston had once panted over. He was married to a vicious, spiteful woman, and there was no way out for him. And she was dragging Connor into the middle of it. He sent her a glare that should have frozen her in place. "I came to see my aunt."

"Is that our dinner?" Aunt Vivian called from inside.

He pushed the door wider and stepped around Louise. "No, Aunt Vivian. It's me."

She was hanging up a dress, and turned just as he walked over to her. "Well, it's about time you returned. I've been waiting all night—and day."

He grinned and did not mention she'd been sleeping most of it. "Sorry."

"So? Where have you been?"

He explained about their proposed trip to the swamps.

"Connor James Westfield, that is the most absurd notion I have ever heard. I will not hear of you going off on some senseless expedition, into some wild, uncharted region where heaven-only-knows-what perils may await, in vague hopes of finding a cure for my illness. Nathaniel is quite capable of working here in St. Augustine. And if he doesn't succeed, then it's my time to go, and the good Lord will take me. If it isn't, then neither of us has anything to worry about."

Connor gritted his teeth. Damned, obstinate, bullheaded . . . "Aunt Vivian, the good Lord often gives *us* a means to do His bidding. Perhaps this is one of those times."

She jabbed a hand onto her narrow hip. "Don't try to use your idea of the Lord's purpose as a means to gain my acquiescence. And do stop that scowling."

"You'd scowl, too, if someone you loved wouldn't let you fight for their life."

A tender look filled her eyes. "I'm fighting, too,

love. I just don't think you going off into some hellish swamp is the answer."

He could feel her softening and took full advantage of the fact. He lifted her hand and unashamedly went down on one knee, knowing she was the only woman in the world he'd do that for, and totally unconcerned that Branden and Louise looked on. His aunt was worth a little humility—and so much more. "I've never asked anything of you. But this time, I am. You're all I have, Nanna," he said quietly. "I can't bear the thought of losing you. Please, don't make a fuss. You'll be perfectly safe here with Louise and Branden to watch after you."

He could see her waver and shot for the heart. "The Lord took my parents and brother. Don't let Him take you from me, too."

Tears welled in her eyes, and she touched his cheek. "Oh, Connor, I don't want to leave you."

"Then help me," he whispered.

A sparkling drop slid down her cheek. "If going on this wretched journey will truly ease your distress, then go." She stroked his jaw. "But don't expect me to stay behind. I'm going with you."

"But your health—"

"Is perfectly normal between those wretched bouts of fever. I'll hear no more arguments. And stop that scowling."

CHAPTER
7

Standing on the wharf in the frigid mist, Ashlee snuggled deeper into her brown velvet cape, shivering against the ocean's morning chill as she stared up at Connor's ship. The three-masted Savannah with its unusual black smokestack groaned and creaked, then swayed to the pull of the outgoing tide.

Seagulls glided overhead, their cries lost in the rumble of the surf, their sleek bodies disappearing into a billow of white smoke rising from the stack.

Suddenly she envisioned herself standing on a ship's deck. But it wasn't the same one . . .

"Beau, I'm frightened."

His arms came around her, holding her against the rail, their warmth a haven against the biting wind. "We're only a few miles off the coast, duchess. Don't worry. The storm will probably miss us. Even if it doesn't, we'll still be able to make land."

He nuzzled the sensitive skin of her neck. "After all the trouble I went through to get you, I'm not about to lose you now."

Loving this man more than life itself, she turned and gazed up into his eyes, then lifted a hand to his cheek. Her movement froze. Panic slammed through her middle. Directly behind him, like an angry demon, a monstrous wave rose up out of the ocean. "Beau, look out!"

"Ashlee? Is something wrong?"

Startled, she swung around to see her father standing on the dock beside her. Her gaze flew back to the ship. Smoke rose at a steady pace from the stack while the massive vessel bumped gently against the pier. Trying to still the savage pounding in her chest, she placed a hand over her heart and gave a winded chuckle. "No, Father, nothing's the matter. I was just amazed at the workings of the ship." She forced a smile. "It's a little unnerving to think that naught but rising steam can propel something that big." *And where the devil were those newest visions coming from?*

He smiled indulgently. "Well, love, I am sure there is a little more to it than that." His eyes gleamed with excitement. "But I am quite intrigued. I cannot wait for Westfield to show me how this new concept works."

At the mention of Connor's name, she felt a sliver of anxiousness. The man hadn't said a mouthful of words to her in the last week.

"Miss Walker?"

She turned to see a boy with a shock of raven curls walking toward her. "Yes?"

"I'm Blackie Snow." He peeled off a gray knit cap, releasing another tumble of ebony rings. "Captain Tesh asked me to show you to your cabin." He nodded respectfully to her father. "You, too, sir. Your rooms is next to each other."

She glanced at her father. "What about Harry and Joe? Shouldn't we wait for them?"

"They will be along soon. I asked them to retrieve

my mice from the farmhouse, and I am certain someone will show them aboard when they arrive."

Blackie looked alarmed. "Mice ain't exactly welcome on a ship, sir." He shifted uneasily from one
foot to another, obviously not wanting to offend, but
concerned.

"I need them for my experiments, son. But they are
in cages and will stay in the cabin with me."

He still didn't appear convinced, but the boy nodded, then directed them to follow.

She couldn't help thinking the youngster, who probably wasn't over twelve, was much too serious for his
age. Still . . . there was a devilish sparkle in those
china blue eyes that proclaimed an impish nature.

The ship's plank floor rocked beneath her feet as she
followed Blackie across the barrel-littered deck to a
door that led below. Just as she started to enter, she
caught a glimpse of Connor standing by the wheel.
Her heart picked up speed. Connor was magnificent to
behold. Wearing only snug black breeches, knee-high
boots, and a billowing white shirt, he resembled a
drawing she'd once seen of a pirate. Dangerous,
frightening . . . and sinfully handsome. The kiss
they'd shared floated through her thoughts, bringing
heat to her cheeks.

Their eyes met for an instant, then he looked away.

Hurt by his cool dismissal, she hurried down the
steps. *She did not care what the man thought of her.
She'd dupe him again if she had to.*

When Blackie opened one of the doors and motioned for her to enter, she stopped just inside and
examined the accommodations she'd use for the next
few days. There was a narrow cot mounted against
one wall below a small window that emitted very little
light. Crude shelves lined most of the walls, and
beneath the bed, to her mortification, someone had

tried to conceal a chamber pot by draping one of the woolen blankets down to the floor.

She flushed and drew her gaze away. Her trunks, which had been loaded when the horses were taken aboard, were stacked against the opposite bulkhead, leaving only enough room for a bureau, mirror, and washstand.

"It ain't much, miss," Blackie apologized. "But the *Summerstar* weren't built for passengers. These rooms is mainly used for linen and food storage and the likes. The other folks' cabins are about the same, except for the mirror—that was Mr. Westfield's idea —and, of course, except for his quarters. All of his ships is built with a 'special' room just for the owner." He stared at the cap he was worrying between his fingers. "I'd be honored to show it to you later—if you like."

He was such a darling, and she really didn't want to hurt his feelings by telling him she couldn't care less about seeing that wretched Connor Westfield's chambers. So she lied. "That would be nice."

A smile brightened his face, revealing adorable dimples on either side of his expressive mouth. "I'll be back after we shove off to escort you to breakfast. Then we can have a peek."

When she closed the door behind him, she took off her cape and hung it on a peg by the entrance, then searched the trunks for her peach morning gown. She had just finished dressing and brushing her hair—no easy feat with the ship lurching as it moved into the open waters—and was still trying to smooth the wrinkles out of her skirt when Blackie returned.

Ever since the animosity had risen between her and Connor, she had spent scant time in his presence, and she didn't relish the idea of doing it over breakfast. Still, she had little choice.

Checking the lace tucker in her bodice one last time, and making sure her hair thoroughly covered her scarred face, she lifted her chin and took Blackie's arm.

Several of the others had already arrived and were seated at a long bench centering the galley. All the gentlemen rose when she entered, including her nemesis. His silver eyes took a rapid inventory of her appearance, revealing nothing of his thoughts, then he politely motioned to a vacant seat almost directly across from him and next to her father.

Connor remained standing after the others had resumed their seats. "Miss Walker, may I present my captain, Franklin Tesh, and first mate, George Acres." He waved his long-fingered hand. "The others, you know."

The others included her father, Joe Longtree, and Blackie. For a moment she wondered why Harry hadn't come with Joe. Then, recalling the older man's sensitivity to his appearance, she knew he had chosen to remain in his cabin.

"How do you do, gentlemen." She nodded as she skirted the end of the bench and sat down.

"Tea, Miss Walker?" her host asked, leaning over to hand her a cup. As she took it, the scent of Connor's spicy cologne floated toward her. He smelled so good . . . so familiar . . .

She held the warm cinnamon cake beneath her nose and inhaled the sweet fragrance. She'd baked it just for Beau. Smiling, she broke off a piece and offered it to him.

"Mmm, delicious," he murmured. His moist lips closed around her fingertips, suckling gently as he took the treat into his mouth.

Fire seared a path up her arm, and she drew in a stunned breath.

His beautiful mouth widened into a smile. His eyes

crinkled at the corners as he boldly began nibbling her fingers, lovingly stroking each with his tongue, then moving higher to savor the tender flesh of her arm, her bare shoulder, her throat. He nudged aside the soft material of the chemise she wore, exposing her fully to his hungry gaze. "So delicious," he whispered, then slowly, ever so slowly, he lowered his head and captured the sensitive tip of her—

"Miss Walker?"

She snapped her head up. Her heart pounded so hard, she was certain everyone at the table could hear it. She crossed her arms over her bosom and focused on Connor. "Y-Yes?"

His eyes, dark with an undefined emotion, rose from her bodice to meet hers. His mouth tightened, and he reached for a steaming teapot. "I asked if you were settled in all right." He filled a cup for her.

"Yes. Thank you. And I truly appreciate the trouble you have gone to in order to make our accommodations comfortable. Especially on such short notice. Not many people would be so considerate." She knew she was babbling, but she couldn't seem to help herself.

"Well, mine are absolutely horrid," a voice rang out from the open doorway.

Connor rose, as did the other gentlemen. "Aunt Vivian," he said, his tone warm. "I was wondering if you were going to join us."

So this was the woman who meant so much to him.

"I was wondering that myself. It was deucedly hard to dress in that closet you call my quarters." She flicked a handkerchief in his direction. "And I may never forgive you for asking Louise to act as my maid." She sent him a meaningful glance. "Nor will she."

Ashlee wondered who Louise was.

A satisfied smile curved Connor's lips as he took his

aunt's hand and led her to the table. "There wasn't enough room for your own maid, Nanna. I told you that."

Ashlee softened at the genuine affection radiating from Connor.

He helped his aunt to sit, then kissed her temple. "And as for your quarters, don't fret. I'll have the situation taken care of immediately."

"Oh? And just how do you plan to do that, pray tell?"

He poured her a cup of tea while Blackie wedged himself between Ashlee and her father, leaving Ashlee perched on the end of the bench across from the first mate.

"I'll exchange rooms with you," Connor offered.

It was plain for anyone to see that he adored the woman. Too, she noticed a tenderness in Vivian's eyes that was at odds with her gruff manner of speech—a sure sign that his feelings were reciprocated.

The woman cleared her throat. "I'll stay where I am, thank you. The space in your chamber is taken up by that gawd-awful monstrosity you call a bed." She shook her head, rustling a feather that was woven into the coiled braid at the crown of her head. "I'd be better off in a musty storage bin."

Connor's low laugh was husky and rich. "As you wish, madam."

Ashlee got the distinct impression that his aunt merely enjoyed grumbling about something, and hadn't truly meant to complain.

"You must be Nathaniel's daughter." Vivian turned to her, then smiled with genuine pleasure. "He's spoken of you often." She inspected Ashlee's features. "You're quite lovely, child."

Guilt stung her after the way she'd disregarded this woman's plight when trying to protect her father.

Fortunately, she was saved from stumbling over a reply when another couple entered the room.

All eyes turned to the door.

Ashlee's widened. Though she'd met Branden Delacorte, she'd never seen the beautiful woman he ushered into the galley. Ashlee fingered the concealing fall of hair covering her left jaw, then shot an expectant glance at Connor.

He addressed everyone at the table. "May I present my friend, Branden Delacorte, and his wife, Louise."

The distaste behind that single name startled her. Ashlee glanced at the woman to see Louise's gaze devouring Connor. An ugly sensation moved through her. The woman looked as if she'd eat him alive.

Connor directed the two newcomers to their places, Branden next to him, and Louise on the other side of her husband. But as the tall woman took her seat, she scooted over as close to Connor as possible. Branden, his mouth drawn into a tight line, sat on the other side.

Ashlee experienced a thread of peevishness at the woman's close contact. From where Ashlee sat, it looked as if Louise's thigh was deliberately pressed against Connor's. *Not that it mattered to her, she inwardly reminded. But the woman was being quite brazen.*

Returning her attention to the cup in front of her, Ashlee stirred in a spoonful of sugar. She saw her father edge a little closer to Vivian. Their heads were nearly touching as they spoke in low tones. Curious, she wondered at their close relationship. Although she was well aware they had known each other for some time, Father had never mentioned Vivian. Ashlee's gaze drifted to Connor, and she noticed that he, too, watched them.

Casual chatter filled the room as the cook and his

helper brought in trays filled with fluffy eggs, fried potatoes, thick slices of ham, plump red strawberries, and steaming scones. But, for some undefinable reason, Ashlee's appetite had deserted her, and she spent a good deal of time chasing a strawberry around her plate.

Something brushed the toe of her slipper.

She looked down over the end of the table, only to discover the first mate's worn boot fondling her foot.

She arched a brow at the impertinent cad directly across from her.

He sent her a sly smirk, then continued to eat and rub her toes.

Of all the nerve. Setting her teeth hard against one another, and without any outward show of movement, she soundly kicked the pompous ass.

George Acres strangled on a strawberry and began to gag.

Her toes throbbed with pain, but she refused to even wince. She merely smiled and nibbled a scone.

Connor turned a murderous glare toward the first mate, while Vivian coughed lightly into her lace handkerchief.

Louise frowned.

Branden gnawed the corner of his lip as if to stop a grin.

The captain rose and pounded the crewman on the back until the spasm passed, then resumed his seat next to Connor's aunt and murmured something about George's too friendly nature going to be the death of him.

Keeping her eyes downcast, and ignoring the man across from her, Ashlee finished her meal, then excused herself from the table. She could feel Connor's still hostile gaze on her as she hurried out the door.

She could hardly believe the first mate's nerve. And

right in front of everyone. Not to mention the way Connor reacted. Why, one would have thought she'd invited the wretch's advances.

Grabbing a book from her trunk, she fluffed the bed pillows and leaned back against the bulkhead. With stiff movements, she opened the tome and began to read William Shakespeare's *Twelfth Night,* hoping to take her mind from the incident—and the lecherous look in George Acres's eyes. Putting both from her mind, she focused on a passage in the second act.

> *She never told her love*
> *But let concealment, like a worm i' th' bud,*
> *Feed on her damask cheek. . . .*

She touched the scar near her ear, then immediately slammed the book shut and tossed it onto the cot. She rose and paced the room. Was it her lot in life to be constantly reminded of her disfigurement?

Her steps slowed. Only Connor seemed unaffected. She snorted. Of course. He wouldn't say anything offensive to the daughter of the man he needed so badly.

Angry all over again, she kicked one of the trunks, then grabbed her toes and hobbled back to the cot, massaging the twice-abused digits.

A sudden pounding rattled the door.

What now? she thought as she rose and opened it. "What do you want?"

Blackie's brow shot up in surprise at her brusque tone. "I came to show you Mr. Westfield's cabin. But if it's a bad time, I can take you later."

Feeling like an ogre, she quelled the urge to stomp her foot at her own abrasive behavior. She gave him a sheepish smile. "No. Now is fine."

A grin split his young face. "Come on, then. The boss man's on deck, and we wouldn't want him to catch us snoopin'."

She froze. "You mean he doesn't know?"

"No, miss. Mr. Westfield, he's a real private sort. This is gonna be our little secret."

CHAPTER
8

Ashlee's nerves tingled as she followed Blackie into the room that sat beneath the bow of the boat, just below the ship's wheel. Connor's private chamber, his masculine world that she had no right to invade. Still . . . she *was* curious.

Taking a fortifying breath, she glanced around at the wide windows, draped in gold velvet, that commanded the two forward walls, exposing a breathtaking view. The third wall was lined with books on either side of the door.

The gargantuan bed Vivian spoke of sat below the windows, allowing sunlight to stream across a lovely flaxen quilt. An image of Connor lying beneath that cover skipped through her mind, and she quickly looked away.

Behind a screen of delicate silk sat a gleaming brass tub. She stared at it, wondering if she might request the use of it one evening.

"Did you ever see anything more fancy?" Blackie

asked in an awed voice. "Every time I come in here, I'm struck dumb."

"It's beautiful," she agreed. "And look at all those maps." She moved to the huge mahogany desk. "He must have traveled all over the world." Trailing a finger down the spine of a leather-bound ledger, she smiled wistfully. She'd always wanted to travel, but her mother had refused to bother with a child on her many voyages to Europe. Or be hampered by a preoccupied husband, for that matter.

"We'd better go, miss," Blackie urged. "The boss was on deck, but you never know when he might need somethin' down here." He grinned. "I'll show you the hold where they got the horses and all that coal stored."

Not sure she really wanted to see the dark, sinister belly of a ship, she nonetheless nodded politely and headed for the door.

Blackie raced to open it for her, then stepped back for her to go ahead of him.

But she couldn't. Connor Westfield was standing on the other side, his hand extended as if he'd been about to turn the latch.

Surprise flickered across his handsome features, to be replaced by wariness. He lowered his hand. "What are you doing here?"

Blackie made a strangled sound.

Connor swung on the boy. "Explain yourself, Mr. Snow."

Terror flashed in the child's eyes.

Unsettled by the youngster's fear, and not in the least intimidated by the man herself, Ashlee quickly spoke up. "It's not his fault. I asked him to show me your cabin."

Blackie looked as if he'd just been saved from the hangman, his shoulders sagging in relief.

Connor didn't appear in the least convinced. "Now, why would you want to see my bedchamber?"

Good question, Ashlee thought. "I, um, was impressed by your aunt's mention of the monstrous bed, and wanted to see it for myself." Heavens, that sounded feeble.

"I see." He glanced at his cabin boy. "Don't you have something to do?"

"Yes, sir!"

"Then get to it."

"Yes, sir!" Blackie shot her a grateful look, then scrambled out the door and closed it behind him.

Ashlee watched Connor turn back to her and was unprepared for the thrill that arrowed through her. He hadn't been wearing those clothes during breakfast, she was positive. There was no way she could have missed noticing the way his tight buff breeches hugged those long, muscular legs and the wicked contour of his boldly outlined masculinity.

Her gaze fluttered upward to the loose blue shirt that clung to his broad shoulders, while its gaping neckline revealed a silken forest of dark, swirling hair and deeply tanned skin.

"If you keep looking at me like that," he warned in a husky voice, "I won't be responsible for my actions."

Her gaze flew to his and collided with bright, quicksilver eyes. "I . . ." She forgot what she wanted to say. She fixed on that sculpted mouth with its slightly fuller lower lip. She tried again. "Connor, I . . ." *want you to kiss me.* Shocked by her own thoughts, Ashlee brought a hand to her chest and nervously fingered the tucker covering her breast.

Connor watched the movement of her slender fingers, wishing he could see the firm, white flesh that surely trembled beneath her touch. He didn't know why she was in his room, but at this point it didn't matter. She was breathtaking.

A warmth seeped into his lower body, and he returned his attention to her face. That was a mistake. The dreamy look in those jewel-bright eyes, and the way her lips were softly parted, warmed him. Nothing could have stopped him from reaching for her.

Suddenly the ship pitched leeward, and she lost her footing. "Connor!"

He grabbed her by the waist and propelled them both against the wall to stop her fall. Their bodies collided from chest to thigh. For a brief instant, neither of them moved. He could feel her heart pounding against his, the firmness of her breasts pressed to his chest. The air in the cabin turned thick, hot. She was so damned soft. Unexpectedly, he found it very hard to breathe.

"Connor—"

"Don't move, Ashlee. For God's sake, don't move."

"But—"

The heat of her breath on his lips snapped his control. Since the moment he'd tasted her sweet lips at the cove, he'd thought of little else. Every cell in his body throbbed, and he took her mouth with an urgency he couldn't begin to explain.

Shocked by his assault, she parted her lips on a gasp, and he plunged his tongue into her velvety, moistness. She shivered, then relaxed.

He couldn't stop a shudder, and it angered him. The strange hold she had on him unmanned him. He cruelly crushed her lips, tightened his grip. He wanted to punish her for weakening him, for trying to dupe him . . . for betraying him.

He pressed her into the bulkhead and took her lips with barely restrained violence. He shouldn't have expected any better from her. But he had. Damn his soul, he *had*.

Ashlee's whimper of pain cut into him like a sword, and against his own reasoning, he gentled the kiss. He couldn't help himself. Couldn't stop the need to protect her . . . even from himself.

With slow, exquisite care, he again parted her lips.

A moan of surrender shimmered over their merged tongues, and she slid her arms up his chest, then encircled his neck. Her delicate, warm body pressed closer, enveloping him in flames of desire. His hands sought the shape of her spine, her waist, her beautiful breast. She filled his palm, tightened into it.

With shaky hands, he edged his fingers beneath the tucker and inched it downward. The feel of her smooth skin was his undoing. He dragged his mouth from hers and nibbled a hot path over the tempting scar she thought was so disfiguring. He stopped to learn its shape, its warmth.

She went rigid. She shoved at his shoulders. "Let me go!"

Coming out of a fog, he lifted his head. "What?"

"How dare you!" she rapped out between short, quick breaths as she righted the lace. Her cheeks glowed bright red. Then she slapped him. Hard.

It was so unexpected, he never saw it coming. Heat shot through his jaw, but it angered him rather than hurt. He lashed out with a few truths. "You vicious little minx. What's your game? You've taunted me from the first moment I set eyes on you, and I'm damned tired of playing the fool. In fact, I'm beginning to think one with any sense would do well to avoid your offensive presence completely."

Offensive presence. Ashlee felt his wounding words all the way to her soul. Cruel words she'd heard in the not so distant past.

She took a breath, but it didn't stop the hurt. "Don't worry, Connor. In the future, my *offensive presence* will avoid yours at all cost." Whirling on her heels, she stalked out of the room and fled back to her tiny quarters. How would she ever endure being confined on a vessel with that insensitive ass? And why did it hurt so much to know he was just like Stephen Frankenburg? What had she expected? That he'd be different?

She removed her gown and flung it on the foot of the cot, vowing never to wear the wretched thing again. The two times she'd worn it so far, she'd come to grief. That night with Stephen . . . and now. She yanked the brush through her hair and slipped into a dressing robe.

Not about to venture out again, and with nothing else to do, she picked up Shakespeare's book and thumbed through the pages. She became engrossed in *Much Ado About Nothing* and smiled as she read a passage in the third act.

Everyone can master a grief but he that has it.

"Especially when you're always reminded of the thing that causes your grief," she added, then continued to read for a time. Soon her lashes grew heavy, and she felt herself slipping into a place where painful insults couldn't touch her. . . .

"A duchess does not paint pillars, damn it."

She smiled up at the horrified expression on Beau's handsome face. "I'm not a duchess anymore. Besides, you've painted nearly the entire building. It's my turn."
She snatched the brush from his loose fingers and quickly dipped it into a bucket of sparkling white paint.

Scrambling down from his perch on a ladder, he stalked toward her, his intent clear. He would not allow her to abuse her station any more than she already had for him.

She backed up, holding the brush out as if it were a weapon. "Oh, do stop. You're making too much of this."

He kept coming—right into the brush. The bristles

folded against his bare chest, and white paint dribbled in a line down his tight stomach until it reached the waistband of his snug breeches.

"Oh, dear. Now look what you've done."

He snatched the brush away and flung it onto the floor of the veranda. Paint splattered on the pane of a large window as the tool bounced noisily. Unconcerned, he gripped her by the shoulders, his eyes serious as he pulled her up against him, uncaring that he'd just transferred the paint from his chest to her dress. "I may not be able to give you servants or fancy balls like you're accustomed to, but I'll be damned if I'll let you lower yourself to do manual labor."

Her heart softened toward the proud man. "Oh, Beau. Don't you see? Those things don't mean anything to me. This is our home, our way of life, and I so desperately want to be a part of it."

He slid his hands down her spine, then covered her bottom with his palms. "You could never be a part of anything, duchess. You are the whole. The whole of my existence, of my love." He brushed his lips over hers, savoring the taste of their mingled breaths. "I need you more than the blood that passes through my heart, more than the air that sustains my very life, but I will not reduce you to peasant labor no matter how much you beg. I've taken more from you than any man has a right. I can't take your pride, too." He traced the shape of her mouth with his tongue. "I would see my own life ended first."

She clutched him to her. "Don't say that. Don't ever say that. I couldn't bear it if anything happened to you."

He smiled against her lips in an attempt to lighten the topic he knew she feared above all else. "Then pray, madam, that your husband never finds us."

A thundering noise shook the cabin.

Ashlee woke with a start and shoved into a sitting

position. She grabbed her head, trying to rid herself of the alien images. Who *were* those people?

A wild pounding rattled her door.

She clutched the front of her dressing gown and swung toward the entrance.

"Miss Walker, come quick," Blackie called out. "There's been an accident!"

CHAPTER
9

"Oh, dear God," Ashlee whispered as she stared at the carnage on deck. The mainsail had broken and crashed to the forecastle deck. Several men were trapped beneath it; others were trying to lift the huge beam.

"Get some bandages!" Connor's urgent voice rang across the confusion.

She whipped around to see him directing the command to her. Her father stood beside him, struggling to help lift the beam. Without hesitation, she gathered the folds of her dressing robe and headed for her father's cabin.

It only took a moment to locate his black medical bag, before she hurried topside again.

She came to a skidding halt when she saw Branden drag one of the seamen from below the fallen mast. The man's chest was crushed.

Connor rushed to his crewman's side. For a moment he held the lifeless body close, then lifted his chin and drew in a strained breath. Agony deepened the lines of his handsome face.

Carefully, as if the dead man were extremely fragile, Connor laid him down, then removed his own shirt and covered the shipmate's face.

Fighting tears, she watched him rise slowly, his features taut as he searched for another friend.

"Bring the bandages!" her father called out.

Snapping out of her frozen stupor, Ashlee raced toward him.

He and Joe held down a crewman who screamed in agony. The man's right leg had been severed just below the knee, and Harry was holding a piece of dirty burlap over the bloody stump.

"Get me some fresh water," Ashlee yelled at Blackie as she knelt beside the fallen man. Taking a clean towel from the bag, she pushed Harry's hand aside and placed the cloth over the grotesque wound.

Joe continued to restrain the crewman while her father and Harry moved on to another mangled seaman.

Seconds later, a bucket of water appeared at her elbow.

Time passed in a blur for her then. So many injuries, so much blood, and very little that she could do. Vivian helped her whenever she could, and so did Branden. She caught a rare glimpse of Santos working on another poor soul across the deck, and Louise standing by the railing with her hand over her mouth, but the man Ashlee was tending again claimed her attention and she set to work.

All in all, eight men had been struck by the topsail. Three were dead, and four were severely injured. Only one escaped with minor cuts. George Acres, the first mate.

When she'd finished tying off the last bandage, she

brushed the tangled hair out of her eyes and looked around for her father. She'd lost track of him and most everything else during the turmoil.

He stood next to Connor, shaking his head in disagreement.

Curious, Ashlee rose and walked toward them.

"This is not some evil omen to plague your research," Connor hissed. "It was caused by carelessness. Nothing more."

"You cannot blame the first mate."

"The hell I can't. I told him to have that topsail mast repaired before I left Charleston. The storm they encountered on the way into port last month damaged it. Acres argued it wasn't that bad, but I didn't want to take any chances. I ordered it replaced. The bloody bastard ignored the command, and now three men are dead." Connor rubbed the back of his neck, his voice now wrought with self-recrimination. "I should have checked it. If I hadn't been so damned preoccupied over Aunt Vivian's health, I would have. But that still doesn't excuse George Acres."

"I am certain the man has already been punished by what happened here today. Perhaps now you should try to forgive his failing, rather than making it worse by condemning him."

"Condemning him, hell. I'm setting him adrift."

"Good God, man. You cannot mean that!" her father exclaimed.

"Yes, Dr. Walker, I most certainly can. I want that rabble off my ship." With a stiff nod, Connor strode off, his spine rigid, his gait determined.

Ashlee felt sick. Setting a man adrift was as close to a death sentence as one could get without actually completing the deed. Even as much as she disliked George Acres, the man didn't deserve to die that way. "Father?"

He swung around.

"Perhaps Connor will reconsider, once he calms down. It's been a trying time for him," she said.

He draped an arm around her shoulder and hugged her close. "You may be right. At least, I pray you are. And, I must say, you did an exemplary job today. I was very proud of you."

Ashlee allowed herself to bask in her father's praise for a moment. It wasn't often he noticed. "Thank you, kind sir." She kissed his cheek. "Now I think you should rest for a while. Connor isn't the only one who's had a trying time."

"If you insist," he teased, but the fatigue in his voice couldn't be disguised. He gave her a quick hug, then strolled off in the direction of his cabin.

She watched until he disappeared belowdecks, then lifted the hem of her dressing robe and hurried after Connor, who now stood talking to Captain Tesh.

Not wanting to intrude on yet another conversation, she stopped short and waited for the men to finish. A moment later, the bedraggled captain nodded, then scurried to an angry group of crewmen holding George Acres captive.

Recalling her recent hostile parting with Connor, Ashlee suddenly became unsure if she should approach him at all.

He turned those quicksilver eyes on her, and she saw no sign of hostility, only gratefulness. "Ashlee. I wanted to thank you for your help this afternoon." Though his tone was more formal than she'd ever heard, she could still tell he meant his appreciation from the heart. "I'm sure we'd have lost several more shipmates if it weren't for you and your father."

It was the opening she needed. "My father took an oath to save lives, Connor. And, though I'm not a doctor myself, I try to uphold the same creed."

"My experience with physicians has been quite the opposite, but I'm beginning to believe your father is an exception."

A little confused by the remark, she paused, then squared her shoulders, determined not to pry into something that wasn't her affair. "Yes, he is. He cares a great deal for his fellow man. Which is why I've come to speak with you."

"What about?"

"You can't set Mr. Acres adrift."

"Yes, I can."

"I mean, you mustn't."

Connor stared down at Ashlee, and his chest filled with admiration for the small woman who gave so much of herself. He knew she didn't realize how she looked at the moment, or how she made him grow warm just watching her. Her hair was wind-whipped around her face in an enchanting disarray. Blood streaked one smooth cheek, and her hands were clutched in death holds on the lapels of her stained dressing robe, pulling the material tight over her gentle curves. Still, no matter how much he wished it otherwise, he couldn't dismiss the first mate's actions. "I appreciate your concern, Ashlee, but I'm afraid Acres will be set adrift within the hour."

She caught his sleeve. "Please don't. That uncharitable act would make your actions no better than his. Men died because of what he did, and he might die because of what you're considering. If you must punish him, then do so when we return, I beg of you."

The warm little hand on his arm was making it hard for him to concentrate. "What is Acres to you?"

"Nothing. But he doesn't deserve to die for a mistake. He didn't intentionally cause the mast to fall. I'm sure after all the orders you inflicted on your men in your haste to leave for St. Augustine when you were so anxious to see my father, he simply forgot or didn't have time." She implored him with her eyes. "His actions don't warrant a death sentence."

With slow deliberateness, Connor removed her fingers from his sleeve. "I wonder if you'd have been so generous if your father had been one of those beneath the mast."

She stared at him, knowing he was right. Since someone close to her hadn't been affected, it was easy to pass impartial judgment. But those men were close to Connor. Very close. She'd seen the grief in the tight lines of his face, in the bitter shadows of his eyes, and knew she wouldn't be able to dissuade him. George Acres would be set adrift, and she was helpless to prevent the punishment.

But she had to make one last effort. "Connor, even public reprimand would be more merciful. I saw a man who died of exposure once. A tavern keeper found him behind his saloon and brought him to Father. He'd been a beggar who had no money, food, or shelter. According to Father's diagnosis, he'd been weakened by lack of nourishment, and the sweltering summer sun had robbed him of his remaining strength. He hadn't even been able to crawl to the horse trough for water."

Her insides knotted at the memory. "I will never forget the sight of his swollen, blistered red face, his puffy lips that were cracked so deeply they bled, or the way his tongue had expanded until it protruded from his mouth."

She pulled her dressing robe closer. "Is that truly the fate you would force on George Acres?" She met his gaze. "If so, then do take pride in yourself. For no one else is going to." Whirling, she hurried below-decks. She couldn't bear to witness the atrocity that was about to take place.

Slamming her cabin door, she flounced down on the

cot. She had never known anyone so heartless. Why couldn't he see what George Acres would suffer because of an accident? Filled with frustration, she punched the pillow. She was sick of accidents. And of men's vicious cruelties.

The thought of food made her ill, but Ashlee had to make an appearance. After overhearing her father's earlier conversation with Connor, and seeing her parent so upset, she needed to make sure he wasn't adversely affected by the day's events. Since her father had openly begun work again, he was nearly back to his old self.

Ashlee shook her head, recalling how she thought her father had been so depressed over his friends' deaths, when, in fact, he'd been almost as devastated over giving up his life's work.

Grimly she tossed off her soiled clothes and headed for the washbasin, hoping his decision to work again had been the right one.

She had just finished dressing when Blackie arrived to escort her to the galley. Excitedly, he babbled the entire way about the accident, the gory bodies, and praised her for her part in the chaotic rescue.

It seemed to take forever to reach their destination.

Taking a seat beside her father, she surreptitiously studied him. He looked a little weary, but not over tired, thank goodness. And he hadn't even noticed her arrival. He was too absorbed with Vivian, who sat on his other side.

Feeling a little left out, she glanced around. Only the captain, Blackie, and Joe were at the table, their expressions somber as they ate. Connor and Branden weren't about—and she assumed Harry had returned to his cabin. She knew Louise had. Blackie had mentioned the woman's bout with seasickness during their walk to the galley.

Straightening a napkin across her lap, she poured herself a cup of tea and took a sip. Her gaze fell on the vacant space Mr. Acres had occupied that morning.

The tea lodged in her throat. How thirsty the poor man must be by now. How hungry. She set the cup down, knowing she couldn't bear to eat while the first mate was doing without.

"Is there something wrong with the tea?"

She snapped around to see Connor standing behind her, and she fought the urge to punch his arrogant nose. How could any man be so beautiful and so cruel at the same time? Well, she wasn't going to hold back her opinion on the subject. "No. There's nothing wrong with the tea. I merely find it difficult to enjoy it knowing a member of your crew may be suffering from thirst or hunger at this very moment."

Her father was clearly surprised by her rude statement. For the most part, Ashlee was usually very dignified in mixed company, even when subjected to a distasteful situation.

Captain Tesh spoke up. "Miss Walker, Acres was—"

Connor held up his hand, silencing the man. "I'm sorry the unfortunate incident has spoiled your supper. Perhaps you'd prefer a tray brought to your quarters later?"

He was giving her an out, and with an apologetic look at her father and the others, she took it. "Yes. I believe I would. The strain of the day has taxed me beyond my limits." It wasn't true, but any excuse would suffice if it released her. She rose and nodded graciously. "I'll say good night, then."

"I'll say good night later," her father said, his expression still puzzled over her behavior, "after I check on the injured."

With a nod, she fled the room.

Connor watched the gentle sway of her hips as she

left. He was torn between the need to shake her for her scathing remarks, and the pride he felt for her unwavering dedication to others. She upset him and pleased him at every turn, which kept him completely unbalanced.

"Why didn't you tell her?" Aunt Vivian asked in that no-nonsense tone she used when irritated with him.

Hating to have to explain his actions to anyone, even his beloved aunt, he shrugged and sat down. "There's nothing to tell." He smiled at Nathaniel. "Pass the scones, would you?"

Vivian's fork hit her plate, her mouth open in astonishment. "Do you mean to tell me that you are going to allow her to believe—"

"Yes," he snapped, wishing his nosy aunt would mind her own business. He already felt bad enough. Never, in his entire adult life, had he ever rescinded a command, and he damned sure wasn't going to give Ashlcc the satisfaction of knowing shc was thc cause of his weakening, or that George Acres was, at this very moment, locked in the cargo hold, *suffering* over a plate of roasted chicken.

CHAPTER
10

Too edgy to remain in her cabin, Ashlee draped a light shawl around her shoulders and took a stroll. A scattering of lanterns cast eerie glows over the darkened deck. Woodsmoke from the stack mingled with the damp breeze, reminding her of her sixteenth birthday.

After much cajoling, she had convinced Father to allow her to have a party down at the cove. Charles had built an enormous fire on the sand, while Tilly had seen to the tables, chairs, decorations, entertainment, and the delicious roasted pig that had been cooked in a pit.

It had been a magical night with the sea wind in her hair and sand beneath her satin slippers as she shared the first dance in her young life with Stephen Frankenburg, the dashing son of a German family who'd recently moved to the area.

She placed a hand on the ship's rail and traced the smooth, polished teakwood with her finger, willing herself not to recall anything beyond that enchanting moment. But it didn't help. Her mind wandered to the last night she'd seen Stephen, just three months ago, to the disgrace she'd experienced . . . and to the vicious way she'd retaliated.

"Care if I join you?"

Startled, she whirled around to find Blackie standing close to the rail. "Good heavens. I didn't hear you approach."

"Sorry. I didn't mean to frighten you."

"It's not your fault. I was lost in my thoughts." She pulled her wrap closer, glad for the interruption. "And I'd be happy to have your company."

He nodded gallantly, but his handsome young face was somber. "I wanted to thank you for what you done earlier today. You saved me a heap of trouble."

"My pleasure," Ashlee said, keeping her expression neutral, not wanting to give Blackie any hint of what took place after he left. Still, her cheeks warmed in remembrance of Connor's fierce kiss.

Something moved off to her left, and she turned, catching a glimpse of Santos standing behind a flickering lantern . . . staring at her. Those dark, glittering eyes sent shivers racing over her flesh. The man frightened her to death. Suppressing a shudder, she returned her attention to Blackie. "So. How long do you think it will take us to reach the beach where we'll disembark to go overland?"

"Heard the captain tell Mr. Westfield it'd take about three days." He braced his elbows on the rail and looked out over the dark water. "Wish I could go with you into the swamps—especially after what I heard at the inn—but the captain won't let me. We gotta take the ship back to St. Augustine for repairs, then come back and wait for your party's return."

"What did you hear?"

"You know. About the ghost."

"What ghost?"

Blackie gave her a look that said she had to be jesting. "Surely you know about the Silver Witch."

"No, I'm afraid I don't."

His young chest puffed out with importance, then he leaned back against the rail and crossed his arms in a gesture usually associated with a more mature man. "You mean that Westfield's gonna take you off into them bayous and hasn't told you about the ghost?" Blackie shook his head. "That ain't right. There could be dangers . . ."

Ashlee was fast losing her patience. "Will you stop skirting the issue and tell me about it?"

His blue eyes gleamed with mischief. "Well. According to legend, there's a deserted house by the lake that's haunted."

A house by the lake? The same one Santos planned to take them to? Her uneasiness returned. "What makes you think it's haunted?"

"The legend."

"What legend?"

Blackie was silent for a long moment, then spoke with genuine seriousness. "It's about the people who once lived there. The story goes that a young woman ran away from her cruel husband, an English duke, to be with her lover. The lover was a man far beneath her class. A carpenter, I think. Anyway, when their ship was caught in a storm and went down, they had to swim for land. Actually, the legend claims that the man held on to her and swam for both of them. And that they came ashore in the same area we intend to unload."

He shrugged. "Anyway, none of the crew was ever seen again, and everyone figured they all drowned. But the two lovers survived. They wandered for days through the swamps, then finally came to a huge lake. Knowing everyone would think they died with the crew, and figurin' they wouldn't have to fear the woman's husband trying to track them anymore, they decided to stay there."

For some odd reason, Ashlee found herself laboring for breath. "What happened after that?"

"They built a grand house and lived in it for a year. During that time, they made friends with the Seminole Indians. The legend comes from them. Anyway, on the day of their first anniversary in the house, they just up and disappeared. Some say the swamp swallowed them for trespassing. But others say the woman's husband came. His men dragged the lover off into the bayous and killed him while the husband stayed behind to slit his wife's throat."

Cold chills swept her. *"Help me. Oh, somebody, please."* Ashlee sucked in a painful breath, trying to ignore the unexplained fear clawing at her nerves. "Wh-Why do they say the house is haunted?"

Blackie shoved his hands into his pockets. "'Cause the woman's ghost has been seen walking the swamps —looking for her lover. The Indians say she can't leave until she finds his body."

"What happened to her body?"

"No one knows."

Tugging her hair more securely over her scar, Ashlee tried to understand why she felt so anxious. "Why do they call her the Silver Witch?"

"Because the woman had silvery white hair, kinda like yours, and the day she disappeared, she was wearing a silver dress to celebrate their anniversary. The Seminole say she's still wearing the dress, even after a hundred years." He crossed his feet. "There's supposed to be more to the legend, but only the Indians know it."

Ashlee had the overwhelming urge to make him take back the tale. "Where did you hear this outrageous story?"

"I told you. In the inn. Me and Acres was having

supper in the common room when some dark-skinned old man joined us. He said he'd lived around these parts his whole life. Said his papa actually saw the Silver Witch once." Blackie shifted uncertainly. "I don't know if I believe it or not, but I could tell he did."

"Most of us would have difficulty believing that tale," Connor's deep voice rumbled from out of the darkness.

Ashlee whirled around to see him leaning against the rail, his arms crossed over his chest, his strong features half-shadowed, half-exposed, in the flickering lantern light.

Blackie snapped to attention. "Mr. Westfield. I didn't see you, sir. And I didn't mean no harm. I was just tellin' the lady . . ."

Connor was only half listening. His thoughts and eyes were on Ashlee. She looked incredible in the wavering light. Molten gold danced over her silver hair, blending delicate rays from the lanterns' flames and the moon in the silky strands. A soft breeze caught one lock and fluttered it against her scarred jaw, guarding it like a jealous lover. Her pale skin radiated against the black sky, emphasizing the long sweep of her throat and giving her an angelic, almost ethereal, appearance.

Those jewel eyes stared up at him from beneath a thick fringe of dark lashes, beckoning him and rejecting him at the same time.

"Mr. Snow, I'd like to have a private word with Miss Walker."

"Of course." Blackie nodded with respect, then sprinted off across the deck, nimbly leaping over coils of rope.

Connor smiled. Then he saw Santos, lurking in the shadows. Something about the man still unnerved him, left him with a compelling need to shield Ashlee from his dark presence. He drew her slim arm through his. "Come along. I'll walk you to your cabin."

She yanked her hand free. "I'm quite capable of walking without assistance."

Wanting to snatch the hand back, and her with it, he reluctantly stepped away. "Miss Walker, in the future, I must ask that you remain belowdecks after sundown. Though my men, for the most part, are a noble lot, moonlight and a beautiful woman would test the restraint of a priest. And I'd prefer not to keelhaul one of my crew for just being a man."

Her chest rose as she took a heavy breath, and he admired the way the material tightened over her soft curves.

"In that case, Mr. Westfield, for the remainder of the voyage, I shall remain in my cabin from sunset until dawn. Far be it from me to cause you to punish yet another man." Lifting her skirts—and her chin— she marched toward the stairs.

Connor clenched his teeth as he watched her walk away, wanting to shake her soundly . . . or make love to her. He just wasn't sure which would give him the most pleasure at the moment.

Ashlee gripped the wood railing as she climbed the steps that led to the deck. No matter how hard she tried, she couldn't stop thinking of Connor . . . especially at night when she was confined to her cabin. That was the worst time. The desolate hours when she could recall every small detail about him, from the way his eyes softened when he watched his aunt to how his smile warmed the day when he bantered with the men. Nor could she forget how exciting his lips had felt on hers, even though she'd been embarrassed to tears.

When she reached the top of the stairs and stepped into the sunshine, her gaze automatically scanned the deck. She spotted Connor standing near the wheel. His head was bent as he spoke to the captain. She noted the way the sun highlighted the mahogany strands in Connor's rich, dark hair.

"Land ho!"

Her gaze shot up to the man pointing from the crow's nest high above the sails.

Ashlee shaded her eyes and squinted. There, off in a hazy distance, a long black shape took form. Their destination. At last.

She moved to the railing, anxiously watching the proceedings that would soon put them on dry land. As the ship neared land, sails flapped, then collapsed, as bare-chested sailors yanked on ropes to lower the heavy canvas. Smoke bellowed from the stack. The engine lurched, then shuddered to a hissing halt.

Excited, she listened to a gurgling splash as the enormous anchor made contact with the ocean's surface.

"Get those longboats lowered and start loading!" Captain Tesh bellowed to no one in particular.

A bevy of crewmen scurried to do his bidding.

The deck burst into activity, and Ashlee took up an out-of-the-way spot near the bow that still afforded her a good view of the operation. At the opposite end of the railing, she caught a glimpse of Mrs. Delacorte, still looking pale from her seasickness.

Ashlee glanced around, wondering where Vivian was. When she didn't see her amid the chaos, she figured Connor's aunt was probably readying her belongings for their departure.

Father, she knew, was tending the recuperating sailors.

At that moment, Harry stepped into her line of vision shouldering a large sack of coal, and she smiled. He'd donned one of the crewmen's knit caps and stretched it down over one ear, concealing most of his scars.

"Over here, Harry!" Joe called out from the first longboat that was about to be lowered into the water. Together they added the sack to the hammers, stakes, and supplies that were already aboard.

Santos, standing beside Joe, steadied the vessel as Harry heaved the lumpy burlap bag over the rail, then climbed aboard. When the longboat was eased onto the water, they pushed off with Joe at the oars.

The sudden whinny of horses drew Ashlee's attention. She turned toward the cargo door to see Connor and Branden leading a pair of geldings onto the deck.

Snorting and prancing, the animals blinked in the sunlight as Connor secured a sling under one of the horses' bellies so it could be lowered into the water.

"Ready!" Connor yelled to a group of men gripping one end of a rope that was draped over a high, heavy beam. The other end was fastened to the sling.

Branden moved back, holding tightly to the other animal.

Awed, she watched Connor's muscles work as he climbed up onto the railing, then stood up, his smooth back gleaming with moisture in the afternoon sunlight. She couldn't tear her eyes away from him. He was magnificent, the image of masculine beauty.

She watched him dive overboard in one fluid motion, barely making a splash as he cut into the water.

He came up, slinging wet hair out of his eyes, then lifted a hand. "All right. Now!"

Branden signaled to the other men.

Amid shouts, curses, and grunts, the first horse was lowered into the water, where Connor quickly removed the sling and swam with the animal, guiding it toward dry land. Branden readied the next mount.

Released from the hold of Connor's presence,

Ashlee glanced up at the afternoon sun. No matter how fast the men worked, with ten horses and all those supplies to get ashore, they surely wouldn't be able to finish this day. She would have to spend another night on the ship—inside that lonely cabin.

She sent one last peek at Connor and was surprised to find him already on the shore, standing near his men, yet not assisting as he normally did. Instead, he had a curious look on his face as he stared across the broad expanse of sand toward a cluster of trees.

Her gaze drifted over the stretch of beach bordered by palm and cypress. Moss hung from the branches in a grayish green splendor. At the bases, flowers stretched toward the sunlight, bursting forth in a lovely array of yellows and lavenders. The beach was beautiful, yet something about it was eerily familiar. Almost sinister.

Uneasiness gripped Connor the instant he set foot on the shore. It was a strange sensation. Relief and terror mixed together, making him apprehensive, yet oddly excited. He couldn't imagine what he had to fear . . . or what it was about this place that gave him such an overwhelming feeling of expectation. Of familiarity. But whatever it was, it held him transfixed. And he knew it had something to do with what lay beyond the trees.

Shaking off the queer feeling, he forced his attention back to the work at hand. There was too much to do for him to stand around daydreaming. Grabbing a stake and mallet, he began pounding the wooden peg into the sand. When he finished, he tied the gelding's reins to the stake, then turned toward the ship.

Seeing Ashlee leaning over the rail, watching intently, he smiled. Even though she was still angry at him, she couldn't hide her attraction. He'd felt her eyes on him when he dove in the water. The warmth from that look had sent him plunging prematurely into the cold water before his body's response became public.

Realizing he was dawdling again, he set to work.

By the time the sun met the horizon, Connor was drenched in sweat and ached in places he hadn't known were part of his body. In desperate need of a bath, he ordered the first hand he saw on deck to bring hot water, then staggered down the steps to his cabin.

Using his shirt to mop at the perspiration coating his face, he opened the door and stepped inside. He froze. Slowly, warily, he lowered the shirt.

Seeing Ashlee sitting stark naked in his tub with her arms shielding her breasts trapped his breath somewhere in his throat. "What are you doing?" he managed in a hoarse croak.

She looked like a frightened sparrow. "I—I—" She swallowed. "I didn't expect you back so soon. And I wanted to bathe before we left for the swamps tomorrow. I-It's going to be several days before we reach the house Santos spoke of, and I knew it would be my last chance to have a decent bath for a while." She sank lower in the tub. "I didn't mean to intrude, and if you'll step out for a moment, I'll be on my way in no time."

Having regained his composure—and humor—while she talked, he dropped the shirt. "Don't bother. I'll join you." He reached for the buttons on his breeches. It was all he could do to keep from laughing when she squealed in protest and put out a hand as if to halt him. She couldn't leave the tub without exposing herself, nor could she stop him from joining her.

It served her right for all the way she'd ignored him over the last few days.

"Connor, please," she whimpered, her eyes wide as she watched him inch his breeches down.

He stopped and arched a brow. "If you really don't want me to join you, then get out."

"I will! Just leave for a minute."

"No." She was beginning to panic—and he loved it.

"Th-Then turn around," she pleaded.

"No."

"Oh, God," she cried, her eyes shimmering with tears as she looked around in terror.

Suddenly the game didn't seem so funny anymore. "Ashlee, I was only teas—"

"Please, Connor. *Please.*" Tears slid down her cheeks. "I couldn't bear your ridicule."

It took him a moment to realize she was talking about her scars. His heart softened. "I wouldn't do that to you, sweetheart. I couldn't. No matter how angry you made me."

She swiped at a tear with her dripping hand. "Don't take me for a fool. I've heard that particular vow before."

Anger held him immobile as the implication of that remark sank in. *Someone had callously taunted her because of her flaws. What kind of heartless vermin could do that to such a lovely woman?*

Furious, he stalked to the door. "You've got five minutes." His rage barely held in check, he stormed out.

He paced the deck for at least a quarter hour, cursing her for arousing instincts in him he hadn't even known he possessed. At last, certain she must have vacated his cabin by now, he headed belowdecks. His quarters were empty—and so was the tub. At its base sat buckets of fresh hot water.

Tired and still irritated, he filled the vessel and peeled off his remaining clothes.

Half an hour later, dressed in a fresh white shirt and clean black breeches, he headed for the galley.

"Well, Connor, I see you've at long last seen fit to

make an appearance," Aunt Vivian remarked, setting down a cup of tea. "For a while there, I wondered if the day's work had been too much for you—or that you'd abandoned me in this hellishly humid country."

He smiled and kissed her perspiration-dampened cheek. "Never, Nanna." He took a seat opposite her. "And as dirty as I was, I'm sure you wouldn't have appreciated my company." Glancing around at the vacant table, he frowned. "Where is everyone?"

"The others have already eaten and retired."

"Ashlee, too?"

"I saw Blackie carrying a tray to her quarters, just like he's been doing for the last few days. What happened between you two, anyway?"

As much as he loved his aunt, he damned sure didn't want her meddling in his affairs. "Nothing. Did Branden eat?"

"Yes. But as usual, he came to the table alone. Louise still claims to feel queasy." She shook her head, causing a springy curl near her ear to bounce. "I will never understand the animosity between those two. They were so happy when they first married."

"I know," Connor said, wondering again what had caused the problem between them. Soon after their wedding, Branden began to change. Uneasy, Connor recalled that it was during that time when Louise first started flirting with him—had formed an attraction to him that enraged Branden and sickened Connor.

The sound of footsteps in the hall drew Ashlee to the cabin door, and she opened it just a crack. Surprised to see Santos standing on the other side, looking as if he was about to knock, she flung the panel wider. "Yes?"

The guide stepped back, then dipped his dark head in greeting but didn't meet her eyes. "The captain asked me to inform everyone we'll be ready to load their personal trunks by ten tomorrow morning."

Everything about the man made her nervous. "I see." She watched him a moment, then decided perhaps a normal conversation with him might rid her of her anxiety. "How much farther is it to our destination, Mr. Santos?"

"There's no 'mister' in front of my name. And we should reach the lake in a day or two, discounting unforeseen setbacks."

"Setbacks? What kind?"

He shrugged, but still didn't meet her eyes. "Thick reeds, bogs, alligators, snakes, many things."

Alligators? Snakes? "Is the house in decent shape? I mean, is it livable?"

"I don't know. I've never been inside it."

That surprised her. "Didn't you say it was deserted?"

"Yes."

"Then why haven't you been inside?"

He flicked a quick glance at her, then lowered his gaze. "It's not a good place for a man of my heritage."

"What heritage is that?"

"Seminole."

Somehow she'd known that. "What could your heritage possibly have to do with going inside a deserted building?"

He looked grim. "Over the years there have been tales of those who entered and what happened. I don't know all of them, but I do know of one." He at last met her eyes. "One brave didn't believe there was anything to fear from the specter and wanted to prove it. So, against the elders' warnings, he went in."

"Did he see the ghost?"

He seemed startled by her knowledge for an instant, then shrugged. "No one knows. He was found on the veranda the next morning. Dead."

She sucked in a sharp breath. "How did he die?"

"Again, no one knows. There were no marks on the body. No visible reason for his death at all."

"Are you certain? Did you see him?"

"I saw him, all right. I found him."

Ashlee couldn't stop the wave of sympathy that overcame her. "You poor man. No wonder you're frightened. But I know there are many factors that could explain the mysterious death that have nothing to do with ghostly apparitions or haunted houses. The brave might have had an ailment for some time that no one knew about."

"No, he didn't."

"How do you know?"

Those black eyes narrowed. "He was my father."

"Oh, Santos. I'm so sorry." In a gesture meant to comfort, she placed a hand on his arm. "I didn't realize—"

He jerked back, his face contorted with horror. "Don't touch me," he half demanded, half pleaded. "Don't *ever* touch me again." With a look of pure terror, he whirled around and fled the corridor as if the flames of hell had reached up to ensnare him for all eternity.

Confused, and just a little concerned, she closed the door and leaned her forehead against the cool wood. It was as though her mere touch had unhinged the man. What on earth was wrong with him? He couldn't possibly fear someone as unthreatening as herself. Could he?

CHAPTER
11

Unnerved by her encounter with Santos, Ashlee found it difficult to sleep, and it was near dawn before she succumbed to the pull of slumber. But it seemed as if she'd just closed her eyes when a loud pounding rattled her door.

"Miss Walker?" Blackie's familiar voice called out. "I brought a tray for you."

Instantly alert, she slipped into a robe and opened the door. "Thank you. That's kind of you. But I'd planned on joining the others this morning."

"The others already ate. 'Bout an hour ago. West-field figured you was packing, so he had me fetch this." He held out the tray.

She took the tray and walked back inside, setting it on the bureau, trying not to feel pleased by Connor's thoughtfulness. "An hour ago? What time is it?"

"Quarter to ten."

"Are you sure?"

"Yes, ma'am."

She tried not to groan in his presence. "I must have

overslept." Glancing at the inviting meal, then to the clothes she'd been too distraught to pack the previous night, she sighed. "Thank you, Blackie. And tell Mr. Westfield my trunk will be ready to load shortly."

"Aye, miss. But I'll tell him to have the men load your things last." With a quirky smile, he left.

By the time the first crewman arrived a half hour later, Ashlee had thrown her garments into trunks and pulled on a lightweight burgundy riding habit. She wasn't very excited about spending the next day or two in the heat that would probably ruin all of her clothes, but there was little she could do about it.

Connor and the others were waiting onshore when the longboat she'd ridden in glided up onto the sand. The odor of brine drifted on the moist wind that dampened her exposed cheek and ruffled the hair covering her scarred one.

"Ashlee, love," her father called, his polished boots kicking up little puffs of sand as he strode toward her. "I was beginning to wonder if you'd decided to stay aboard the ship."

"I'm afraid I overslept." She cast Connor a fleeting glance, but he had his back to her, staring at something farther up the beach.

"Well, come along, daughter. We're ready to leave." With a steady hand, her father gripped her waist and lifted her over the side of the longboat, setting her feet firmly on the sand.

Warmth seeped into the satin slippers she'd chosen to wear for the sake of coolness, and she turned to follow. She stopped and stared.

Only one horse remained without a rider. "Where's the other one?"

Everyone glanced at Connor for a response.

He busied himself tightening a cinch on the riderless horse. "I sent a man up north with it. The, er, animal didn't fare well on the voyage."

"But how—"

"We'll ride double," he answered.

Those wretched tingles quivered through her belly. Ashlee didn't want to ride with Connor. The mere idea made her dizzy. "Let Vivian ride with you. I'll ride with Father . . . or Joe . . . or Harry."

"If I had my way, Aunt Vivian wouldn't be on a horse at all, especially in this damp heat."

"Stop scowling," his aunt scolded. "I've ridden horses all my life, and the humidity here isn't any worse than in Charleston." She glanced at Ashlee. "And I prefer to ride with Nathaniel so we can . . . discuss my illness."

Ashlee looked to Joe for support.

Connor stepped in her way. "We've spent the last half hour sorting out the riding arrangements, Ashlee. We're not going to change them now to suit your whim. Now, come on." He took her arm and marched her to his horse, then grabbed her waist and lifted her sidesaddle over the pommel. He turned to the others. "All set?"

Her father nodded, then mounted behind Vivian.

Ashlee fumed at Connor's high-handedness, but kept her mouth shut. Besides, what could she say? Evidently the others were in complete agreement with the bossy Mr. Westfield.

Santos eyed the group, then headed across the sand in a slow trot.

As he looped his arms around either side of her to gather the reins, Connor's chest pressed into Ashlee's side. The close contact was nerve-racking. Her riding habit all of a sudden became too warm, and she could feel beads of moisture tickling the valley between her breasts.

In an effort to take her mind off her discomfort, she trained her eyes on the scenery just ahead, on the dark, forbiding swamp they would soon enter.

How different the southern Florida territory was from St. Augustine, she thought with a blend of unease and amazement. The region was so pure and clean, so unspoiled. So beautiful yet intimidating. And the trees—every one, from oak to cypress, had strings of pale olive moss hanging majestically. The spongelike streamers made the trees look as though they were weeping. Around every bend, there were small lakes or eerie algae-infested pools speared with limber reeds.

"I'm not going to survive this," Louise grumbled. "I'll be nothing but a mass of bumps and bruises by the time we arrive." She shifted on the saddle in front of her husband, then slapped at a mosquito on her neck.

Ashlee tried not to smile when she saw Vivian place a hand over her mouth as if to hide a giggle.

Joe and Harry, riding behind the Delacortes, made no effort to hold their grins in check.

Ashlee didn't agree with Louise. In fact, the rocking motion of the horse against the cushion of Connor's thighs made her quite comfortable. Too comfortable. In the sultry heat, she was beginning to feel drowsy and was fighting the urge to lean into Connor's broad chest. . . .

"This is scandalous. Why, in London, I'd be banished from the ton for swimming with a gentleman in nothing more than this bit of silk." She plucked at the wet chemise clinging to her skin. Warm water lapped at her ribs. "And with a naked gentleman, at that."

Beau laughed. "Oh, little witch. After what we did, this is quite tame." He nuzzled her ear with his wet mouth. "But I'm not."

Shivers rippled along her flesh, and she leaned her head back to more fully enjoy his wicked meanderings. Below the water, his hands felt like velvet as they lovingly stroked up and down her thighs, gaining ground under her chemise with each upward swipe until his thumbs brushed the swell of her breasts. Tiny wings fluttered through her most vital parts.

She could smell the moist, spicy scent of his hair as he bent to gently nibble her neck. Water swirled erotically between the small space separating their lower bodies.

His hands glided down her naked sides, then up again to fully encompass her bare breasts beneath the silk. Fire shot through the tips, then arrowed down to ignite a low flame in the smoldering place between her thighs. It burned with pleasure. "Love me, Beau. I want to touch heaven with you."

An indrawn breath and the gentle tearing of cloth was his answer. He slid the useless chemise from her shoulders, exposing her breasts to his starving gaze. With a low, masculine groan, he caught one tight peak in his mouth and ravished it with tender savagery, while his fingers disappeared below the water to explore the shape of her bottom . . . and the sensitive valley beneath.

The feel of his hot mouth nursing so eagerly made her weak. But when his water-slick fingers stroked her secret place, she cried out at the exquisite torment.

"Burn for me, sweet witch," he moaned against her aching crest. "Burn until the fires of pleasure consume us both." He eased a long, slender finger inside her.

It was too much. Her back arched as sweet pain stabbed her center. "Beau!" She erupted in a scalding explosion of honey-coated lava.

Her cry of fulfillment wasn't enough for him. He mercilessly worshiped her again and again, with every part of his beautiful body, bringing her to peak after magnificent peak until she lay limp and breathless in his arms.

"You've given me heaven," he murmured against her lips, his breath ragged yet husky. He lifted her from the *water and laid her on the sand. "Now I want to explore the mysteries of hell." With hungry intent, he slid down her quivering form, leaving a trail of hot little kisses before he lowered his mouth over the valley between her thighs.*

Her body burst into flames.

Ashlee gasped and blinked, only then realizing that Connor had wrapped one of his arms around her waist, and her cheek was nestled against his chest. She shot into an upright position.

He chuckled. "Having a nightmare, sweetheart?" His gaze slid down to the tight peaks of her breasts jutting against the bodice of her jacket, and his eyes darkened. "Or maybe not."

She crossed her arms protectively. "Stop calling me that, and let me off this horse," she demanded through gritted teeth. "Right this minute."

"I can't."

"And why not, pray tell?"

He shifted, and a firm warmth nudged her thigh. "I'm afraid the little moans and whimpers you made in your sleep affected me sorely." He brought his lips closer to her ear. "I'd give a handful of gold to know what you dreamt of." He brushed his thumb over the underswell of her breast.

Flames licked up her cheeks, and she closed her eyes, praying for death to rescue her from the killing humiliation. It didn't. Grasping a shred of courage, she slapped Connor's hand away and stiffened her spine. "Don't ever speak to me again."

"Talking isn't always necessary," he murmured warmly, then brought his palm back to her belly, easing his long fingers upward.

Ashlee's breath caught at Connor's audacity—and her body's own traitorous response. Fire speared through her nipples. Heat slithered into her lower stomach. Frantically she sought a way to stop him without causing a scene in front of the others. "Please," she pleaded urgently. "Don't do this to me."

He stopped the movement of his finger just short of the peak he wanted so badly to explore. But her plea cooled his lust quicker than a dip in the North Sea.

He withdrew his hand, angry at her for enticing him, however unintentional. "If you don't want to invite my advances, Miss Walker, then move forward and keep that seductive little body of yours out of my reach. I'm only a man, after all—not some saint."

He felt her gasp of outrage all the way to his bones, but he refused to take back the words. Because he knew they were true. She did tempt him at every turn.

"What is it, dear?" Vivian asked as she and Nathaniel rode up next to them.

"I-I . . . something must have startled me." Ashlee's cheeks grew bright, and she clasped her hands to stop their trembling.

Connor felt a stirring of shame at the callous way he'd treated her—and for the way she was having to explain herself now because of him.

"I guess I was daydreaming. . . ." She gave a weak smile. "About our destination."

"Must have been some dream," Branden remarked, riding up on the other side of them, his eyes on her chest.

She again folded her arms over her front. "Yes, it was. I was swimming . . . in *cold* water."

Branden's teeth flashed in a disbelieving smile.

Connor wanted to rearrange them for him.

"That sounds more like a nightmare," Aunt Vivian said, giving a delicate shudder.

Louise gave a low snort and shifted farther away from her husband. "The notion you have about water being unhealthful, Vivian, especially bathwater—is absurd. If that were the case, your beloved nephew would be dead by now." She cut her eyes to Ashlee. "Both of us know how much he enjoys a long, hot soak."

Connor tensed.

A muscle in Branden's jaw started to throb.

The implication that Louise had firsthand knowledge of Connor's intimate routine made Ashlee want to pull the woman's hair out, with excruciating slowness.

"Men have much stronger constitutions than women," Vivian said in an attempt to calm the explosive situation.

Louise gave a bark of laughter. "In old wives' tales, perhaps." She flicked a sultry glance at Connor. "Men may have much stronger muscles, but women are stronger inside. How else could they endure the ordeal of childbirth and survive?" She lowered a hand to her stomach and gave a smug, secret smile.

Branden's eyes glittered dangerously.

Connor frowned.

Ashlee was at a complete loss. She had no idea what was going on between Connor and the Delacortes. And she wasn't sure she wanted to know.

Connor waited until the last of the tents was set up before he grabbed a towel and headed for the pond he'd found. The day's ride with Ashlee so close had wreaked havoc with his control. Just the faintest scent of her warm woman's flesh made him break out in a sweat. Thank Providence they'd arrive tomorrow. He couldn't last much longer.

Seeing the other men busy with the fire, and the women preparing supper, he slipped into the trees and made for the pool.

Unsure what lay beneath the surface of the reed-infested basin, he removed his clothes and waded with caution into the green, tepid water. Finding nothing threatening, he sat down and leaned back on his elbows, admiring the diamond-studded sky.

Crickets, frogs, and an occasional crow filled the night with nature's sounds, and he let his mind wander back to the events that took place before Ashlee had joined them on the beach that morning.

He had ordered a pair of crewmen to bring George Acres from the hold. As hateful as Ashlee had been over the man's supposed punishment, he wouldn't give her the satisfaction of seeing the bastard set loose, nor could he bear to see her gloat over the fact she'd bent him, Connor, to her will.

Acres had still been squinting in the sunlight when the crewmen brought him ashore. After this day, Connor never wanted to set eyes on the son of a bitch again.

"Take this horse," he'd ordered, shoving the reins at the former first mate. "Leave it in St. Augustine. And from this day forward, stay out of my way."

Acres's hate-filled eyes met Connor's. "You bloody coxswain. After what ye put me through in that rat-infested hold, the next time I see ye, I'll cut your black heart out."

Connor was surprised. He figured the man would be grateful. "Then we'll make it a point to avoid each other. Now, get the hell out of here."

Awkwardly the man dragged himself onto a saddleless horse, then whirled the animal around and rode off.

Connor stared after him.

"I'd watch my back if I were you, Mr. Westfield," Joe warned as he strolled up beside him. "That man has a real mean streak, and you've made an enemy of him."

"By not setting him adrift?"

"By putting him in that hold. He hates dark places.

I heard tell that his papa used to punish him by locking him in a cellar. Acres killed him for it. And I think he plans to kill you, too."

"He said he murdered his father?" Connor couldn't keep the disbelief from his voice.

"No. Blackie did. Seems him and Acres talked when the lad took him his meals. Acres confessed to the deed, then made his displeasure and intentions toward you quite clear. The boy asked me to make sure you knew."

Connor considered Joe's tale, then lifted a careless shoulder. "Thank you—and Blackie—for your concern, and I'll certainly watch my back if I ever see him again, which I doubt." He watched Acres a moment longer, then turned to see a longboat gliding toward them, carrying Ashlee and her trunk. "At last." He smiled, then motioned to the group. "Mount up. We're just about ready . . ."

A crow screeched, jarring him back to the present, and he sat up. Scanning the night-darkened pond, he dipped his hands in the inky water and began washing. When he'd finished, he straightened and shoved the hair out of his eyes. It took a while for him to realize something was wrong. The night sounds . . . they had all stopped.

An anxious shudder swept over him, and he slowly rose out of the water, his naked body tightening with chills. It became hard to breathe. His heart picked up speed as he watched the trees. Waiting.

Then he saw it. The transparent figure of a woman . . . dressed in silver.

CHAPTER
12

Held motionless, Connor could only stare. His thoughts suddenly became disoriented, distorted. . . .

"I love you, Beau. I love you so deeply, it frightens me." She stood with her back to him, her naked body flushed from their lovemaking and bathed in moonlight, a shimmering silver against the dark, moss-draped cypress. *"I've never known such complete happiness, such fierce pleasure. But those feelings terrify me. I'm so afraid of losing them. Of losing you."*

"Nothing will ever separate us, duchess. It can't. We ceased being two people the day our eyes first met. In that moment, our souls touched, and we became one. We are, and always will be, inseparable."

She faced him, her eyes bright with tears of joy.

His own stung, and he lifted a beckoning hand. There weren't enough words to describe his love for this woman.

Their fingers touched, then entwined. Neither of them moved. They were one. One heartbeat, one breath, one soul.

"Connor, darling, where are you?" Louise's voice cut into the stillness.

Whirling around, Connor saw her just as she stepped from behind a cluster of wild coffee bushes.

"Oh." Her eyes widened, then drifted over him with blatant interest. She smiled. "Waiting for me?"

He shot a glance back across the pond, to the place where he'd seen the ghost, wondering if his mind was playing tricks on him, or if there really was an inkling of truth to the legend of the Silver Witch.

The wraith was gone—whether real or imagined.

Disappointed, and completely ignoring Louise, he stalked to the shore and dragged on his breeches, then faced his friend's wife. "What the hell do you want?"

"You," she said brazenly. "Why else would I traipse through this ghastly bog, if not to spend a fleeting moment alone with the man I desire above all others?"

Connor had met a lot of bold women in his life, but this one far surpassed the others. And it was time she received the setdown she so well deserved. "Louise, you are without a doubt the—"

"Wife of another," Branden injected, his voice frosty, his eyes alight with battle as he stepped from the shelter of a shaded copse. "And you, Westfield, would do well to remember that." Grabbing her arm, he marched her back toward camp.

Fury skipped through Connor at Branden's refusal to see that he was not enticing Louise, but he couldn't hold on to the thought. Not now. His gaze again searched the trees. Had he really seen the Silver Witch? Or was it a trick of the moonlight?

Ashlee watched as Branden stalked into camp, dragging Louise along with him, his expression murderous. They had come from the same direction she'd seen Connor disappear earlier. Her fingers tightened on the tent door covering. *Connor and Louise?*

"What are you staring at, dear?" Vivian asked.

"Nothing. I was just wondering where Connor had gotten off to."

"Mmm. Bathing, most likely. That man has an obsession with cleanliness."

So did she, but she'd made do with a pail of water from the rain barrel. Of course, she hadn't planned a rendezvous with anyone, either. She dropped the netting back into place, then crossed to her own pallet and sat down, dragging a pillow over her lap. She rested her arms on the softness. "Have Branden and Connor known each other a long time?"

"Almost a score of years. They met in their youth and have been fast friends ever since."

Some friends. "I imagine they've known Louise a long time, too."

"No. Branden met her last year when her family moved to Charleston. She had him entwined around her finger before he could pronounce his own name. He was besotted with her." She lowered her mending to her lap and stared at the doorway, her voice filled with dismay. "He wouldn't listen to well-meaning companions who tried to tell him of her family's dire financial straights, and how desperate she was to marry someone of consequence." Sadness deepened the fine lines of Vivian's face. "He was so sure she loved him as much as he did her."

"But she didn't love him, did she?" Ashlee ventured. "She was in love with Connor."

"I couldn't say. But I do know that she and Connor never met until the day of the wedding. Connor was Branden's best man." Sadness shadowed her eyes. "Those two have gone from best friends to enemies in the scant six months since."

"Enemies?" Ashlee wasn't surprised. She'd felt the tension between them. "Why?"

"I don't know. But whatever the problem is, it's very real. They were going to duel the day I had my attack."

"Duel?" Visions of Connor lying on the ground, his shirt covered in blood, unsettled Ashlee. "That's barbaric."

"Dear, when men are hurting, civilized behavior doesn't enter into it." She traced the row of neat stitches on her skirt. "I'm only glad the good Lord saw fit to stop the nonsense before I lost one of those I love so dearly."

"But it isn't over yet, is it?"

"No. And it won't be until their differences are settled—whatever they are."

Ashlee had a fair idea, but kept silent. After all, she could be wrong about Connor and Louise. Maybe.

Connor would rather face the gallows than ride the rest of the distance with Ashlee so close at hand. The sweltering, muggy air was like trying to breathe soup, but it didn't stop her intoxicating scent from seeping into his lungs and stirring unwanted images.

Even though her perspiration-stained clothes were ruined, and her hair so damp it curled, it didn't matter. She was still the most beautiful woman he'd ever had the misfortune to desire. He could only thank Providence she'd tried to keep her distance from him.

With her spine rigid, and her bottom scooted as far up on the saddle as humanly possible, they might as well have been riding separate horses . . . if it hadn't been for her dizzying scent. That was driving him crazy.

Needing a moment away from her, he abruptly halted his mount and swung down.

"What's wrong?" Nathaniel asked, reining up beside them. Curious, the others came to a stop.

Connor waved them on. "I just need to make some adjustments. We'll catch up in a minute."

"What kind of adjustment?" Ashlee asked as the rest of their party rode past.

Connor tried to come up with an explanation, while noticing a trickle of perspiration trailing down her throat. She looked damned uncomfortable—just like she was making him. At least he could do something about her problem, if not his own. He offered her a hand. "Come on. Get down."

When she stood next to him, swiping at the dust on her skirt, he withdrew a knife from his bedroll and cut a strip of leather from one of the ties on his saddle. "Take off that riding jacket," he commanded.

"What?"

"Just do it, Ashlee. It's too hot to debate the matter."

Keeping her wary eyes on him, she unbuttoned the lightweight linen and slipped it off.

"Now turn around."

"Why?"

"I'm going to tie your hair up off your neck."

She crossed her arms and took a step back. "No."

He advanced, the leather draped across his palm. "Yes."

Her hand flew up to ward him off. "C-Connor, please. I can't."

The anxiety in her tone stopped him cold. Then he knew why she was so concerned. The scar on her face. His voice softened. "I'm not going to let you roast to death because of a small imperfection."

"It's not sm—"

"Turn around."

"Connor—"

He spun her around and gathered a handful of silky hair. The strands came to life beneath his fingers. "Don't say another word," he warned, fighting his own demons. He wanted to bury his face in the silvery curls, spread them out on a pillow. . . . Furious at his own wayward thoughts, he quickly tied the leather around the hair high on the crown, then gathered the ends and tucked them under the strip.

He inspected his handiwork. "That's better."

Tears of embarrassment shimmered in her blue-green eyes.

Compassion filled him, and he gently traced the scar from temple to jaw. "This doesn't take away from your beauty, sweetheart. Nothing could do that."

Her lips parted in a soundless gasp.

His pulse picked up speed. All he could think of was taking that tempting mouth. Again and again. He snatched his hand back. "We'd better go before the others start worrying."

Ashlee was withdrawn and quiet when he tucked her jacket into his bedroll and helped her mount. Her vulnerability tugged at his heartstrings. He wanted to hold her, comfort her . . . and so much more. Hoping he could keep a rein on his desire until they reached their destination, he eased back a bit, trying not to inhale her sweet fragrance—not to want her.

But it wasn't to be. Every hour, every plod of the horse's hooves, tested his restraint. Even the chatter of the others just ahead of them didn't distract him from the tempting curves just inches from his hands, the slim throat just a breath away from his lips. Swallowing, he reminded himself it was only a few more miles.

"Stop!" Santos's voice erupted.

Startled, and grateful for the disruption, Connor hauled in on the reins.

The guide's hand was in the air to halt the party as

his horse reared. Only Santos's expert handling kept the gelding in check.

"What's wrong?" Nathaniel called out.

"What is it?" Branden demanded from where he'd ridden up beside them.

Santos glanced at the women and seemed to hesitate. "A few obstacles in the path." Dismounting, he motioned for the men to join him.

"Well? What is it?" Branden demanded.

"Alligators."

Connor slapped a mosquito on his bare forearm. "You stopped because of alligators when we could just go around them?"

"There is no around."

"What the hell do you mean?" Branden grumbled.

Santos gestured for them to follow.

Nathaniel, Harry, and Joe tagged along.

When they reached the reeds they'd been about to enter, the guide separated the willows with his hands. "See that narrow strip of dry land bordered on either side by swamp? That's our only way through this part of the bayou without going several miles out of our way."

Connor shaded his eyes and squinted into the shadows. The finger of land Santos had indicated was there, all right, but it was blocked by the slow, squirming bodies of a dozen alligators. "Couldn't we fire our weapons and frighten them off? Or kill them?"

"Gators don't frighten easily," the Seminole countered. "And there are too many of them. Others would return before we could cross."

"What are we going to do?" Joe asked anxiously.

"Wait them out. We'll try it after they've gone back into the water."

"How long will that take?" Branden inquired, his eyes still on the menacing reptiles.

Santos shrugged. "Could be minutes . . . or days.

Either way, we'll have to wait. I'm not about to antagonize one of them."

"When they leave the path, will it be safe to cross?" Harry wanted to know, his single eye wide with apprehension.

"No. We'll have to walk the horses over as silently as possible, and pray we don't rouse one of them from the water."

Connor sent a glance toward the women. Ashlee stood near Vivian, with her flushed face turned away from Louise, a hand covering the scar on her jaw.

Louise's mouth was tilted into a taunting sneer.

It didn't take a genius to know Louise had said something insulting to Ashlee. Furious, Connor swung back to the men. "It might be a good idea to keep this quiet until it's time. No sense worrying the ladies." Ashlee had endured enough upset.

Nathaniel nodded in agreement, then peered again at the alligators. "They look to be set for the night, and since it is so late, perhaps we should make camp."

"Not here," Santos countered. "We'll go back a half mile or so, to the dry forest we just came through."

"Won't we still be in danger?" Joe asked.

"I doubt it. The alligators probably won't wander far from the water."

"What'll we tell the ladies?" Harry asked.

Connor glanced at Nathaniel. "The truth. The path is blocked, and we can't move until it's cleared—and it's too dangerous to camp near water."

"We'll need wood," Branden remarked, waving a mosquito away from his face.

"When we reach the campsite, I'll get it while you and the others set up the tents," Connor offered. With everyone in agreement, they headed back to the horses.

Ashlee met him as he approached. "What's going on?"

Noticing the way she kept her scarred cheek turned away from him, he sighed. "Nothing. Just some debris that needs to be cleared from the trail. We'll take care of it tomorrow. And since it's so late, we're going back a ways to make camp."

Once they'd chosen an area, and started preparations, Connor grabbed an ax from the mound of supplies and started for the woods.

Ashlee clutched his arm. "Where are you going?"

His skin grew hot where she touched him. "To cut wood." The warmth was seeping downward, and he had a sudden desire to be alone with her. Completely alone. His eyes sought hers. "Come with me."

As if she'd read his thoughts, she sucked in a breath and jerked her hand away. "I-I've got to help Vivian." Whirling around, she raced to join the others.

He watched her swaying skirt, then hoisted the ax over his shoulder and strolled off toward the trees. With each step, he reminded himself he was glad she'd rejected his hasty offer.

With her hair again in place and replete from the evening meal, Ashlee watched her companions from where she sat by the dying fire. The Delacortes and Joe had already retired, thank goodness. Another taunt from Louise would have broken Ashlee's restraint. She should have never listened to Connor.

Beneath a lantern hung from a post, Vivian was perched on a log, while Connor sat on the ground nearby, his legs folded in front of him as he watched Harry and her father play checkers.

Light from the lantern danced over the lean lines of Connor's handsome face. Although he wore a shirt, the front hung open almost to his navel, revealing a healthy portion of his sweat-dampened chest. Droplets played through the silky forest coating his bronze skin, before the dark trail disappeared. She was very, very glad she'd refused to accompany him into the woods alone earlier. She just wasn't strong enough to ignore all that blatant maleness.

Unconsciously she fingered a lock of hair covering her scar, recalling Connor's gentle words and easy acceptance of the disfigurement. She'd been in a euphoric daze most of the day, thinking about how his reactions had been so different from Stephen Frankenburg's. Memories of the night she broke off their engagement rose, but she forced them away. She didn't want to think of that ever again. She lifted her gaze . . . only to have it collide with Connor's.

Without a word spoken between them, she knew what he wanted. It was there for everyone to see. That smoldering look cried out his need to touch her, to make her his in every way.

Her body gave an answering throb. Startled by her own reaction, she rose. "I-If you'll excuse me—" she nodded to the others "—I find I'm quite exhausted." Not waiting for a reply, she hurried to the tent she shared with Vivian. It was her sanctuary. The one place Connor's powerful presence couldn't reach her.

Striking a flint to a lantern, she stripped off her clothes, trying not to think about Connor. Damp air moved over her bare flesh, giving her a moment's relief. She lifted her arms over her head and stretched, then blew out the light and slid between the cool sheets on her pallet.

For a long time she lay there, trying not to notice how the linen felt against her naked skin. How every breath she took shifted the material over the tips of her breasts, reminding her of the way Connor's hand had felt. The memory sent pricks of desire straight to the area between her thighs.

She closed her eyes, trying to ignore the sensations,

but it only served to heighten them. Curse Connor for looking at her like he had and making her want what he was so obviously offering.

A small noise, almost imperceptible, pierced the darkness of the tent.

She clutched the sheet to her chest and sat up. "Vivian?"

"I've been mistaken for a lot of things in my life," Connor said quietly. "But never a female."

"What are you doing in here?" she hissed. "Where are Vivian and the others?"

"Everyone's retired except your father and my aunt." He knelt beside her, so close she could feel the heat radiate from his skin. "They're in Nathaniel's tent . . . enjoying a private game of checkers."

Her nerve endings went crazy. "C-Connor, why are you here?"

He leaned over, his mouth so close to hers, she could feel the moistness of his breath. "I think you know the answer to that, little witch—especially after that enticing display."

She pressed back, trying to gain some distance from the tempting mouth so close to her own. "What display?"

She felt more than saw his smile. "Let's just say your come-hither look, along with your naked silhouette on the wall of your tent, served its purpose."

The breath left her. "I didn't— You can't come in here and— *You can't do this.*"

"Do what?" he asked, his tone too innocent. "Touch you?" He laid his palm on her stomach over the sheet, spreading fire through every inch of her body. She fell back onto her elbows, too shaken to speak.

His hand slid down her thigh, then upward, stopping just below her breast. "Caress you?"

Flames licked through her, and she couldn't breathe. Couldn't form a thought.

"Kiss you?" he breathed against her lips.

Tingles exploded through her nervous system. "Connor, no," she managed in a weak plea.

It was no use. He took her mouth, then gently, oh so gently, filled her with his tongue. "You make me burn, Ashlee," he whispered against her lips. "Every time I get near you, my body goes up in flames." He trailed his thumb over the tip of her breast.

Her mind screamed for him to stop, but her lips refused to form the words. Pleasure streaked from her nipple to spots much lower. At last she found her voice. "Connor! Stop! I—mmm."

He took her mouth again, his kiss fierce, erotic, while his thumb continued its devastating torture.

The game was lost. She knew it, and he knew it.

As passionate in defeat as she was in battle, she slid her arms around his neck, parted her lips more fully, and met the fiery pressure of his tongue with her own.

"Connor? Connor, where are you?" Louise's voice penetrated the canvas walls. "Branden's finally asleep, and I was able to get away."

Every muscle in Ashlee's body went rigid. She whipped her head to the side and shoved at Connor's chest. "Get out of here."

"It's not what you think. I—"

"Get out," she hissed. "Right now." What a fool she'd been. He hadn't wanted her. He'd used her. He probably even made sure someone saw him go into her tent to cover up his real assignation. "Please, just get away from me." She hated how that sounded like a plea, but she had to get him out of there before she broke down completely.

He cursed, then shoved away from her. Without a word, he slapped the netting aside and stormed out of the tent.

CHAPTER
13

Connor didn't know how he managed to keep his temper in check when he rounded Ashlee's tent and saw Louise lounging against a tree, her smile triumphant in the wavering moonlight. "It's about time."

His first impulse was to strangle her and be done with it. Then his common sense took hold. If he planned to stop this madness, he had to find out what she was about, why she kept instigating trouble between him and Branden.

Not wanting anyone to overhear their conversation, Connor gripped Louise's arm and led her toward a stand of pine. "Let's get out of here."

When he reached a secluded spot only a few yards away, he spun her around to face him, his fingers digging into the flesh of her upper arms. "Explain this lunacy, woman. What's going on inside that empty head of yours? What vicious scheme are you planning now?"

She pulled away from him and rubbed her arms.

"What was I supposed to do?" Louise demanded. "I saw you go into that slut's tent. Did you expect me to just stand idly by while you bedded her? Ha! Not hardly."

"What I do with Ashlee is none of your concern."

"It most certainly is."

What was the matter with the woman? She acted as if she believed there was something between them. It was on the tip of his tongue to set her straight, but the odd look in her eyes stopped him. It wasn't madness, but something very genuine. He proceeded with caution. "Why are you trying to destroy my friendship with Branden?"

"I couldn't care less about your friendship."

"Then why are you doing this, damn it? Why do you want Branden to think there's something between us?"

"Because there is." She sent him an indulgent smile. "Whether you admit it or not. No man could have held a woman the way you did when we danced and not felt the attraction between us. Not wanted more."

He was at a loss. "Danced? You mean at your wedding?"

"Yes. I knew the moment your body pressed against mine that I'd made a mistake." She drew her finger over the rise of one breast, tracing the well-defined contour beneath her dressing robe. "And I know you felt it, too. The power between us made the air come alive, turned it hot." Her hungry gaze traveled down his length. "If only I'd met you first. Before I sacrificed my happiness—my life—to insure financial security for my family." She stepped closer. "But it's not too late."

Connor recalled the single, obligatory dance, but he certainly didn't remember charging the air with life or heat. "Louise, this thing you claim is between us is a product of your imagination. We shared one dance, nothing more."

That indulgent look was back in her eyes, making him damned uncomfortable. "Connor, darling. I wouldn't have expected you to say anything else. You are such a loyal man. You won't even admit your feelings to yourself because I'm the wife of your friend."

Connor believed he was beyond being shocked by anything a woman could say. But that statement knocked him off balance. "You're talking nonsense. I've never given you any reason—"

She gave a throaty laugh. "Spoken like the honorable man you are." She trailed her tongue over her lower lip. "But we both know the truth, my love."

"Damn it, Louise. Will you listen to me? I—"

A twig snapped nearby.

Louise gasped.

Connor jerked around and squinted into the darkness.

Nothing was there.

"I've got to go," Louise whispered. Whirling around, she raced toward her tent.

Watching her go, Connor sighed, then laced his fingers through his hair, wondering how he'd gotten himself into such a mess over one lousy dance.

After a fitful night, with images of Louise and Connor in each other's arms, Ashlee wasn't in the best of moods when she emerged from her tent the next morning and stepped smack in the middle of a mud puddle. As if she didn't feel wretched enough already, now she'd ruined her slippers. Curse the tropical downpours in this area, anyway.

Expelling a frustrated oath, she lifted the hem of her skirt and trudged out of the puddle. Now she'd have to find her boots, packed somewhere in the mounds of luggage and supplies the men had unloaded into a heap when they made camp.

Water squashed through her toes as she began rummaging to find her carpetbag.

"What are you looking for, love?" Vivian asked as she approached.

"My boots. I've destroyed my slippers."

"While you're about it," Louise chimed in as she walked up on the other side, "would you locate mine, too? I really would like to remove myself from the saddle today."

Ashlee would like to see her removed from the earth, but was too much of a lady to say so. Still, she couldn't stop a small jab. "Too much riding, Mrs. Delacorte?"

Louise lifted a pencil-thin brow and sent her a slow smile. "Mmm, yes. Much more than I bargained for."

The innuendo set fire to Ashlee's blood, and she restrained the urge to claw out those smiling eyes. "Which bag is yours?"

"The one on the bottom."

Where else? Ashlee barely kept from snapping. Holding her tongue in check, she unearthed her own boots and dry stockings, then began the laborious search for Louise's.

Vivian made for the open supply sack next to the campfire.

It took Ashlee nearly a half hour to find Louise's footwear, and when she did, it was all she could do to keep from shoving the high-heeled leather in Louise's gloating face.

"Thank you, Miss Walker," she said, though her eyes gleamed with satisfied malice.

Not trusting her own response, Ashlee sat down on a trunk and pulled off her soggy slippers and stockings, then toweled her feet before setting about to don dry footwear. She felt a measure of relief when Louise sauntered off toward her tent.

"Shall we start breakfast?" Vivian called out.

Stamping into her boots, Ashlee glanced up. "Where are the men?"

Vivian lifted the metal coffeepot from the mound of rocks where it had been left the night before. "They went to clear the path ahead, I believe." She filled the pot from a canteen and dumped in a handful of coffee. "I imagine they'll be back soon."

"I'll make the biscuits." After locating the flour, lard, salt, and pearl ash, she measured the ingredients into a pan, then reached for the canteen of water.

Louise chose that moment to stroll by, carrying several pillows.

Surprised, Ashlee watched her plump each, then place them against the base of a palm. When all were situated to her satisfaction, she lowered herself regally amid the cushions to watch Ashlee and Vivian prepare the morning meal.

Wanting to strangle her, Ashlee set the canteen aside and walked over to a tree liberally strung with moss. With as much flourish as she could muster with rage-tightened limbs, she sat down and stretched. "Why don't you finish up for me, Louise? I'm exhausted."

Louise's eyes flashed with anger. For a moment she looked as if she were going to refuse, but her gaze drifted upward to fix on something overhead, then quickly lowered again. "I'd be happy to."

A little shocked by her acquiescence, yet knowing how well she'd irritated her, Ashlee had a devil of a time restraining a smile. "Thank you." Still holding on to her grin, she watched Louise saunter toward the fire.

Suddenly the fork Vivian had been turning the ham with hit the edge of the skillet. "Ashlee, don't move," she said in a too soft voice that fairly screamed danger. "There's a water moccasin directly above your head."

Terror gripped her. *So that's what Louise had seen, and she hadn't even tried to warn Ashlee.* Afraid to move her head, she cut her eyes to Vivian to see that she'd set down her cooking implements. "What do I do?" Ashlee's own hoarse whisper was nearly as frightening as her predicament.

"Stay dead still."

She wished Vivian hadn't put it just that way.

"Don't move," she reinforced. "I'll get help." She disappeared out of Ashlee's line of vision.

Barely able to breathe, Ashlee clenched her hands to stop their trembling and slanted her gaze to Louise.

"You've landed yourself in quite a mess, haven't you, puss?" she taunted. "It would be really horrible for you if someone should make a sudden movement and startle the snake, wouldn't it?"

Ashlee's nerves began to tingle. She wouldn't. Unable to move, and reach for Louise's throat, she answered the only way she could—in a very soft voice. "Yes, Louise, that would be horrible. But if I survived, you can wager your life, I'd dismember the spiteful culprit who did the deed, one—piece—at—a—time."

Louise's indrawn breath gave Ashlee a fleeting moment of satisfaction before a booted foot appeared on her right. She raised her eyes to see Connor standing in front of her, his gaze fastened on the snake.

He lowered his eyes to hers, and she saw the spark of fear in their depths.

That frightened her more than the snake.

"I'm going to hold out my hand," he said in a quiet, strained voice. "You do the same, but very, very slowly. Do you understand? No. Don't nod."

She instantly checked the reflex.

Connor inched his large, secure palm forward, and she noticed a slight tremor. "Give me your hand. Easy now. Slow."

Almost paralyzed with fear, Ashlee could barely lift her arm, much less do it quickly.

At last his fingers closed around her wrist. Without warning, he jerked her forward and into his arms. For several seconds he just held her, his heart thundering against her own.

The snake slithered off deeper into the branches, out of sight.

After several long moments, Connor at last eased his hold and turned his mouth to her ear. "Don't *ever* scare me like that again," he whispered harshly. "Or, I swear, I'll take you over my knee."

What did he think? She'd done it on purpose?

"Are you all right, love?" Vivian came up beside her and placed a frail hand on her shoulder.

"Just a little frightened," Ashlee lied. She was a lot frightened, but she didn't want to concern Vivian, nor give Louise a moment's satisfaction.

"Why didn't you shoot it?" Vivian demanded.

Ashlee turned to see Santos standing next to Joe and Branden, holding a gun in his hand.

"She could have been killed," Vivian raged.

The man shrugged. "The moccasin was only protecting his home the way you or I would. As long as no one trespasses, there's no danger."

"And just how is one to know when they're trespassing on a snake's domain?" Connor's aunt clipped in outrage.

"One doesn't, madam. One just has to keep an eye out for peril." Santos made a sweeping gesture with his hand. "There are several animals and reptiles in here that take offense to intruders—like alligators."

Louise snorted. "Those ugly creatures aren't all that treacherous."

Realizing she was still in Connor's arms, Ashlee quickly stepped away, then turned on Louise. "Oh, yes. I hear they're quite dangerous, especially when *someone* gets too close. You know, if they should stumble into the gator's path by accident, for instance."

When Louise went pale, Ashlee smiled complacently. "Of course, that sort of thing would never happen with anyone in our party, would it, Mrs. Delacorte? We're all much too careful."

"Yes, yes. We certainly are." Louise hurried to Connor's side. "But after such a frightening experience, I fear I simply must retire. Just the thought of the dangers out here makes me anxious." She lifted her eyes to Connor. "Would you walk me to my tent?"

Branden reached Louise in quick strides. "I'll escort you, my dear." Though the words were polite enough, Ashlee heard the underlying fury.

Louise's lips thinned. "Of course."

"What about your breakfast?" Vivian called after them.

"We'll eat later," Branden assured, then with a brisk nod, he steered his wife in the direction of their sleeping quarters.

Feeling just a little guilty over the way she'd taunted Louise, Ashlee cast a glance at the branch where the snake had been, thankful it was no longer visible. Relieved, she returned to the fire to finish the biscuits. Connor, she ignored. He may have saved her life, but she refused to overlook—or forgive—his behavior last night. Even knowing he'd been frightened for her a few moments ago didn't lessen her anger one whit. Still, a tiny little part of her was pleased.

She was so deep in her thoughts, she didn't hear Joe approach until he was right beside her.

He placed a hand on her arm. "Are you all right?"

Touched by his concern, she nodded. "I'm fine, thank you."

"Did you manage to clear the path?" Vivian asked.

Ashlee looked to Connor for an answer, but he was gone.

"Most of it," her father said, strolling toward them with Harry. "We should be able to cross . . . er . . . we'll leave by noon."

"Providing we don't encounter any more snakes," Vivian added.

Her father's brows shot upward. "Snakes? What snakes?"

Ashlee groaned, wishing Vivian hadn't been quite so informative.

Connor leaned against the base of an oak, staring at the dim outline of the trees, still unable to rid himself of the fear he'd felt for Ashlee. For the life of him, he couldn't understand how he, who had never experienced genuine panic, could have become so unstrung. But he had. When he'd seen that snake coiling over her head, paralyzing terror had held him immobile for a split second, and it had taken every ounce of his control to keep his voice steady when he spoke to her, though he hadn't been able to do the same for his trembling hands.

He would never forget the relief he felt when he crushed her to him, then how angry she'd made him for losing control. He smiled, recalling his threat of a spanking.

The humor left him when he remembered how Louise had gloated over Ashlee's plight. It was almost as if she'd enjoyed seeing her frightened, and he was damned glad when Branden hustled his wife off— before Connor gave in to the urge to turn *her* over his knee.

Rubbing his neck, he braced his head against the bark, wondering what he should do about Louise, if anything. And what had dissolved twenty years of friendship between him and Delacorte without confirmation? If only Branden would talk to him, tell him why he so readily believed Connor would cuckold him. Why he'd believe another's tale without even giving Connor a chance to defend himself.

A low, eerie wind whipped around Connor, ruffling the loose shirt he wore. It was a bizarre wind that teased his senses—and moved right through him.

Then he felt it. An overwhelming presence.

Startled, he sprang to his feet and spun around, expecting to find someone standing behind him.

No one was there.

He narrowed his eyes, peering into the shadows, and for a fleeting second, he could have sworn he saw a flash of light material through the trees, but it was gone before he could be certain.

"Damn." He would never understand the peculiar effect this swampy region had on him. Bewildered, yet not ready to return to camp, he sat back down.

Although the humidity undulated through the air in waves, and mosquitoes buzzed noisily, he felt a strange kind of peace, but as always, lurking in the background was the prickling sensation that needled his nerves. He could feel the danger here. Almost touch it. He closed his eyes and tried to put the thought out of his head.

"What are we going to do, Beau? We lost everything in the storm, our clothes, the jewels I was going to sell, everything."

He touched her damp hair, so grateful she was alive. A chill swept him as he remembered how frightened he'd been when the ship went down. He'd fought like a madman to reach her, then held on, swimming for shore with every ounce of strength he possessed. He refused to let the sea take her from him. Not now. Not ever.

"We haven't lost everything, duchess. We have each other." He smiled. "And the hefty purse at my waist— compliments of Samuel."

Her eyes grew wide. "You stole it?" A delighted laugh bubbled up. "Oh, Beau, you're wonderful." She flung her arms around his neck and smothered him with kisses.

"Whoa, hold on. Don't get too excited. We still don't have a place to stay yet."

She snuggled closer, curling onto his lap like a child. "We have a bed of the softest grass, a ceiling of black velvet, and nature's orchestra to lull us into slumber. As long as we have each other, that's all we'll ever need."

Happiness infused him, and he pulled her closer. "We might need to eat once in a while."

She nipped his neck. "Come to think of it, I'm hungry now." She pulled his head down and nibbled his ear. "For you."

A noise jolted Connor. His eyes shot open, and he blinked, trying to focus.

Anxious, he scanned his surroundings—looking for his companions only to find that he still sat beneath the oak. Alone.

CHAPTER
14

Unnerved by the visions that had plagued him from the moment he'd laid eyes on Ashlee Walker, Connor rose and headed for camp. He would never understand them—and he was tired of trying.

Just as he started around a group of palms, he heard someone talking, and halted.

"The bastard doesn't deserve to live," Joe hissed, keeping his voice low. "Look what he's done to you. And to me. He mutilated you, destroyed your life, and he killed my twin sister. The bloody whoreson murdered our beloved Charlotte."

"He'll get his, one day," Harry predicted, his jagged teeth slurring his words.

"And he's prepared to do it again," Joe went on. "He doesn't give a damn about what happened to Charlotte and David. Even his own daughter. All that matters is that experiment. I tell you, the bounder deserves to die."

"By your hand?" Harry asked disbelievingly.

"Of course not," Joe denied. "I'm not going to add a hangman's noose to my already shattered existence. But someone should cut the bastard's throat. And someday, I might just find that person."

Connor arched a brow. He had no idea Joe had such vicious thoughts. Thank God he didn't plan to act on them. Still, he would keep an eye on Joe just the same.

Coughing to alert them to his presence, he stepped around the palms. "Breakfast ready yet?"

Joe nodded nervously. "I-I think so."

Harry shifted and avoided Connor's eyes.

Studying their faces a moment longer, he dipped his head courteously, then went on to camp.

"Well, it's about time you found your way back," Aunt Vivian remarked as he walked into the clearing. "You certainly took your time. Breakfast is almost ruined." She waved a spoon. "Where do you keep wandering off to?"

His gaze drifted to Ashlee where she knelt in front of the fire, her shoulders tense. He frowned, then turned back to Vivian. "I fear I'm guilty of daydreaming. I saw an inviting oak and gave in to the impulse to relax beneath it for a time." He avoided mentioning the rest of his experience.

Ashlee gave a disbelieving snort.

Scowling, he stared at her. Then he saw the reason for her reaction. Louise stepped from the trees he'd just left and wandered toward her tent, patting her hair.

Vivian cleared her throat. "Well, do try not to wander off again so close to mealtime."

"Of course." Connor nodded absently, wondering if Louise had overheard the same conversation he had.

Joe and Harry ambled into view just as Branden emerged from his tent, blocking Louise's entrance. Delacorte said something to her, his expression stony.

Louise gasped, then stormed inside.

"I don't know about the rest of you, but I'm starving," Nathaniel remarked.

Smiling, Ashlee handed him a plate.

Experiencing a rumble of hunger himself, Connor forgot the Delacortes and turned his attention to breakfast.

After they'd finished and loaded the majority of the supplies, Connor remembered he'd left his towel and razor by the pool the night before. Trying not to swear, he went after them.

Folding the razor and shoving it into his pocket, he shook out the damp towel, then draped it around his neck and started back.

Something rustled the reeds up ahead.

Wary, he darted behind a tree.

Ashlee picked her way nervously through the tall grass, scanning the overhead branches as she walked.

He couldn't help but wonder if she'd followed him. Pleased by the notion, he waited until she drew abreast of the tree, then stepped out. "Were you looking for me?"

She gave a frightened gasp and leapt back, then her eyes narrowed. "Don't *do* that."

"What?" he asked, all innocence.

"Jump out at me," she hissed. "I don't appreciate having the life startled out of me. Blast it all, Connor, I've had enough upsets during this wretched journey."

"Why are you following me?"

She looked uneasy. "Because I wanted to talk to you alone."

"About what?" *Making love in the shade, he hoped.*

"Your aunt. I'm worried about her. She was very distraught when you disappeared this morning, though she hid it well. I just wanted to ask you to stay close, not wander off like that again. She doesn't need that kind of distress."

Knowing his aunt better than anyone, Connor hid a

smile. His wanderings were as much a part of him as the way he talked or walked. Nanna knew that, and she'd never been concerned before. She just liked to grumble. Still, he couldn't help but taunt Ashlee. "What about you? Were you distressed, too?" He moved closer, so close he could smell her clean jasmine scent. He expected her to step away.

Instead, she lifted her chin and stared boldly into his eyes. "Yes. I was concerned." She arched a brow. "If you'd gotten lost, we'd have had yet another delay."

"Witch."

"Scoundrel."

He laughed. She was a treasure. One he'd like very much to stuff in his pocket and keep close to his heart. "Come on, I'll walk you back."

"One more thing," she said in a solemn voice.

"What?"

"I'd like to apologize for interfering in your business aboard ship—with the first mate. The only excuse I can offer for my meddling is my concern for other people." She glanced up. "I'm sorry. And I'd like very much to be your friend."

He wanted her to be a helluva lot more than that. "Is my friendship that important to you?"

"No. But this constant unrest is giving me hives."

One of these days her honesty would be his undoing. "I see. Well, for the sake of your well-being, I accept your apology . . . and I have a confession. I didn't set Acres adrift. I gave him a horse before you came ashore and sent him on his way."

"You did?"

"Yes."

Those beautiful eyes softened. "Thank you."

The steamy swamp surrounded them, stoking the fires he'd tried so hard to bank. His gaze met hers, and he knew he'd lost the battle. Without thought to the consequences, he slipped his arm around her waist and bent to take her tempting mouth.

"Ashlee! Ashlee, dear, where are you?" Vivian's voice bounced through the trees. "We're ready to leave."

She jumped back, startled, then spoke quickly. "I-I'm right here, Vivian. I'll be there in a moment." She shoved Connor back when he reached for her. She glared at him, daring him to reveal his presence to his aunt—and explain.

In mock surrender, he lifted his hands, then spoiled it by giving her an impish wink. "Go," he whispered. "I'll wait a few minutes." He nudged her forward.

When Ashlee reached camp, she forced lightness into her tone. "Is everything ready?"

"Almost, but Nathaniel wanted to know where you put his jar of healing salve. He scraped his knuckle on a rock when he was dismantling his tent."

"Come on," she said brightly, looping her arm through Vivian's. "I'll get it."

When everything was in readiness, Ashlee waited by the horse she would share with Connor.

He strolled into view, but instead of approaching her, he went straight to Santos. "Are they gone?"

The guide shook his head. "But they're off the path."

What on earth were they talking about? Ashlee was saved from asking when Connor turned to address the group. "Up ahead there's a narrow strip of land we must cross to reach our destination. Yesterday it was the resting place of several alligators. That's why we camped here. They're gone now, but they're probably still nearby in the water. We're going to have to walk the horses over the path and remain as quiet as possible." He met her eyes. "Are there any questions?"

When no one spoke, he nodded. "Good. Santos will

go first, then Nathaniel and Aunt Vivian, the Delacortes, Joe, and Harry. Ashlee and I will bring up the rear." He glanced at Santos. "Ready?"

As the troop neared the bayou, Ashlee stared at the trail Connor had spoken of and felt a prick of fear. The path was only a few feet wide, and several yards long. Inky, green-black water, speared with reeds, pooled on either side, hiding the dangers that might lurk just beneath the still surface.

She didn't want to do this. Clasping her hands to still a nervous tremor, Ashlee held her breath as Santos inched his way across, his eyes darting from one edge to the other, his dark hand in a stranglehold around his horse's reins.

When he reached the other side, everyone took a relieved breath, then he motioned for the next party.

Her worried gaze slid to her father as he handed his horse's reins to Vivian, then he swooped her up into his arms. They shared a reassuring look, then her father slowly stepped forward, like Santos, ever watchful of threats, the horse plodding lazily behind.

Ashlee's heart pounded so hard, she feared the loud thundering would disturb the hidden beasts.

Branden moved forward next, but he wasn't so considerate of Louise. He placed her between himself and the horse, holding on to the reins and her arm at the same time.

As much as Ashlee disliked Louise, she was frightened for her, and she felt her heart wrench when they reached the other side and Louise dropped to her knees to bury her face in her hands.

Joe, evidently not trusting the reins, gripped his horse's bit, then tiptoed onto the path, his free hand clenched, his eyes wide, alert, his fear so tangible, she could have touched it.

Harry was even more nervous—not that she blamed him. Sweat beaded on his brow, and his hands shook as he led his horse onto the narrow strip, his eye darting wildly.

Without warning, monstrous jaws shot up out of the water.

The horse shrieked and bolted for the other side. Harry lost his grip and bounced sideways, crying out as he tumbled into the water.

Huge jaws clamped around his arm, and he wailed in terror as the beast dragged him under.

"No!" Ashlee screamed, and lunged forward.

Connor caught her around the middle and tossed her back, then dove in after their companion.

Scrambling to her feet, her body shaking with fear, Ashlee watched the water churn as Connor fought to free Harry from the alligator.

Both men disappeared.

Branden charged forward to help, but her father and Joe wrestled him to the ground.

Louise screeched, while Vivian stood frozen in horror, watching.

Several heartbeats passed before Connor burst from the water and dragged himself ashore, gasping for air, his clothes torn and bloody. "I c-couldn't s-save him," he whispered brokenly. "The a-alligator was too fast. Harry was d-dead before I got to him."

Shaking and crying, Ashlee dropped to her knees and cradled Connor's head in her lap. "Oh, God. Oh, sweet God . . ."

"Nooo!" Joe bellowed from the other side. "He can't be dead!"

Branden was holding Joe as he fought savagely to reach her father. "This is your fault! He's dead because of *you,* you son of a bitch!" His struggles increased to where Branden could barely restrain him. In desperation, he drew back his fist and struck a blow that rendered Joe unconscious.

Ashlee wished for the same relief from the wrenching ache in her chest. Oh, Harry. Kind, gentle Harry. Tears streamed down her face, and she bent over Connor, crying and rocking back and forth in her sorrow.

"Connor? Damn it, Connor, listen to me." Branden's urgent voice carried over the distance.

Ashlee lifted her head as Connor raised up.

"You can't cross now," Delacorte said in a defeated tone. "The alligators are stirring. You're going to have to wait until they settle back down."

Nervous tingles skittered over her skin as she slid her gaze to the narrow strip of land.

Three alligators had crawled onto the path, their slitted eyes watchful, their mouths half-open as if in anticipation of another feast.

"Damn it," Connor swore as he rose, bloody water dripping into puddles at his feet. He studied Ashlee for a long moment, then glanced back to Branden. "You go on to the house. Santos said it's only another couple miles. We'll be there as soon as we can."

Branden nodded. "Be careful, Connor." Then, turning to the others, he motioned them forward, watching Ashlee's father comfort the women as they followed Santos. Branden then lifted Joe's limp form and eased it over the saddle. With a last long look at Connor, he joined the group.

Folding her arms over her middle, Ashlee stared after the retreating party. "How long will it take before we can cross?"

Connor placed a hand on her shoulder, its warmth steady and reassuring in a world that had suddenly gone mad. "I don't know. Perhaps only a few hours. Then again, it could be several days. There's no way to tell."

She drew in shaky breath. Days? With no food or shelter? Alone with *him?* God couldn't be that cruel.

CHAPTER
15

Connor tried not to show his pain as he led the horse back to their recently cleared campsite. An alligator's razor-sharp teeth had cut into his side while he'd been trying to free Harry, and the blood was oozing through his shirt. He glanced at Ashlee, hoping she wouldn't notice. She had been through enough for one day. He knew the soul-stripping pain of watching someone close to you die.

Unsaddling the gelding, he tossed the saddle on the ground, then handed her the horse blanket. "Here. Spread this out and make yourself comfortable. I'm going to change into dry clothes, then see what I can find to make a shelter . . . just in case."

Ashlee's aquamarine eyes grew wide with concern. "Do you truly think we'll have to stay here all night?"

"I hope not." Connor didn't think he could stand the temptation. Grabbing a clean shirt, breeches, and a cloth for a bandage out of his saddlebags, he stared at her. "Don't leave this spot. I'll be back in a few minutes."

As soon as he was concealed by the trees, he wiped his wound with his wet shirt, then tied the cloth securely around his middle. After pulling on the clean clothes, he went in search of branches and palm leaves that might serve as a lean-to.

He found Ashlee sitting on the blanket with her knees drawn up to her chest. Tears stained her smooth cheeks.

Seeing her like that caused a surge of empathy. The compassion she felt for others was genuine. There was an astounding depth to Ashlee Walker, a childlike vulnerability, that nearly unmanned him. He could feel her deep, tormenting hurt, and it was the most natural thing in the world for him to set the branches and wet clothes aside, then kneel and, without a word, draw her into his arms.

She didn't protest as he'd expected. She just slumped against him and cried . . . and cried. He held on, trying to absorb some of her pain and soothe the anguished sobs that tore out pieces of his heart.

But her effect on him was great. He swallowed, forcing down his own tears, the deep-rooted grief he'd never allowed to surface. But God, it was hard not to give in to the ache clawing at his gut.

After several long minutes, she spoke in a trembling voice. "Perhaps Father's right about this experiment being cursed. He said it was an evil omen when the ship's mast fell." She knotted her fists in the folds of his shirt. "Maybe he's right."

How easy it was to blame something, or someone else, when you were hurting, just as he'd blamed the physician. For the first time, Connor wondered at the motive behind his distrust of doctors. "You're much too intelligent to believe that," he said gently, rubbing his chin against her soft hair.

"Perhaps I'm not as smart as you think I am," she murmured, snuggling closer, her warm cheek finding his naked flesh in the opening of his shirt. For several minutes, she didn't move, then he felt the flutter of her lashes and knew she'd closed her eyes.

Content just to hold her, he sat listening to the rustle of leaves, the twitter of a sparrow, and the low hum of nearby mosquitoes. The muggy air dampened the skin where their bodies met, but he didn't release her. Not yet.

A rustle of the tall reeds up ahead forced him to move. They couldn't remain here if the alligators were lumbering in their direction.

Seeing Ashlee had fallen into healing sleep, Connor eased her down onto the blanket, then rose, his senses alert as he crept toward the path. A lizard slithered through the weeds, and he smiled, relaxing as he walked on. But when he reached the swampy pools, he came to an abrupt halt—and stared at the strip of land with disbelief. Not a single alligator was anywhere to be seen.

His first thought was to wake Ashlee, then he considered what might happen tonight if they were forced to stay. But his honor wouldn't let him. He would not take advantage of an innocent, no matter how much he wanted to. Still . . . on the brighter side, perhaps he could save her from more upset.

Returning to camp, he saddled the horse in silence, tied the reins to his waist, then picked up a sleeping Ashlee.

She nuzzled his shoulder and groggily slipped her arms around his neck. "Where're we going?"

"Shh." He brushed his lips over her ear. "Just for a little walk."

"Mm, nice," she slurred, then again slumped into exhausted sleep.

Temptation to stay for the night reared again, but he suppressed it and hurried to the path. He scoured the area, then slowly, oh so slowly, inched across the dangerous strip, his heartbeat as loud as the thud of hooves behind him.

When he reached the other side, he mounted, holding Ashlee close, then followed the others' trail in the soggy soil. Nearly an hour later, he slowed the animal in a clearing where a huge house sat surrounded by trees, near the bluest lake he'd ever seen.

Smiling, he knew that was the sight he wanted Ashlee to wake up to. He dismounted at the water's edge, then carefully lowered her to her feet in the tall grass, but held her close.

She blinked and raised her lashes. "What?"

It was all he could do not to kiss that full, sleep-softened mouth. "I have a surprise for you."

For a full second she stared at him, then her eyes grew wide and she came fully awake. "The alligators? Are they gone? Can we leave?"

He brushed a finger over the tip of her nose. "They're gone . . . and behind us." He turned her around. "We made it."

Filled with awe, Ashlee stared at the lake. The rippling indigo water seemed to go on forever, a sea of shimmering sapphire. She had never seen anything so beautiful. "It's magnificent," she whispered almost to herself. Her breath caught, and she whirled around. "How did we get here? What happened to the alligators? The path? The camp?"

He smiled down at her, melting her with that boyish grin. "You slept through the whole journey."

"What?"

"Connor! Ashlee!" her father's voice rang out, and she whipped around to see him sprinting toward them. Santos strolled behind at a more leisurely pace.

"Oh, thank God," her father said, drawing her into a bear hug, then setting her away from him to examine her. When he was satisfied she was unharmed, he pumped Connor's hand in gratitude. "I knew I could trust you to see to her safety."

Vivian and Branden came rushing over to them. For a second Ashlee was startled by the sheer relief flooding Branden's eyes, before he swiftly shuttered them.

"I see you made it," he said matter-of-factly.

"Oh, child, I was so worried." Vivian grabbed her in a hug, then smiled at Connor. "Look at the house!" she exclaimed. "It's exquisite."

Disengaging herself from the woman's arms, Ashlee automatically turned to the left. "Oh . . ." Her eyes widened as she stared at the two-story white mansion. It was overgrown with moss and wild foliage, but the stately English elegance couldn't be disguised. Like a rare, perfectly formed pearl lying in a bed of rich emerald satin, the house shone in the afternoon sun like a crown jewel.

The lower floor was encompassed by a veranda, while a graceful balcony encircled the upper level, supported by tall, proud columns of glistening alabaster. Even from this distance, she could tell by the painstaking craftsmanship that someone had loved the house very much. A surge of inexplicable pride fluttered through her chest. "It's breathtaking."

"Such a fine piece of workmanship," Father said, his voice overflowing with appreciation. "The fateful couple must have been quite proud of their accomplishment."

Recalling how Blackie had retold the legend at supper aboard ship, Ashlee wondered if the others were as inclined to believe the story as she was.

"I'm sure they were very proud," Connor said solemnly.

"I wonder what really happened to them," Vivian queried.

An uncomfortable iciness crawled over Ashlee's flesh.

"No one knows for sure, but the Seminole have their own ideas," Santos offered.

Assuming he, too, referred to the legend, Ashlee flicked an uncertain glance at Connor.

He was staring at the ground, little furrows creasing his smooth brow.

"Shall we set up our laboratory here?" Father asked, directing his question to Santos. He sent a glance at Connor. "We just arrived ourselves since Louise's decision to walk slowed us, and Joe's horse threw a shoe, so we haven't settled anything yet."

Santos's gaze fixed on Ashlee for some reason. "This would be a good spot for your experiment location, with the water so close, and far enough away from the main house. But I think you'd all be better off sleeping inside."

"We can't just barge into someone's home," Louise argued, sauntering up behind the guide.

Santos turned to her, his expression cool. "Mrs. Delacorte, there are no owners. Until today, this house hasn't been seen by a white man for nearly a hundred years, and the Seminole keep clear of it. Believe me, there's no one to object."

Ashlee silently agreed. Although she'd never been here before, she felt a strange welcoming presence.

"I think Santos is right," Father seconded, sending Vivian a concerned look. "We'd all be better off sleeping indoors." He pointed to a small, tree-lined spot bordering the water's edge about two hundred yards from the house. "We can set up a tent there for my work."

Ashlee stared at the clearing, mesmerized by the familiar spot. . . .

"A gazebo by the lake? Oh, Beau, how lovely."

He stroked the backs of his fingers across her cheek, sending rivulets of warmth down her spine. "Not nearly as lovely as you are."

She hugged him soundly. Without mention, he had somehow known how much she missed having a gazebo. "I will love it almost as much as I do you."

He chuckled and kissed her, savoring her lips as a child would a sweet. When he'd tasted his fill, he pulled her into the circle of his arm, then turned again to the lake. "We've accomplished a lot in the last year, duchess, but there's so much more I want to do." There was a ring of pride in his voice that tightened her heart. "As soon as I finish the stables, I'll start on the gazebo, then I want to—"

"Are you coming, dear?" Vivian's voice jolted her.

Ashlee whirled around to see Connor and the others waiting for her. "Yes. I'm sorry, I was . . . entranced by the lake."

"Come along, then." Her father motioned with his hand. "I'm anxious to see inside the house."

When they reached the front entrance, she noticed Joe standing sullenly by his horse, and her heart went out to him. He'd lost his best friend.

Branden opened the dusty, cobweb-encrusted door, drawing her attention, and peaked inside. "Someone better have a broom."

Louise twisted her mouth in disgust.

"There's one on the back porch," Ashlee announced, then clamped her mouth shut. How could she know that?

Everyone turned to stare.

Ashlee's cheeks grew hot. "Um, at least, there should be. Shouldn't there?"

Vivian cleared her throat. "Well, let's hope so. Then we can set to work."

"No, Nanna," Connor countered. "Branden and I

will sweep up. You ladies direct Joe where you want the supplies and your things put." He glanced at Santos. "And since you don't want to enter the house, why don't you start setting up Nathaniel's tent."

"I'll help sweep," Ashlee spoke up, somehow feeling it was her right. And, for some reason, no one objected. Not even Connor.

Everyone set to work, and filled with excitement, she hurried up onto the ivy-strewn veranda, but stopped short to stare at the two massive cedar doors.

"Why won't you let me go to St. Augustine with you to bring back the cedar? I get so lonely when you're gone."

"I know, sweet, but you know we can't chance anyone recognizing you. If the duke ever found out . . ." He pulled her closer, trying to conceal the tremor that rippled through his strong arms. "I couldn't bear to lose you."

Ashlee's gaze focused again on the door, and a pulse pounded in her temple. The memories that kept stealing into her head were unnerving. But they weren't as unsettling as the fact that she knew exactly what lay beyond those enormous cedar panels: a large, circular entry with gleaming white tiles; a staircase that started on the right, then swept upward in an arc until it merged with a railed landing that overlooked the entry; in the center of the floor, a white pillar rose to the roof, its base encircled by curved, cushioned seats of red velvet; twin gold chandeliers of the finest crystal hung on either side of the center column.

Taking a breath, she went in. A damp, musty odor assailed her, and she brought a hand to her nose as she looked around. Finding the entry not only dusty and laced with cobwebs, but also just as she'd imagined, didn't comfort her one whit. Or the fact that she somehow knew the exact location of every room, every piece of furniture—and the broom. Then the most unnerving sensation of all struck. *She had lived in this house.*

As Connor stood looking out the smudged window, he felt as if he'd come home. Yet there was a sadness, too. When he looked at the overgrown yard, he could visualize how it once was, with thick, wide lawns, roses, jasmine, lilacs, orchids, borders of white rock, and so much more.

Too, he had the strangest feeling of possession about the house. As if he were responsible for its very existence. He walked through the rooms, touching, exploring. When he came to the other end of the manor, he glanced out the dirty rear windows. Beyond the yard, dark, eerie swamps filled his vision.

The unexplainable fear he experienced in this strange land grew at a vicious rate. A ripple of terror slithered through him. Damn it. He would not be cowed by some unknown demon.

Angered, but not sure at whom, he reflexively grabbed for an iron-handled ax off the back porch and stalked off into the trees. They needed firewood, and he would be happy to get it. But as he strolled through the trees, a thought hit him, and he stopped. How had he known where the ax would be?

Irritated all over again, he spotted an aging oak, and stripped off his shirt. He winced when pain shot through his injured side, but he ignored the annoying twinge and hefted the ax onto his shoulder. He approached the decaying wood trunk and studied it for a moment, then, picking his spot, he swung.

The rusty blade bit into the bark, sending forth a shower of dry chips.

As he worked, his thoughts turned to Ashlee, and how right she'd looked in the house. He had watched her from the stairs for several minutes as she lovingly dusted each piece of furniture, each vase, each candleholder and statue. He wondered, what was it about the woman that warmed his blood every time he thought of her?

He swung again.

From the first moment he'd seen her in her father's parlor, he'd wanted to taste that full, pouting mouth, caress her soft skin.

The ax cut into the wood. Again. Again.

He'd envisioned himself making wild, primitive love to her, taking her—and himself—to unimaginable heights. Even now he could almost smell her heady jasmine scent.

"Look out!" a woman screamed.

Startled, he glanced up. The enormous oak splintered and plunged toward him. He dove to the side— just as the tree crashed to the ground, barely missing him.

Connor sprang to his feet, his heart slamming into the walls of his chest, and swung around to confront the woman who'd saved him.

There was no woman. There was no one at all.

Ashlee stared at the beautifully furnished parlor she'd just finished sweeping. Wiping her arm across her damp brow, she leaned the broom against the wall. She still couldn't believe that every dish, every vase, every piece of valuable furniture, that had belonged to the previous owners was still there. Nothing had been touched for a century.

"I've managed to prepare four rooms upstairs," Vivian announced, coming in from the entry.

Ashlee smiled, recalling the fuss the older woman had put up when Branden wouldn't allow her into the house until the upstairs had been swept. "Did we bring enough linens?"

"Thankfully, yes. Devil of a time I had, though. The sheets on the beds were so old and rotten, I had to tear them away one strip at a time before I could replace them. Fortunately, the feather ticks were in fair shape, but I couldn't imagine what to do with all the clothes in those armoires. So I left them." She sat on a newly dusted settee. "I wonder if anyone knows what happened to the poor souls."

"Perhaps the legend Santos's people believe is the truth, that the woman's husband found the couple and killed them."

"Possibly. But I find it difficult to believe anything he says. That one's afraid of something." She brushed at a streak of dirt on her lavender skirt. "Besides, his smile's too cynical." Vivian stared at the front window. "Just like that Joe's."

What in the world did that have to do with anything? Ashlee wondered. Maybe Connor's aunt had been working too hard. "Would you like some tea? I believe I saw Father carrying a tin toward the cookhouse a short while ago."

Vivian leaned into the high-backed cushion and rested her head against a rim of mahogany beneath the cover. "That would be lovely, dear."

Realizing Vivian was much more exhausted than she'd let on, Ashlee picked up the broom and headed for the cookhouse.

One entire side of the frame building was made of brick. Two ovens were built into the masonry, while an open hearth centered the massive wall. An iron rod extended from the side of the hearth and held a rusty metal pot over cold ashes, as if something had been left cooking when the owners vanished.

"Mmm, that smells delicious. What is it?"

"Fish stew." She poked the mushy blob, and sent *him a satisfied smile. "I wanted to use up all the fish you caught this morning. Besides, this is our celebration dinner."*

*A comical expression crossed his handsome features.
"You used all ten of them in that one pot?"*

"Of course not. I used one for the garden."

*A rumble of laughter shook him. He came up behind
her and slid his arms around her waist. "Oh, Amanda,
what am I going to do with you?"*

*A blush stole over her face. "Nine was too many,
wasn't it?" She stared at the thick gob, wondering if
she'd ever learn to cook a decent meal. "I'm sorry."*

*"No," he said. "It doesn't matter. I'd eat tree bark if
it meant keeping you by my side." He took one of her
hands and tenderly massaged the palm. "You were a
gently born lady," he rasped in an embittered voice.
His hand tightened around hers. "You shouldn't have
to do this. You should have a string of maids and cooks,
a housekeeper. . . ."*

*Her heart ached for him. He wanted so much to give
her all the luxuries he imagined she missed. Lavish
comforts that their funds wouldn't allow. She touched
his cheek, loving the feel of his strong, smooth jaw. "I'd
rather have you than all the servants in England."*

A thud on the wooden walkway outside pulled
Ashlee from the uncanny vision, and she turned to see
her father set down a trunk she knew was filled with
cooking pots, pans, and kettles. Wishing she could
understand the strange illusions that kept creeping
into her mind, she went to find a cauldron for Vivian's
tea.

As soon as she found what she needed, she carried
the kettle inside and built a fire. An instant later, thick
black smoke boiled out of the hearth opening.

"Oh, no." She heaved a sigh. Either the damper was
closed, or, more likely, the blasted chimney was
plugged with debris.

An hour later, Ashlee handed Vivian her steaming
cup.

"Is there enough of that for me?" her father inquired as he came in and took a seat beside Vivian.

A warm look passed between the older couple, then Vivian smiled. "Ashlee just made a full pot. I am quite sure we could spare a smidgen for you." Her eyes twinkling with amusement, she rose and got another cup from the newly polished sideboard.

"Did Santos manage to raise the tent?" Ashlee asked, sipping her own drink.

Father nodded, yet his attention didn't waver from Vivian's graceful movements as she filled his cup and sat down.

"Ashlee and I made modest headway in here." Vivian sent him a sideways glance. "But I am afraid we only managed to ready four bedchambers. Connor and Joe will have to sleep in the stables, I fear."

Father smiled into his cup. "They might as well sleep outside, then. The stable roof is nothing more than a frame."

"As soon as I finish the stables, I'll start on the gazebo." The words rang in Ashlee's ears. Whatever happened to the previous owner must have happened while he was constructing the livery. The gentle woman of her dreams had never gotten her gazebo, and for some reason, the thought made Ashlee sad.

"Actually, I believe I will sleep right here," Father continued, patting the settee. "Connor can have my chamber."

"What about Joe?" Ashlee asked. "Santos won't set foot in here, but it isn't right to leave Joe outside while everyone else sleeps indoors."

"She's right, Nathaniel. It's not proper."

Father cast them a complacent smile. "Perhaps there is room in the study."

"Room for what?" Connor asked, strolling in with an armload of wood.

Nathaniel explained.

Setting the wood on the hearth, Connor straightened and then turned his back while he buttoned his shirt. "Joe and I will stay in the study, and we can use the cots in the attic. They should have weathered the years."

"I'm sure they did. They're made of iron," Ashlee added. She felt a cold chill run through her. No one, including herself, had been in the attic. Yet she knew the cots were there—just as she had everything else.

And Connor knew.

Their eyes met in a sudden, eerie understanding.

CHAPTER
16

Connor carried a candle to light their way to the attic. Neither of them spoke as they ascended the narrow stairs and entered the spacious upper room.

Setting the holder on a crate by the door, he glanced around the dusty, cobweb-covered storage area, then fixed on the two iron beds stacked against the north wall. "You knew they'd be here, too, didn't you?"

Her gaze followed his. "Yes."

"How?"

"I swear to you, Connor. I don't know. But ever since I set foot on this place, I've felt as if I'd been here before." She rubbed her scar. "No. It's more than that. I feel as if I've *lived* here. And I know whatever's happening started the moment I met you in St. Augustine." She touched his wrist. "I can't explain it exactly, but I think all this has something to do with the dream."

"What dream?"

"The one I've been having since childhood." She

moved to stare out a cloudy window. "It's always the same. I'm scared and running, trying to make it to the safety of the cypress. But I stumble, and I'm trying to crawl when a man grabs my hair." Her hand trembled as she brought it to her throat. "There's something terrible out there. Something that wants to hurt us both."

"I've felt it, too."

Brushing a cobweb from her sleeve, she turned. "Why is this happening to us? Is it some kind of curse? Why do I feel threatened, yet strangely at peace? And what about the house? Is it possible we've both dreamed of this type of home, and had visualized it so many times in our minds, we only think we've been here?"

"I've got a hell of an imagination, but not with such detail that I know the exact location of an ax, or that two iron beds were stored in the attic . . . or that those beds were once placed side by side with a large feather tick over them until we finished the new one. . . . Damn. See what I mean?"

"I see something else," she said softly. "You said 'we,' Connor. Not I or you, but *we.*"

He took her hand, loving the feel of her satiny skin. "I know. It's as if you're as much a part of this house as the foundation."

"What are we supposed to do?"

He brought her hand to his lips and kissed it. "I wish I knew."

She shivered.

"Cold?"

"I'm frightened. There's so much happening that I don't understand. And always, in the back of my mind, is the fear that something horrible is going to occur."

"I've sensed that, too. But short of leaving, which isn't possible for my aunt's sake, there's nothing we can do but take each day, each unsettling sensation, one at a time and try to sort it out."

"How?"

"Damned if I know."

"What about this thing I'm feeling between us?"

He smiled. *"That,* I can explain." He massaged her palm with his thumb. "It's attraction. The desire to touch and explore." He traced her lower lip, and watched her eyes darken. His body responded instantly, and he pulled her to him. His senses absorbed her warm jasmine scent. "It's the urge to fulfill a desperate need as only a man and woman can."

Her small pink tongue slid out to wet her lips. "How do we stop it?"

He fixed on her mouth, on the gentle curve, the lush fullness. "Like this." He lowered his head and captured her lips. They trembled, then parted beneath his. Fire raced through his body, and he hungrily took what she offered. But it wasn't enough. He needed to touch her, each glorious inch.

He sought the firm fullness of her breast, kneading gently as he learned the shape and weight. Her nipple tightened, and so did he.

"Connor, I'm scared." Her breath feathered his lips and set fire to his blood.

"Don't be. Not of this." His kiss was long and thorough, his breath heavy with passion as he eased his fingers inside the bodice of her gown to find the hard little crest he so urgently wanted to explore.

She trembled and made a cry of protest, but he absorbed it with his mouth as he freed her from the material and reverently caressed the silken flesh.

A moan vibrated against his tongue, and she arched into his hand.

His sex sprang to life. He pressed against the juncture of her thighs. The need to sink into that sweet haven staggered him.

Unable to control the impulse, he dragged his mouth from hers and kissed a hot trail down her throat, over the hammering pulse at the base, then lower, sampling the shape of her scar, then, at last, the stiff little peak he hungered for. He drew her into his mouth and suckled greedily. She tasted like potent wine. So intoxicating.

A whimper rose from her throat, and she slid her fingers into his hair, holding him to her, arching her neck as she offered him her intimate treasure.

And he took it, like a hungry babe at his mother's breast. Nursing, savoring, satisfying his ravenous appetite.

Still, it wasn't enough. He gathered her skirts and with slow deliberateness worked them upward until his palms could glide beneath, over the soft chemise and sweet curves. But soon the material became a barrier he couldn't tolerate, and he dragged it up, exposing her naked flesh to his desperate hands.

He explored her woman's curves, then gently bit her nipple while he sought the warmth between her thighs. Soft curls and delicate folds teased the tips of his fingers, sending fire straight to his shaft.

"Connor . . . oh, God . . . I can't!" She shoved away from him, her chest heaving as she frantically pushed her skirts back into place. Like a frightened child, she worked to right her bodice, her eyes darting about for a means of escape. "I-I can't," she whispered again, then raced through the door.

Ashlee ran down the hall to the opposite end and stopped to catch her breath. She couldn't go downstairs and face the others until she calmed herself. Dear God. Why had she allowed him such liberties? She closed her eyes and crossed her arms over her tingling breasts, certain that she'd just made a complete, scandalous fool of herself.

Curse this house. And curse the sensations that stripped her of control.

"I should kill you now and be done with it!"

At the sound of a man's voice, her eyes shot open, and she nervously scanned the dim corridor.

"And release me from your loathsome presence, darling? Go ahead. That's all I want." Louise's purring voice filtered through the doorway behind Ashlee. "That's all I've ever wanted."

Startled, she jerked forward and spun to stare at the closed panel.

Branden's voice resounded through the cedar. "Get out of my sight."

Feminine laughter rumbled. "My pleasure. All you have to do is grant me a divorce."

"Damn you! You know I can't." Branden sounded so tired, so defeated.

"You're going to have to make a choice sooner or later, darling. Either denounce your beliefs in the church and set me free . . . or spend the rest of your life claiming the child I carry as your own." Silk rustled as if she'd moved closer to him. *"Connor's* child, Branden."

The beds were set up, and everyone situated, by dusk, but Ashlee wasn't ready to retire. Everything that had happened rode on her mind. Harry's death, the house, the strange familiarity, the indefinable fear . . . and Louise's disgusting accusation.

Ashlee drew her hands into fists at that last thought, wanting to flatten the haughty Mrs. Delacorte's nose. Ashlee didn't believe for a moment that Louise spoke the truth. Connor would not cuckold his best friend. She knew that with all her heart. Still, she had the horrible feeling that Branden did believe it.

The thought angered her. Why would he take

Louise's word over Connor's? As hateful as Branden's wife was, even a saint would have trouble accepting her tale.

Glancing around the empty parlor, Ashlee recalled how she'd avoided Connor after the trip to the attic, trying to sort through her muddled thoughts. It hadn't taken her long to exonerate him.

She slid a peek at the door leading to the study he was sharing with Joe, trying not to visualize Connor lying there beneath a blanket, and wearing very little clothing, if anything at all.

Her body warmed at the thought, and visions of their encounter in the attic came back to haunt her. She shoved the scandalous images away. One would think, after the way Stephen had reacted to her scars, she'd have been more cautious.

But, for the life of her, she couldn't imagine Connor ridiculing her the way Stephen had. Connor was gentle and sensitive, so genuinely kind.

One of the doors eased open, and Connor peeked into the parlor. He smiled. "I figured you were still up."

That was not the face of a man who could ridicule —or impregnate his friend's wife. "I wasn't sleepy."

He edged into the room. "I can't sleep either."

The sensual look in his eyes made Ashlee uneasy, and she retreated a step, wanting to run and stay at the same time. The feelings he evoked frightened her.

"Why couldn't you sleep, Ashlee? Is it because of what happened in the attic?"

Her stomach grew tight. "Of course not. I hadn't given it a moment's thought."

His mouth stretched into a slow smile. "Liar."

He was so handsome, he took her breath away. She cleared her throat, trying for some sense of normalcy —and a definite change of subject. "Um, where's Joe?"

"Asleep in the study, snoring like a contented hound."

She chuckled. "So that's why you couldn't sleep."

"No. I was thinking of you."

Those softly spoken words reduced her to a gooey lump, and she felt warm. "Why don't you sit down? I'll pour you a cup of tea." Shakily she reached for the pot.

Connor's hand covered hers. "Tea isn't what I want."

His sensual gray eyes told her exactly what he did want. Her.

He rubbed his thumb over the back of her hand. "Why did you avoid me tonight?"

She didn't think he'd noticed. For a brief instant she considered telling him about the conversation she'd overheard between Branden and Louise, but decided against it. He had enough to worry about with his aunt's illness and the strange things going on around them. Still, she didn't want to lie. "I needed time to think about what happened upstairs."

His hand swept up to cup the back of her neck. "You mean this?" He covered her lips with his, then pulled her into his arms, his movements slow and gentle.

With the low table between them, she almost fell. She reached for his waist to steady herself. Beneath his shirt, she felt the outline of a band of cloth. She'd had enough experience with makeshift bandages to identify one by touch. She wrenched back. "What happened? Why is your stomach wrapped?"

He let out a breath and shifted away from her. "It's not my stomach. It's my side. And it's nothing. Just a scratch."

"From what?"

For several seconds he didn't answer. Then he glanced away. "An alligator."

Shock reverberated through Ashlee for a split second, then she darted around the table. "Let me see."

"I told you, it's just a scratch. I cleaned and wrapped it right after it happened."

"Humor me." In this humid climate, infection could set in within a matter of hours.

Sighing, he unbuttoned his shirt and took it off, then dropped it on the settee. His nimble fingers made short work of the knotted cloth and he slowly eased the material from his wound.

Several red, razor-thin cuts marred his tanned flesh. But none of them appeared to be infected. Still . . . "I think my father should take a look at this."

"No."

"But—"

"I don't need a damned physician."

Her own anger rose. "What is this ridiculous aversion you have to doctors?"

He tossed the bandage on the table and sat down. "Let's discuss something else."

Sitting onto the settee beside him, she placed a hand on his arm. "I just want to understand."

"It's not something I like to talk about."

She didn't comment but just arched a challenging brow.

With a weighty sigh, he slipped on his shirt, then leaned back and draped his arm behind her. He stared into the cold fireplace for several long moments before he spoke. "When I was seven, my father decided to expand his shipping business. After he received a contract to haul goods to China, he wanted to make the first few trips himself. I was too young for long sea voyages, so he left me and took my older brother, David."

Unconsciously he slid his hand up her arm, massaging her shoulder with his thumb. "Mother and I went to stay with Aunt Vivian until their return. A week before Father and David were due in port, my mother became seriously ill."

His fingers tightened. "On my eighth birthday, we received word that my father and brother were drowned in a storm at sea. You could imagine what that type of news did to such a young child. Anyway, in my sorrow, I wanted to see my mother. I guess I just needed to feel her arms around me, for her to tell me everything would be all right again."

His throat worked and he looked up. "The physician attending her wouldn't let me in. He said she was too ill to bother with a whimpering child." His voice turned harsh. "The bastard forcibly shoved me out and closed the door. I remember standing there, staring, fighting tears, and desperate to see my mother, if only to look at her."

He laced his fingers through his hair and leaned forward. "I sneaked into the adjoining bedroom and eased open the door just enough to see her. She was crying, her voice so weak, I could barely hear her, begging that bastard not to bleed her anymore. She was so pale, so thin. And there was so much blood in the pail beside the bed. I tried to get to her. God, how I tried. But he caught me and threw me out, kicking and screaming. Then he locked the doors. I was still sitting there when he told me she was dead."

Ashlee felt the depth of his pain. "I hope Benjamin Rush rots in hell."

Connor glanced up. "Who?"

"Benjamin Rush. He was a rebel among physicians who claimed purging, blistering, and bloodletting would remove the poison from an ill person's system and cure them. And he taught his methods to others. Evidently your mother's physician was one of them." She touched his hand. "Believe me, Connor. Any practitioner worth his salt wouldn't use those barbaric measures." She looked directly into his troubled eyes. "And my father never has."

"Thank God for that."

A thud sounded from the entry, and they both turned toward the door.

"What was that?" Ashlee whispered.

"I don't know." Rising, Connor went to the parlor door and opened it.

Ashlee was right behind him, searching for the cause of the disturbance. Then she saw it, and her knees went weak.

Vivian stood halfway up the steps, clutching the rail. She was drenched in perspiration and shaking, her skin an unhealthy red.

"Aunt Vivian!" Connor cried, rushing to her.

She opened her mouth but couldn't speak for the shudders that racked her thin frame.

Connor swept her up into his arms, then bellowed at Ashlee, "Get your father!"

"Put her to bed," Ashlee commanded, racing up the stairs. "And bathe her in cool water."

"D-Don't make a fuss," Vivian ordered between chattering teeth. "It w-will pass."

Ignoring her feeble command, Connor stalked toward her room, while Ashlee hurried to her father's.

Not bothering with a robe, Nathaniel dashed into Vivian's bedchamber and promptly ushered Ashlee and Connor out.

Ashlee's concern wavered between Vivian and her nephew. Connor looked ready to collapse.

He paced the hall. "This has got to stop. "Damn it. I can't watch her die."

"She'll be all right," Ashlee tried to soothe. At least she hoped she would. "Come on, let me fix you a drink."

"Make that two," Branden said softly, his white-knuckled hand gripping the rail. He looked to Connor. "The fever again?"

Connor nodded, then, with a last glance at his aunt's door, he went downstairs.

In the parlor, Ashlee hurried to the sideboard and poured both men a straight whiskey.

Branden met her halfway and took a glass.

Connor had dropped into a chair.

"Here, take this," she ordered, shoving the goblet into his hand.

He shot her a grateful look, then, clutching the glass like a lifeline, he tossed back the contents in one swallow.

Knowing neither man was in the mood for talk, she took a seat across from them, but didn't attempt conversation.

After what seemed like hours, her father appeared in the parlor.

"Is she all right?" Connor and Branden asked in unison, both coming to their feet.

"I need a brandy." At the sideboard, her father downed the drink, then poured a second before taking a seat. The lines in his face were more pronounced, and there was a concerned look about him that he didn't usually allow to show.

"Is it bad?" Connor asked anxiously.

Her father nodded. "The quinine helped some, but Dr. Ramsey's earlier diagnosis was quite correct. Vivian's heart rate has slowed considerably from when I examined her myself in St. Augustine. It is weakening with each attack. And the voyage did not help. If I do not find a cure soon—" He swallowed the rest of his words and rose. "I am going to sit with her tonight. Would you bring my notes from the lab?" he asked Ashlee. "I would like to go over them again."

Branden didn't say a word, he just went to the window and stared out at the night.

Connor paled and sank farther into the chair, his unseeing gaze fixed on the floor.

Ashlee wanted to comfort him, but didn't know how. "I'll bring the notes in a few minutes, Father."

Nodding, he left the room.

She moved to Connor. "Are you all right?"

"No. I'm scared. Goddamn it, I'm so scared of losing her, I'm sick with it."

Branden made a choked sound but didn't turn.

"She's going to recover this time. Both of you, remember that, and stop torturing yourselves before it's time."

Connor sent her a half smile. "Is that what we're doing?"

"Yes. Now, why don't you gentlemen get some rest? I'm going to get those notes for my father, then find my own bed."

"I'll look in on her first," Connor conceded.

"We'll both go," Branden voiced, turning from the window.

Having done all she could, Ashlee headed for her chamber to get a cloak. Securing the ties on the way downstairs, she lit a torch and slipped out the front door. But her thoughts remained inside as she walked through the tall grass toward the tent. Trying to dispel her own worry over Connor's aunt, she focused on the structure a few yards away, barely visible in the small circle of light.

A shadowy figure darted from the opening and disappeared into the trees.

Startled, she stopped. "Who's there? What do you want?" She waited. Listened.

Nothing.

Her chest pounding, she ran to the tent and lifted the torch high so she could see inside.

White mice, the ones Father used to test the effects

of various elixirs, scrambled in every direction. Someone had let them out of the cages.

"No. It can't be." But it was, and no matter how much she wished it otherwise, the horrifying fact remained . . . someone had deliberately sabotaged her father's work.

CHAPTER
17

Ashlee jammed the torch into a holder and frantically tried to corral the mice. Without them, Father couldn't continue. She tore off her cloak and tossed it over several little white bodies. A dozen more scrambled to the other side of the tent. "Blast."

Ripping off a petticoat, she threw it over the second cluster of squirming, squealing rodents.

"Ashlee? What are you doing—" Connor inhaled. "What the hell!"

"Help me put them into their cages," she ordered, trying to scoop up a bundle of mice without losing any. Thank Providence the canvas sides had been staked down to prevent snakes from getting inside.

Connor gathered up her petticoat and its occupants, then carried them to an open crate and placed her undergarment and all inside before closing the lid.

Ashlee did the same with the mice under her cloak. When the majority of the mice had been caged, she drew in a sigh of relief, but as she turned to Connor, another image wavered before her mind's eye.

"The chickens are dead? All of them?"

Beau shook his head. *"About half."*

"How? Why? Who would do something like that?"

"I don't know, duchess. Maybe someone doesn't want us here."

"The Seminole?"

Beau took the cooking pot from her grasp but held on to her hand. *"It's possible. Although they've never given an indication. No,"* he rescinded. *"They've been too kind to us. I don't think it's them."*

"Then who?" They'd found a place to be happy, to be together, and now someone was trying to take it away. Tears stung her eyes. Why couldn't people just leave them alone? They weren't hurting anyone.

"I don't know who did it, Amanda. But I won't let it happen again. I promise you."

"Is that all of them?" Connor asked, breaking into her thoughts.

Ashlee snapped back to the present. "I think that's all we'll be able to catch." She faced him. "Thank you. I'm afraid several more would have gotten away if you hadn't shown up when you did." She stopped, staring. "Why did you come out?"

"I was coming down the stairs from seeing my aunt when I heard you call out. What happened?"

She told him what she'd seen.

He gripped her arms. "You mean it wasn't an accident?" A low hiss whispered from him, then he spun around and grabbed the torch from its holder. "Come on, I'm going to see if everyone's accounted for." He shoved the light into her hands, then raced out the door and sprinted through the weeds ahead of her to the manor.

When she reached the veranda, she snuffed the torch in a pail of sand by the entrance and hurried inside.

"Joe is still asleep, I saw Santos lying beneath a

tree out back, and I know your father and my aunt weren't responsible. That only leaves Branden. He only peeked in on Aunt Vivian, then left right away."

Recalling how she'd gone upstairs to get her cloak, Ashlee knew Branden had been afforded enough time to go out to the tent. The thought made her uneasy.

Connor headed for the Delacortes' bedchamber.

Ashlee raced after him.

Without knocking, he flung open the door.

Branden, fully clothed, spun around. Louise sat straight up in bed, clutching a quilt to her chest, the scarlet neckline of her gown a bold slash against the amber bedcover.

"What's the meaning of this?" Branden demanded.

"Why are you still dressed?" Connor asked suspiciously.

Ashlee didn't point out that Connor himself was also still dressed.

Branden's eyes narrowed. "That's none of your business."

Connor's fists drew into knots. "Did you by chance pay a visit to Nathaniel's laboratory?"

"What the hell for?"

"Just answer the question."

"No."

His jaw tight, Connor spun around and stalked out.

Branden started after him, but Ashlee stepped into his path. "Don't," she urged. "He's just upset."

"What's going on?"

She explained about the mice.

Branden paled at first, then turned angry. "He thinks I would do something to hurt Vivian? That I sabotaged the experiment?"

Ashlee could feel the depth of his outrage. He had suffered as much as Connor over Vivian's illness. She touched Branden's arm. "Connor's just trying to account for everyone. The only reason he questioned

190

you was because you were the only other one not abed."

His eyes blazed. "Damn him. He knows me better than that. He knows I'd never do anything to harm her."

"I'm sure he does," she soothed. "He's just agitated at the moment. When he comes to his senses, he'll realize—"

"That Branden simply lives to see people suffer," Louise supplied hatefully.

Branden stiffened.

Ashlee ignored Louise. "Connor will be all right, and perhaps even apologetic, when he calms down." She gave Branden a reassuring smile, then started to leave, but her gaze landed on his shiny boots. Pieces of grass clung to the muddy sides.

Not lifting her eyes, she continued on as if she hadn't seen anything, but inside, her heart was pounding. *Branden couldn't have.*

No, she instantly admonished. He wouldn't. There could be a dozen reasons why he was dressed in the middle of the night—*and* why he had mud on his shoes. For Vivian and Connor's sakes, she had to give Branden the benefit of the doubt. This time.

When she reached the foyer, Connor had a blanket slung over one broad shoulder, and was just opening the front door.

"Where are you going?"

"To sleep in your father's tent." Sending her a look that vowed there wouldn't be any more mishaps this night, he slammed out.

"What's all the ruckus?" her father called from the top of the stairs.

Realizing in the excitement she'd forgotten his request, and not wanting to upset him anymore tonight, she lied. "Nothing. I was just going out to get the notes you wanted."

He frowned, but didn't comment. "Do hurry."

"Yes, of course." Gathering the folds of her gown, she scampered out the door.

Picking her way through the dark weeds, she'd almost reached the laboratory when she collided with an immovable chest. "Oh!" She jumped back in shock.

"Ashlee? What are you doing out here again?" Connor's voice penetrated her fear.

"You nearly frightened me to death." She placed a hand over her heart. "Why are you lurking around in the dark?"

"Watching for intruders." He took her arm and headed toward the tent. Light wavered over the planes and angles of his striking face, over the fall of rich, dark hair that played on his brow. He tilted his head and flashed a smile. "Did you come out to keep me company?"

The brilliance of his teeth against his bronze skin turned her insides to water. She could drown in the man. "I-I forgot Father's notes."

As if he'd sensed the truth of her thoughts, Connor released her and nodded toward the laboratory. "Get your father's papers, and I'll watch until you reach the house."

The next morning, after a night of restless twisting and turning, Ashlee peeked in on Vivian, and seeing her sleeping peacefully, headed downstairs to prepare breakfast.

As soon as the meal was finished, the men set to work, her father poring over his notes at Vivian's side, and Joe separating the mice by tags that identified the medicine they'd been injected with. Connor and Branden set out to restore the grounds.

Santos, Connor had related over breakfast, had gone to visit the Seminole village.

Ashlee saw little of the men for the next few days, only at meals, and they were so engrossed in their various projects, they talked of little else.

Fortunately, Louise kept to herself, and Vivian had improved. Ashlee found herself spending a lot of time with the vibrant woman.

"And when Connor was ten," Vivian said as Ashlee sat at her bedside mending a sheet, "he tried to catch a fawn. He chased it through the woods for hours, barefooted."

Ashlee couldn't help smiling as she pictured a dark-haired boy racing through the pines, bent on capturing a young deer. "Did he ever catch it?"

"Oh, yes. After he sliced open his foot. I had to feed the blessed thing for a week while he recovered."

Somehow it didn't surprise Ashlee that he'd succeeded. Connor didn't strike her as a man who accepted defeat—even while impaired. "What did he do with the fawn?"

"He nurtured it and raised it with all the worshiping love only a young child can give."

A tender spot grew in her breast for the boy who could love so thoroughly. "Does he still have it?"

"No. After the first few weeks, he refused to keep Halfpenny—that's what he called him—confined any longer. But by that time, the animal had grown so attached to Connor, he wouldn't leave. For over two years they were the best of friends. They did everything together, from fishing to wishing on the moon."

"What happened to him?"

Vivian twisted a gray curl at her shoulder, a sign Ashlee had come to recognize as distress. "Halfpenny was killed by a hunter's arrow while Connor was away at school."

"Connor must have been devastated."

"Yes." She lowered her gaze to her lined hands. "It was just one more agony for the boy to endure."

Ashlee grew silent. He had suffered so much. "He told me about his family."

Vivian's head came up, her eyes filled with a mixture of wonder and pleasure. "He did?"

"The night of your attack."

A weak smile crossed the older woman's lips. "That's encouraging. Up until now, he's never mentioned that day to anyone." She waved a hand. "Oh, I tried to talk to him about it several times, hoping he'd come to terms with his grief, accept it, then let it go. Unfortunately, all I accomplished was watching him walk out the door and disappear for days on end. I was beginning to fear it was too late." She studied Ashlee, then she smiled. "But, evidently, it's not. At least, not with you around."

Vivian's revelation stunned Ashlee. Connor had never told anyone about his grief. But her. It was an unsettling fact—one she wasn't sure she knew how to take. That sort of intimacy was usually shared by people who cared very much for one another. Not people who were so mismatched.

"I think you're putting too much store in the conversation. It's more likely that your illness has been wearing on him and he just needed someone to talk to." Rising, Ashlee tugged the light cover up to Vivian's shoulder. "And speaking of talking, we've done enough of that for a while. You get some rest."

Closing the door, she hurried down the stairs and out the back, trying not to think about Connor's peculiar behavior.

"Is it dinnertime already?" Branden asked as she rounded the corner of the house en route to the lake.

"No. I was just taking a stroll. Why? Are you hungry? I could fix a snack."

He didn't pause in his attack with the hoe. "No. I just never see you unless you're ready to summon me for a meal."

She smiled at that, then sought a chair on the veranda near him. Though it had been days, she needed to know the answer to a question. "Branden, why was there mud and grass on your boots the night the mice were set loose?"

He paused midstroke and stared at her. After a long moment, he released a breath, then rested the hoe on the ground and leaned on the handle. "Before I learned of Vivian's attack, I'd had a row with Louise. I was on my way to the lake, to walk off some anger, when I met you and Connor in the hall. After the upset with Vivian, I needed that walk even more. I had returned only minutes before you and Connor came to my chamber."

Knowing what they must have argued about, she offered him a tentative smile. "I'm sorry I suspected you."

"Don't be. I'd have done the same if I'd seen mud on your slippers. After all, there're only two places around here to acquire it. Either in the swamps or at the lake. And we both know how close the laboratory sits to the lake." He sent her a quirky grin. "But I do thank you for not mentioning it to Connor."

She nodded. "Did you see anyone while you were down there?"

Resuming work, he shook his head. "If I had, I'd have reported it immediately."

"Yes. I'm sure you would have." Watching Branden swing the hoe, Ashlee was consumed with the need to help him and Connor settle their differences. A sightless person could see how much the two men cared for each other. Perhaps if she could get Branden to talk to her, explain why he believed his wife's word over his lifelong friend's. But she didn't want him to know she'd overheard his discussion with Louise. "Branden? Why are you and Connor at loggerheads?"

He paused and arched a brow. "At the risk of

sounding rude, Miss Walker, that is none of your business." Smiling to take the sting out of his words, he continued hoeing on around the other side of the house.

Her cheeks stinging from embarrassment, Ashlee wished she'd kept her mouth shut.

She didn't know how long she sat there damning herself before she saw Connor, shirtless and gleaming with perspiration, step from the trees. He carried an armload of newly cut logs to finish the stable with, his muscles bulging from the task.

Connor glanced up, startled to see Ashlee sitting idly on the porch. It was so unlike her. He started to say something, but lost the words. . . .

He set the logs down and stepped up onto the veranda, drinking in the sight of Amanda wearing only a clinging dressing robe, her skin damp from a recent bath. The pail she'd been about to dump rested at her feet.

"You're all sweaty," she teased when he reached for her. But her eyes were warm with desire. "I should have waited for you to join me in the bath."

He pulled her against him, loving the feel of her woman's body. "It's not too late."

A spark of mischievousness lit her eyes. "No, it isn't, is it?" She squirmed out of his hold, and before he knew what she was about, she'd grabbed the pail and dumped the water down his chest.

"Why, you little—"

She squealed and darted around a chair, her hands on its back, keeping it between them. "Now, Beau, I was only having a little fun."

He straightened. "That's all I intend, duchess."

Her eyes darkened as they roamed his bare chest.

Smiling, he eased his breeches down over his hips, then kicked them aside.

Her breath caught. "Beau, not here! Someone might see us."

He jerked the chair out of the way. "There is no one else. We're completely alone." He untied her belt and opened the robe, feasting on her naked beauty. His hands became unsteady as he eased it off her shoulders and let the silk pool at her feet.

Sunlight speared through the leaves and touched her satin body. "Oh, duchess." Desire rushed him, and he dropped to his knees, nuzzling her smooth stomach with his cheek, his mouth. "You take my breath away."

Her fingers entwined in his hair, and she sank to her knees in front of him. "Make love to me, Beau. Show me another side of heaven."

A groan ripped from his throat, and he took her with urgency. . . .

Connor blinked away the erotic images, yet he couldn't slow the pounding in his chest. He set the logs down and stepped up onto the veranda, his eyes never leaving Ashlee. "What are you doing out here?"

"What?" She looked up. She blushed to the roots of her hair and glanced away. "I was just getting ready to start dinner." She scrambled to her feet and turned to go.

He put out a hand to stop her. "You saw it, didn't you?"

She kept her eyes straight ahead. "What?"

"The vision of them making love on the porch."

She drew in a sharp breath, and their eyes collided. "You saw it, too?"

"Every detail."

"This is lunacy." She moved out of his grasp and rubbed the place where his hand had been on her arm. "Were you just in the swamps?"

"I was cutting some logs because I want to finish the stables. I'm careful, Ashlee, believe me. I don't know what's out there, but I don't let my guard down for an instant." He started to raise his hand to touch her **again**, but swiftly lowered it.

"Blast it, Connor. I wish you wouldn't go in there. This thing is too real to ignore." She faced him, her concern genuine.

Their eyes met. Locked. He was held immobile as time wavered in and out. The air turned thick. Musky. He was transfixed by her beauty, the sensual heat radiating from her body so close to his own, her arousing scent, the smoldering look in those hypnotic, blue-green eyes. It was becoming hard to breathe.

Without realizing he'd moved, she was in his arms, his mouth on hers.

For just an instant, she resisted, then, like a candle too close to a fire, she melted against him.

Their surroundings faded away, and he lost himself in her softness, the warmth of her body pressed so intimately to his. Though he'd kissed her before, something about this kiss was different. It was as if she had no control over her actions. She gave her passion fully, holding nothing back.

A low moan escaped, and she slid her arms up to encircle his neck, her lips parting for the slow thrust of his tongue.

His body went up in flames, and he deepened the kiss, grinding his mouth against hers with an urgency that shook his soul.

"I want you," she cried with the same desperate need. "Oh, Beau. I want you."

His blood iced over, and he jerked back. *"What did you say?"*

She stared as if coming out of a daze. "What?"

He gripped her upper arms. "Damn it, Ashlee. You just called me *Beau.*"

CHAPTER
18

Ashlee shuddered at the feel of Connor's powerful hands gripping her arms. "What's happening to me? To us? *Why* is it happening?" A lump clogged her throat. "I feel as if I'm teetering on the brink of insanity."

His hold softened with his words. "I know. Sometimes I feel the same."

The compassion in his eyes was Ashlee's undoing. Tears spilled onto her cheeks. "I don't know what to do."

"Neither do I," he whispered, pulling her into his arms.

"Don't cry, angel, you're tearing me apart." Beau *stroked her back. "We'll have children someday. I promise."*

"No, we won't." She tightened her fist in frustration. *"Before we even met, that bastard I married destroyed any chance of that. From the first, he took me with brutality, savagery, uncaring that the act was so painful, I screamed in agony. I was certain he damaged me*

on our wedding night, and when I didn't conceive after the first year, the beatings began." She shook with remembered fear. "*Every time my monthly came, he knocked me to the floor. He'd call me a barren bitch and kick me in the stomach, again and again. Merciful heavens, how I would bleed afterwards.*

"*Oh, Beau, don't you see? Either I was barren from the beginning, or he ruined me. But no matter which, I'll never be able to have your babe.*" Tears flowed freely. "*I'll never hold in my arms the sweet proof of our love.*" She buried her face in his shoulder and wept in bitterness.

His loving arms encircled her. "*I won't lie to you and deny I'd like a child of our union, because I would. But a babe isn't the whole of my existence. You are. You're my entire life. With you at my side, I'll be content with or without children.*" He kissed her tenderly. "*Just as long as you love me, sweet witch.*"

"*I'll love you for eternity.*" Her tears increased, but this time from overflowing joy. She savored the taste of his mouth as she pressed into the warmth of his long body. "*No,*" she whispered. "*Eternity isn't long enough.*"

Ashlee struggled back from the vision, and stepped out of Connor's hold.

"What is it?" he asked with concern. "What's wrong?"

"They couldn't have children. Her husband beat her until she was barren."

"What?"

Ashlee pressed her fingers to her temples, trying to rid herself of the images and words, but it didn't help. It was becoming hard to breathe. "I-I'm not feeling well." Without another word, she turned and raced indoors.

Connor stared after her, his gut tight with concern and despair. *They couldn't have children. Her husband beat her until she was barren.* Anger surged through his veins until he shook with the force. But he didn't know who to direct it at. The husband of the long-ago lovers? Or at the presence that kept torturing Ashlee? And himself.

"Connor!" Joe yelled. "Come quick!"

The man raced around the corner of the house, then skidded to a halt.

"Hurry!" Joe screeched, then whirled around and ran back the way he'd come.

Connor was in motion instantly, running for the laboratory. When he reached the entrance, he came to an abrupt halt. "What's wrong?"

Nathaniel gestured toward several test tubes and the clay oven he used to bake the coal. All of them had been destroyed. His face drawn, he tried to explain. "We went into the house, assuming dinner would be ready. When we found it wasn't, we stayed for a brandy, then returned." He clenched his fist. "We weren't gone but a few minutes. Yet someone did this in that short space of time."

"What's the problem?" Branden's voice rang out from behind Connor.

"Did you see anyone near the tent?"

"No. I was working on the other side of the house. Why? What happened?"

Connor flung his hand toward the destruction. "Damn."

"What about you?" Connor directed the question to Joe and Nathaniel. "Was there anyone about when you went inside?"

"I didn't see anyone," the assistant denied.

"There wasn't anyone," Nathaniel voiced. "Since the incident with the mice, I've kept a close watch."

"It looks as if someone else is watching, too," Branden concluded. "Waiting for the opportunity to strike."

"Well, he won't get another one," Connor vowed. "From this day on, I want someone inside this place at all times. Even if we have to eat in shifts." He explored the wreckage. "Is any of this salvageable?"

"Some," Nathaniel answered. "And I have others in my trunks." He motioned to Joe. "Help me clean this mess up, will you? Then we'll get one of them."

Joe reached for an empty bag.

"What's going on?" Santos asked as he strolled up.

"When did you get back?" Suspicious, Connor turned on him.

"Just now. Why?"

Connor explained. "Have you seen anyone around who doesn't belong?"

"No."

"What about the Seminole? Would they find cause to disrupt Nathaniel's work?"

"The Seminole won't come within a mile of this place," Santos answered evenly. "Even I'm nervous about getting this close. I'm afraid you'll need to look elsewhere for your villain."

Knowing how much he himself hated to be wrongly accused, Connor softened. "I apologize. It's just that this is the second occurrence in a week, and I'm afraid the next time may call a halt to the experiments altogether. Everyone's under suspicion at this point."

"I understand. And if it'll help, I'll sleep inside the tent at night."

Having done that himself for the last few days, Connor was glad to give up the chore. "I'd appreciate it." Nodding, he made for the house. There was one person who wasn't accounted for. Louise.

He found her in the bedchamber she shared with her husband, sorting through the ancient clothes hanging in the armoire.

"What are you doing?" Connor demanded, inexplicably angered over her touching the garments.

She spun around, her eyes wide. "Connor." She placed a hand over her heart. The movement separated the neckline of her robe, allowing him to glimpse the swell of one white breast. "You frightened a score of years off my life." She trailed her nails over the exposed flesh, and smiled. "Dare I hope this is a rendezvous?"

He ignored the sultry invitation. "Where were you ten minutes ago?"

Her smile widened, and she waved her hand toward a tub filled with sudsy water. "In my bath." She walked toward him, her hips swaying provocatively. "Too bad you didn't come a little sooner." She traced a finger down his bare, sweat-dampened chest. "You could have joined me."

He brushed her hand aside and moved to the window overlooking the lab. Santos and Nathaniel were helping Joe carry debris from the tent. "Did you see anyone enter Nathaniel's laboratory a few minutes ago?"

"No. I told you, I was in the tub . . . having a very erotic daydream." She pressed against his back. "We were in Paris—"

He reeled around, almost knocking her over.

She grabbed for his arms to keep from falling.

Reflexively he caught her.

"You don't ever quit, do you, Connor?" Branden's voice rang ominously from the doorway.

He released Louise. "This isn't what you think."

Louise laughed. "Darling, don't try to worm your way out. We're caught."

He sent her a glare that could have frozen the entire ocean, then shoved past her to face his friend. "She was the only one who wasn't accounted for, so I came up here to question her—and to see if she saw anyone. If that isn't explanation enough, then perhaps we'd better get that duel over with here and now."

Branden's gaze slid from him to Louise, then back again. "I can wait." Then he turned on his wife. "Don't push me too far, woman, or you may not live long enough to enjoy the end to your game."

Louise paled.

Connor left the room, in complete agreement with his friend, and wanting to strangle Louise with his own hands. Women! he mentally cursed as he descended the stairs. He would never understand the lot of them. Or why God put them on this earth to torment men.

When he reached the foyer, he caught a glimpse of the silver apparition, standing in the parlor archway. She was pointing frantically, Connor swung toward the entrance just as the front door burst open. "Fire! The tent's on fire!" Joe screamed.

What else could go wrong? Connor raged. "Get the others and all the buckets you can carry," he ordered, running for the door. "Branden!" he bellowed toward the stairs.

"Connor?" Ashlee asked, coming in from the cookhouse. "What's all the shouting?"

"Come on," he commanded, gripping her arm. "We need all the help we can get."

Charging across the just cut lawn with Ashlee in tow, he tried to stop the fear racing through his blood. This could very well be the end of Nathaniel's experiments. No! Damn it, he wouldn't let it be!

When they reached the burning tent, he shoved Ashlee toward the water. "Get a bucket. Hurry!" He had to save what he could. Taking a breath, he shielded his eyes with his arm and charged into the flames.

He gathered Nathaniel's notes from the table and shoved them into a pair of hands just outside the opening. Returning, he grabbed the two crates of mice and tossed them out, then headed for the bags of coal stacked in the corner.

A loud roar filled his ears. The table flew toward him. It slammed into him, knocking him backward. Then everything took on an eerie quality of slow motion. He could feel the pain in his head, the blood dripping down his jaw. His knees folded, and he felt the table pressing down on top of him, then he was falling. . . .

From far, far away, he heard Ashlee's tortured cry. "No! Oh, God. *No!*"

Ashlee's lungs felt as if they'd collapse from lack of oxygen by the time she saw Branden pull Connor from the burning rubble. When they'd heard the explosion, Branden had nearly gone insane trying to get through the flames to his friend.

But Connor was unconscious.

Panicked, Ashlee dropped down next to him. "Oh, Connor," she cried, barely able to stop herself from touching the charred flesh on his lower back. Then she saw his breeches. The fabric had melted to his left thigh. "Someone get me a knife. Quickly!"

"How bad is he?" her father asked, coming down beside her. He sucked in a breath when he saw Connor's breeches. "I'll get some cold mud." Lunging to his feet, he grabbed an empty bucket and charged into the lake.

A knife was shoved into her hand, and she set to work, cutting the material away from Connor's skin. The odor of scorched flesh permeated the air, but she didn't slow her tedious work.

When she'd at last freed the garment and began pealing it away, raw flesh and blood followed in its wake. Her father was there in an instant, slapping the cool mud on Connor's thigh. She knew there was a risk of infection from the wet dirt, but stopping the burn from going any deeper was vital.

Relinquishing the care of his leg to her father, she scooted to Connor's shoulders. Fortunately, his upper torso had escaped injury. Somewhat relieved, she glanced down at his face. Then she saw the blood.

A line of crimson trailed from his temple to his jaw. With a trembling hand, she touched his coffee-colored hair and parted the silken strands. A bloody gash split his scalp. Something had struck him.

"Is he all right?" Branden asked worriedly.

"I don't know. He's been hit on the head."

Branden paled.

"Let's get him to the house," her father ordered.

She rose and stepped back. "Be careful."

When Connor was situated facedown on the feather tick, Ashlee set to work cleaning the mud from his back and thigh. It didn't occur to her that they'd stripped away the rest of his clothes until her father placed a stilling hand over hers. "Under the circumstances, I think it is better I tend him, love." He squeezed her fingers. "Make us some tea, would you?"

Realizing her hand rested on a smooth, naked buttock, she snatched it back and lurched to her feet. "Certainly." Mortified, she rushed from the room.

She'd just about reached the kitchens when she saw Santos standing in the trees, his gaze fixed on an upstairs window. She started to call out to him, but at that moment he turned and slipped into the woods.

Not sure what to think about the odd expression she'd seen on his face, Ashlee dismissed him from her thoughts and went inside.

By the time she'd prepared tea, fixed a tray of cheese and scones, and informed Vivian of the fire, Ashlee was exhausted . . . and worried. Her father still hadn't come down.

Tired, she rested her head on the high back of a chair, ignoring the other occupants of the parlor. But every time she closed her eyes, she saw a fiery canvas collapse on top of Connor.

She rose and walked to the window, her heart heavy, her concern deepening with each passing moment. What if he died?

"Ashlee?"

Hearing her father's voice, she whirled around and rushed to him. "How is he?"

Joe and Branden rose, their expressions expectant.

Louise looked ready to collapse, her features tense, deeply concerned. The woman's feelings for Connor couldn't have been more plain if she'd written them on parchment.

Ignoring the sting of jealousy, Ashlee directed her attention to her father.

A lock of white hair fell onto his forehead as he poured a cup of tea and sat down. "I am not sure how he is. The burns are not serious. We got to them in time, but the injury to his head has me worried. I will not know exactly how serious it is until he comes around."

Having seen many head wounds while helping her father, Ashlee knew Connor's return to consciousness could take an hour or months . . . if he woke up at all. "Maybe you should tell Vivian."

He shook his head. "She has enough to worry about. If it can be helped, I do not want her to know about this until she has fully recovered." He rose. "Speaking of which, I had better get back to her. Will you stay with Connor awhile?" At Ashlee's nod, her father gave a halfhearted smile. "Thank you."

"I'll sit with him first," Branden countered. "Ashlee needs to get some rest."

Knowing how frightened Branden had been for

Connor, she didn't argue. "I'll relieve you after I've bathed and changed." A clock on the sideboard behind her chimed three times. Startled by the fact that she'd been up most of the night, she glanced out the narrow window next to the door. A man's silhouette was outlined by the lake's moonlit water. Santos.

She'd forgotten all about him. She felt a flicker of sympathy. Santos must be concerned, but he wouldn't come near the house, not even to ask about Connor. Well, that was one problem she could rectify, she decided as she reached for the door latch.

He was bent over, looking at something, when she approached. "I thought you might like to kn—"

Santos rose abruptly. "Do you know what started the fire?" It was more an accusation than a question.

"Well, no. I don't. I assumed gas ignited from the broken coal oven."

"You figured wrong." He shoved something in her hand. "Look at this."

She glanced down at the club she held. It had charred rags tightly wound around one end. "What is it?"

"One of the torches. I found it in the rubble. Someone deliberately set the fire."

"But how? Surely someone would have seen an intruder sneaking around the tent."

"Maybe it wasn't an intruder," he said, taking a step away from her.

"That's absurd. Everyone was about. Branden told me so." Her eyes narrowed with sudden realization. "Except you."

Those bottomless black eyes stared into hers. "I was answering nature's call. And if it had been me," he stressed, "then I damned sure wouldn't have pointed out the fact it wasn't an accident." He curled his upper lip in a gesture of contempt. "No, Miss Walker. It wasn't me." He sent her a meaningful look. "Perhaps you'll have to look a little closer to home." With that, he dipped his head and walked off.

She gaped at his retreating form. What did he mean, a little closer to home? That couldn't be. Everyone had been accounted for.

According to Branden.

CHAPTER
19

No. Ashlee would not believe Branden had anything to do with the fire. And she wasn't about to let Santos's remark go without explanation. Gathering the folds of her gown, she raced after him. "Wait!" she cried. "What are you talking about?"

He stopped, then glanced around as if taking note of their isolated surroundings in the predawn darkness.

Suddenly uneasy, she retreated a pace. "What do you mean, closer to home? I don't understand. Are you talking about the Seminole?"

"My people aren't to blame."

"Then who?"

His eyes drifted to the house, then slowly returned.

In the moonlight, she could just make out their shape, but his expression was visible—and incredible. "You couldn't possibly believe this was caused by the ghost that some say haunts the swamps. You strike me as much too intelligent."

"Then you come up with the answer."

"Don't you think I would if I could? Besides,

assuming there is such a thing as the Silver Witch, what possible reason could a hundred-year-old specter have for upsetting Father's experiments?" Ashlee shoved aside memories of the haunting visions she'd experienced.

"Maybe she doesn't like you staying in her home."

That likelihood hadn't occurred to Ashlee. Not even once. In fact, she'd felt just the opposite—as if they'd been warmly welcomed.

Her gaze fluttered back to the manor, and for the first time, she felt a stirring of uneasiness. Could he be right?

No, her soul cried out. It's not true. "It isn't that. I don't know how I know, and I won't try to explain the sensation, but I'm certain we're not intruding."

"Perhaps you're not, at that." He broke off a long, limber branch and twisted the ends around his hands, then drew it taut, as if testing it for strength. "How's Connor?"

Her attention remained fixed on the limb. "H-He hasn't regained consciousness yet. As a matter of fact, I was getting ready to sit with him when I saw you."

"That's good." His gaze slid to her neck, and he tightened his hold on the limb. "A woman belongs with her man. Always."

She swallowed nervously. "I-I've got to go." She whirled around and raced through the darkness, back to the safety of the house. Though he hadn't really done anything threatening, Santos frightened the stuffing out of her.

After a soothing bath, she went to relieve Branden. She was anxious to check on Connor. As she strolled around the landing, she noticed a strange stillness to the house, an unearthly silence.

She gripped the banister, knowing she was being foolish by letting Santos's suspicion affect her. Of course the house was quiet, she rationalized; no one but she and Branden were up and about. It was bound to be still. Even so, she couldn't shake the feeling that the mysterious silence was somehow different from normal. Almost eerie.

Not about to let her mind start wandering along that particular vein, she attributed the unsettling sensation to her own fatigue, and opened the door to Connor's bedchamber.

She froze.

The misty figure of a woman stood beside Connor's bed.

A nervous skitter rippled through Ashlee's midsection. *This is not happening.* It had to be her imagination. She closed her eyes and rubbed the lids with her fingers, then opened them again, blinking rapidly.

The ghost was gone.

A relieved breath slid past her dry lips. She was more tired than she thought. Now she was seeing phantoms to go along with her mysterious daydreams. Certain that all of Santos's talk about apparitions was to blame, she scolded herself for allowing him to influence her.

Branden sat in a chair next to the bed, sound asleep.

Smiling, and not wishing to disturb him, she retrieved another chair, then pulled it up on the opposite side of the four-poster.

Connor still lay on his stomach, his powerful arms drawn up on either side of his head. A sheet had been draped over his lower body. Through the thin material she could see no outline of bandages, only firm, masculine contours.

Father had told her that a light dusting of dried aloe and ample ventilation would speed the healing process, but she couldn't help worrying about the wounds being so exposed.

She examined his head wound. He lay with his face turned to the side, toward her, his wavy, overlong hair spilling onto the pillow. The rich, dark color contrasted with the bandage at his temple.

For a timeless moment, she stared at his perfect features, the healthy tanned skin, long, black lashes resting in quarter-moon crescents on his high cheekbones, while his beautifully shaped mouth remained half-open, allowing her a glimpse of straight white teeth.

A light growth of beard shadowed his jaw and chin, which always held a trace of arrogance. Everything about him bespoke self-confidence. As did his high-handed manner.

She smiled at that, but lost her humor when she thought of the seriousness of his condition. He still wasn't out of danger. And until he regained consciousness, they wouldn't know the extent of damage the blow had caused.

Unable to sit still, she rose and paced the large chamber, her nerves strung so tight, they could be used for bowstrings.

"Ashlee?"

She jumped and whirled around.

Branden, too, jerked awake and looked about in confusion.

"May I have some water?"

Stunned, she stared down at Connor. He was awake —and speaking to her. Elation filled her. "O-Of course. Right away." She was so shocked, she almost stumbled in an attempt to get him a drink. "You startled me," she blurted. "I thought you were still out."

"Are you all right?" Branden asked.

Connor propped himself up on his elbow and turned onto his side as she handed him the glass. "What happened?" His brows rose sharply. "The fire."

"Yes," Branden affirmed. "The tent was destroyed,

and you were burned. Not to mention nearly having your skull crushed."

The baffled look on Connor's face sent waves of tenderness through Ashlee. She shot Branden a warning glare.

"What are you talking about?" Connor asked.

"Branden's referring to your injuries. The burning tent fell on you. The flames burned your waist and left thigh, and something struck your head."

"That large table your father used. I remember it slamming into me." Connor touched the bandage, wincing. "It is a little sore, but not too bad."

Because you have such a hard head, she wanted to retaliate for his scaring her. "Father gave you a dose of laudanum to ease the ache."

He nodded as he laid a palm on his left leg, then drew in a slow, hissing breath. "Damn."

Ashlee stared at his strong hand lying on the sheet. The contrast between light and dark was startling. "You're very fortunate not to be in worse pain. Your wounds could have been quite severe."

He gingerly massaged the area, then yanked the sheet back for a look.

"Connor!" Branden blurted.

Without thought, Ashlee gazed at the injury. Her breath stuck at the sight of a naked thigh. She spun around, presenting him with her back. "For heaven's sake, cover yourself."

Branden chuckled. "If you'll excuse me, I'll go fetch Nathaniel."

Though she was glad for Branden's departure, the fire in her cheeks still seared her skin.

"You can look now. I'm decent."

Ashlee had her doubts that anything about this man was decent. Wary, she peeked over her shoulder. True to his word, Connor was covered.

Wondering how his head wound fared, she cleared

her throat and gestured toward his other injury. "Would you remove the bandage?"

"I thought you wanted me to remain covered."

"I do. At least, from the waist down."

He smiled and pulled the gauze away from his skin, wincing as strands of hair clung to dried blood.

Ashlee lifted unsteady fingers to separate the vibrant strands and leaned forward for a better look. They were so close, she felt the heat of his breath moving over her throat. His masculine scent touched her senses. He smelled of mint, exotic spice, and clean soap.

She traced the healing gash. "It's going to be sore for a while."

His fingers came up to close over hers. "I'm past the point of caring." His eyes were fixed on her mouth.

Her insides fluttered around. The heat from that smoldering look made her shiver. She moved back. "I've got t-to see what's keeping my father."

Breathing hard, more from their encounter than her hurried exit, Ashlee raced to Vivian's room, where she almost collided with Branden and her father as they emerged from the doorway.

"I-I think he's better," she babbled.

Her father sent her an odd look, then nodded and hurried down the hall.

Branden was right behind him.

Ashlee made for the parlor to gather her senses—which took considerable time. Nearly an hour passed before she at last felt steady enough to return to Connor's bedchamber.

Her father had just finished examining Connor and drawn much the same conclusion as she. "He's fine."

Only half listening, she glanced uneasily about the dim room. She hadn't mentioned the ghost—and doubted she ever would. Still, she scanned the bedchamber . . . just in case, then returned her attention to the conversation. "Well, I, for one, am quite pleased." Ashlee hadn't meant to sound so sincere, especially after the way Connor had embarrassed her earlier. She glared at him. "Yes. I'm pleased, indeed. I have enough to do around here without tending a careless oaf who should have had more sense than to run into a burning tent."

Connor's lips tightened. "It seems that fortune has smiled upon us both. For I have no wish to be subjected to the malicious whims of a tyrant." He stared at her full mouth, wishing he didn't feel the urge to kiss the little vixen senseless.

"Well, it's been a long night," Branden said on a yawn. "If you'll excuse me, I'm off to bed." Nodding, he left the room.

Nathaniel coughed lightly. "Since you no longer require my services, I believe I'll rejoin Vivian."

"How is she?" Connor asked with concern.

"Better. She should be up and around in a day or so." Nathaniel's eyes twinkled. "Time enough for a few strong men to rebuild my laboratory."

"Yes," Ashlee interjected. "Your foolishness did have one passable benefit. You managed to save Father's notes and the mice. And since he hadn't yet retrieved the new clay pot and tubes from the other trunk, he can still carry on his work."

"Thank God for that," Connor said, relieved. "Vivian can't afford more setbacks."

Nathaniel dipped his head in agreement as he left.

As soon as the door closed, Connor turned his attention to Ashlee. "What? No rejoinder? No biting remark about someone's carelessness causing the accident in the first place? Possibly even myself?"

Her aquamarine eyes met his for the first time without rancor. "Connor, it wasn't an accident."

He stared at her, praying he hadn't heard her

correctly. The fire *had* to have been an accident. "What did you say?"

"It was not an accident," she repeated. "Santos showed me the torch used to set the blaze. I didn't mention it earlier because I didn't want Father to know. I hope he'll just assume that, since the clay oven had been broken, gas escaped and a spark ignited. I don't think we need to worry him further with the knowledge that someone is determined to stop his work."

Connor swallowed his anger and took her hand. "Your common sense never ceases to amaze me." He gave a light squeeze, then released her. "Did Santos have any idea who might have set the blaze?"

"He thinks the ghost did it."

Connor didn't voice his own thoughts on the subject. He wasn't even sure what they were. "And what do you think?"

"I don't know. I think it's possible that the Indians are involved, though Santos swears they aren't."

She had a point. "Have you seen any around?"

"No. But I did see someone the night the mice were released. It could have been a Seminole. Or someone who isn't a member of our party."

Connor considered her words as he watched her smooth the fabric of her rose-clustered apron. Was it possible someone else was about whom they weren't aware of? One person came to mind, but he didn't want to say anything until he could give a thread of credibility to his suspicions. He sat up and started to toss the covers aside, but stopped. "I'm going to talk to Santos, so unless you want to watch me dress, I suggest you leave the room."

"You can't. You're—"

"I'm fine. Now, are you going or do you wish to help?"

Her only wish was to choke the cur. She rose stiffly. "Don't be absurd."

Amused, he watched her strut regally from the room. She tried so hard to be prim and straitlaced, but there was an undercurrent of warmth and passion that couldn't be disguised by that haughty air. He had seen the vulnerable side of her too many times, the side that hurt for other human beings and revealed the depth of her sensitivity. The side that burned with passion. No matter how cold and aloof she tried to make herself appear, it wouldn't work. He knew the real Ashlee. And he wanted to know her better.

A little unstrung by the thought, he shoved back the quilt and carefully swung his legs over the side of the bed. He still needed to see Santos.

The sun winked between rustling, moss-draped cypress overhead when Connor found the guide kneeling near the tent.

Santos touched a ridge of spongy soil, tracing the outline of a man's footprint. "It doesn't belong to anyone here. I checked."

Staring at the first real piece of evidence they'd found, Connor knelt beside Santos, wincing when his breeches brushed the burns on his thigh. "This shoots your theory about apparitions all to hell."

The guide arched a brow, but didn't comment.

"You know, there may be someone we've overlooked," Connor said, voicing his earlier thought. "George Acres."

Santos came to his feet. "We saw him leave."

"True. But he could have doubled back." Connor rose. "Anyway, it's a possibility that can't be dismissed. I want to search the area thoroughly. If we don't find anything, I'd like for you to return to your village, question the Seminole. See if they've seen anyone. In the meantime, I'm going to guard this place so close, a snake couldn't get in without being spotted."

"I'll do what I can."

Connor offered his hand. "Thank you."

Santos nodded, but didn't touch him.

Ashlee saw little of Connor and the others for the next two days because they were totally engrossed in building the new laboratory.

Vivian had improved and was up and about, but she still needed a great deal of rest.

Occasionally, Ashlee caught a glimpse of Louise lounging in the parlor, but she avoided her whenever possible. Instinctively, she knew they would never be friends.

Not wanting to think of that situation, she headed for the back of the house and the wash tub.

Connor stared at Santos. "They haven't seen anyone but the members of our group? That doesn't make sense. You said the footprints didn't belong to any of us."

"They don't," the guide reiterated. "You saw them. They're too small."

An ugly thought crept in. "Could the culprit be a woman?"

Santos rose from his cross-legged position on the ground. "No. The impression was too deep. The man weighed twelve stones or more."

Connor frowned. Nearly a hundred seventy pounds? "Are you sure? That particular weight doesn't fit any of us. Even George Acres was smaller than that."

Santos shrugged and dusted off his breeches. "Have you considered yours or Nathaniel's enemies?"

No, he hadn't. "I'll give it some thought, ask a few

questions. Meanwhile, keep an eye on the laboratory. Report anything suspicious to me immediately, no matter how minute."

Anxious to talk to Ashlee, Connor strode toward the manor. He found her behind the house, leaning over a steaming tub, and up to her elbows in soap suds. "What are you doing?"

She raised a dripping hand to brush the hair out of her eyes, not even realizing she'd exposed her scarred cheek to the morning sun. "The wash."

Seeing her working like a slave sent an unexpected wave of rage through him. "That isn't your duty."

She straightened and placed her hands on her slim waist. "Oh? And who, pray tell, do you expect to do it? Your aunt? Or perhaps the elegant Louise?"

"Of course not."

"Then who?" she demanded.

"I'll do the damned wash," he grated. Anything was better than seeing her reduced to this level. She was a woman of breeding. . . . The thought was eerily familiar. *A duchess does not paint pillars. . . .*

A little unnerved, he set Ashlee aside, then rolled up his sleeves and grabbed a shirt from the tub. He slapped it against the rub board and scrubbed vigorously. "Don't go," he commanded when she started to leave.

"Why? Do you need instructions?" she taunted.

He smiled at her wit. "No. Information." He met her eyes. "Does your father have any enemies?"

Her brows rose at his offhanded question, then she grasped his reasoning. "I'm certain he does. No man grows to the age of fifty without gaining a few. For that matter, neither does a woman. But if you're asking me to name them, I can't. Still, I doubt there are any who'd follow him into the swamps to exact revenge when they could have done so in St. Augustine."

"You have a point. Too, that same situation applies

to all of us. Why would anyone follow—or wait—until we were in the swamps?"

"Perhaps the need for revenge just happened recently."

Recently? As in the discord between him and Branden? No, his heart immediately defended. Branden wouldn't do this. He was angry and upset over Louise, but he's not underhanded. And he'd never do anything to hurt Vivian.

"What about Joe?" Connor asked.

"What about him?"

Connor recounted the conversation he'd overheard between Joe and Harry.

Ashlee crossed her arms and stared off into the distance, her delicate features in profile. Sunlight winked in the silver-gold locks that brushed her creamy cheeks and finely sculpted jaw. Mounds of smooth flesh covered by a sheer tucker rose above the low, square bodice of her gown.

Connor had trouble paying attention to the subject.

"I had no idea they blamed my father for Charlotte's death," Ashlee said softly. "But I can't imagine Joe instigating something like this on his own. Charlotte and Harry were the leaders. Joe followed." She shook her head. "No, I think it's someone mentally stronger, more vicious. Someone like Louise Delacorte."

CHAPTER
20

Ashlee headed back to the house and left Connor to do the wash. She wanted to give more thought to the identity of the saboteur. Although she'd remarked on Louise, somehow she didn't really believe the woman capable of the deeds. But if it was someone else, what reason could the person have for waiting until now?

"Who do you think destroyed our garden, Beau? And why now, after nearly a year?"

He pulled her down beside him on the settee and drew her against him. "Since there's no one else in the area but Seminole, it's reasonable to assume the culprit is one of them. Yet the only reason I can imagine for them waiting so long is, just perhaps, they didn't expect us to stay."

"But we haven't done anything to make the Indians angry with us. For heaven's sake, we're practically hermits."

Beau stared into the fireplace, his expression thoughtful. "Perhaps it's not something we did as much as who we are and what we represent. The white man. The intruders."

Ashlee stopped. *Not something we did. Who we are and what we represent.* Could it be the problem arose from who they were? It was a thought, but the more logical explanation of unknown enemies still couldn't be discarded.

"Well, well. Aren't you a sight," Louise's sultry voice rang from a chair by the window. "What have you been doing, puss? Wallowing in the shallows?"

Knowing the front of her gown was wet from doing the wash, Ashlee seethed. "No, I haven't been wallowing in the shallows. I've been with Connor."

When those ruby lips tightened, Ashlee felt a burst of smug satisfaction. "Actually, we were doing the laundry together." She tried her best to appear innocent.

Not waiting for the woman to respond, Ashlee left the parlor and made for the laboratory. Still, she couldn't suppress a rush of gratification as she sauntered over the thick grass. Louise was overdue for a good setdown.

When she entered the new thatch structure, her father was bent over a microscope, while Joe was noting the behavior of a pair of mice that had been separated from the others.

Father glanced up and smiled. "Good morning, love."

Ashlee smiled, then eyed the mixture in front of him. "Anything?"

"Have a look." He gestured toward the magnifying instrument.

Pressing her eye to the round cylinder, she squinted at a glass slide. Blood had been smeared on the glass, and she could see hundreds of little squirming organisms in the matter. "That's amazing."

"Now look at this." He slipped another glass wedge into place.

It looked the same, except this smear had long, sticklike organisms the other sample hadn't contained. "What are those odd-looking ones?"

"The malaria. That blood sample is from Vivian's finger. The first one was mine."

Ashlee was amazed at her father's progress. "Have you found a way to destroy them?"

"I will have to run more tests. But this latest elixir does look promising."

"What's in it?"

He checked his notes. "I have used a coal tar base, then combined opium salt and liquid oxygen." He shook his head. "But there is still something missing. An ingredient, or combination of ingredients, I cannot quite grasp."

Ashlee's excitement grew. He was getting very, very close. She could feel it. Still, there was the possibility of more delays if the saboteur wasn't caught. "I'm sure you'll find it, and when you do, everyone will be green with envy. Even your enemies."

Joe glanced up and frowned.

Her father lifted a white brow. "Enemies? Fortunately, I stopped making those when I gave up doctoring to do research."

"You made quite a few enemies back then, as I recall."

"More than I care to count. If I could not save a patient, I was sometimes blamed for the death."

"That's not fair."

"No, it is not. But when a man watches a loved one die, in his grief, he will lash out at the closest target. That is usually the physician." He gave her a small smile. "It is human nature to strike out when you are hurt."

Ashlee could certainly understand that. And too

much time had passed since then for someone to seek revenge now.

Joe, she noticed, had turned his back to them, his shoulders stiff.

After watching a few minutes longer, she bid them good-bye, then went to check on Connor's progress with the laundry.

Ashlee nearly tripped over her own feet when she saw Louise's shapely bottom wiggling as she bent over the tub, diligently scrubbing one of Connor's shirts. Tears of laughter almost blinded her, and she hurried into the house.

In her haste, she ran smack into Branden.

He stumbled backward and automatically grabbed for her waist, then held on until they both righted.

"What's the rush?" he asked, not yet releasing her.

She fought for something to say. She couldn't tell him she was trying not to laugh at his wife's attempts to wash his friend's clothes. "I . . . um . . ."

"What's the meaning of this?" Connor said from the dining room doorway.

Ashlee's gaze flew to Connor.

Branden's hands tightened on her waist. "I was just enjoying the lady's company." His eyes narrowed. "As you've often enjoyed my wife's."

Connor tensed.

Branden's fingers dug into her sides.

Ashlee wished she were anywhere else at the moment. The strain between the two men was so tangible, she could cut it with a feather.

"Let her go," Connor said in that dangerously soft voice that sent chills up her spine.

"Sure." Branden set her away from him, then gave a wicked smile. "There's always another time." Dipping his dark head in mock salutation, he strode out the rear door.

Connor stared after his friend, then turned that

hostile gaze on her. "Stay away from him, Ashlee. He's only using you to get to me."

"Why would he do that?" she asked in an innocent tone.

He watched her for a moment, his expression uncertain, then he released a breath and brought a hand to the back of his neck. "Let's go into the parlor. I need a drink."

The sudden defeat in his tone worried her as she followed him. He looked as if he carried the weight of the world on those broad shoulders.

She waited by the window while he poured himself a drink.

When Connor at last turned to her, he didn't meet her eyes. Instead, he stared down into his drink, watching the amber liquid move as he swirled the glass. "Before we get into a discussion about Branden, tell me about the explosion in your father's laboratory in St. Augustine."

Uncertain, Ashlee frowned. "What do you want to know?"

"Everything you can remember about that day. Where everyone was, what your companions were like, how the explosion happened."

Perching a hip on the window seat, Ashlee stared out at the thick lawn still damp with morning dew. "It was just like any other day, so I don't recall much until right before it happened. Father had gone into the library to check his notes against a report he'd just received from a scientist in Italy. Joe was on the far side of the room, injecting serum into one of the mice. David and Charlotte were at the table next to the coal oven, labeling vials."

"Where were you?"

"Standing in the doorway. I'd just returned with clean smocks. Harry was leaning against the end of the table where Charlotte and David were, getting ready to strike a flint to his cigar."

"Is that what caused the accident?"

"I believe so."

Connor braced his arms on the back of a chair, rolling the glass between his palms. "Were all your friends close?"

She smiled. "Yes. Joe and Charlotte were twins, and, of course, Harry was Charlotte's husband. David was the only outsider, but he got along well with the others." Remembered grief clogged her throat. "Harry and Charlotte were so much in love. The sparks between them charged the air when they were in the same room. I miss them terribly, but I'm happy they're together again."

Connor tilted his head and looked at her curiously. "Again?"

"In the hereafter. I've always believed that only the body dies, not the soul. At least I hope so. I want to believe there's something better after we pass on, that Charlotte and Harry are together in some beautiful, divine place for all eternity."

Connor gave her a little smile. "It's a nice thought, but not very practical." He sipped his drink. "How did Joe take their deaths?"

"Hard. Charlotte was his life. Their parents died when they were young, and they were raised in an orphanage. Even though they were the same age, she was like his mother. She doted on him. Spoiled him. Coerced him into getting an education . . . Understandably, he went a little crazy after she died. He wouldn't eat. Wouldn't talk. He'd just sit beside Harry's bed and stare at the wall. When Harry recovered, he took Joe under his wing. They bought an apothecary shop and shared the upstairs living quarters."

"Why do you think Joe blames your father?"

"Because he's hurting. But he's a good man, Connor. He really is. Why can't you see that? He wouldn't seek revenge." She shook her head. "Not Joe."

"I didn't mean to upset you. I'm just trying to find out who's responsible."

"Well, look somewhere else." Ashlee met his eyes, daring him. "What's wrong between you and Branden?"

He straightened and finished his drink. "He thinks I bedded his wife."

"Did you?"

Connor's mercurial eyes sharpened, then without a word, he set the glass down and walked out.

Folding her arms over her stomach, Ashlee turned back to the window, wondering if she'd just made a horrific mistake.

"That was a cruel thing to say, you know." Vivian's voice floated across the parlor.

Ashlee glanced around to see Connor's aunt standing motionless in the doorway. "I know."

"Do you also know that he'd never, ever, betray a friend?"

"Mr. Delacorte doesn't seem to think so."

Vivian took a seat. "I've known Branden for more than a score of years. Believe me, he doesn't mean what he's saying. Deep down, he knows Connor wouldn't cuckold him. But at the moment, Louise is hurting him, and—"

"He's lashing out at the closest target." Ashlee repeated her father's words.

"Exactly." Vivian's voice gentled. "But you've just hurt my nephew. Honor means a great deal to Connor, and when it's questioned, it cuts him to the quick."

"I'll apologize at once."

Vivian smiled. "Actions speak louder than words, child. Remember that when you do."

"I will." But Ashlee wanted to know more. "Why does Branden believe Connor would betray him?"

"I wish I knew. But I do know this: Whatever it was, Branden, who is usually quite rational, believed the tale. And, until it's proven otherwise, or he comes to his senses, he'll continue to do so."

Ashlee smiled at Vivian's unshakable faith in her nephew. "Isn't there a chance Louise told the truth?"

"Not even a small one."

"Your trust in Connor is remarkable."

"It's been well founded. You'll know that one day. And Branden already knows it. He's just suppressed the knowledge beneath his pain."

Ashlee knew in her heart everything the woman said was the truth.

Ashlee's dislike for Louise grew. "Someone should teach Mrs. Delacorte a lesson."

Vivian stood and brushed down her white skirt. "Oh, I'm sure someone will, dear. One of these days." Smiling, she ambled out the doorway.

Ashlee had the strangest feeling she'd just been manipulated. Which, of course, was a ridiculous notion. Making certain the hair covering her scar was in place, she headed for the door, anxious to find Connor and set things right.

He stood in the shadows of a pine, his troubled gaze fixed on the lake. Unconsciously he snapped a branch into small pieces. Anger was revealed in every taut line of his stance, in the rigid set of his shoulders. Even the lock of dark hair that touched his brow didn't soften his harsh features.

A little nervous, she approached him.

A breath of air swept through her. . . .

"Beau, please don't be angry with me. When I said I missed my sister, I didn't mean I wanted to leave you. Surely you know that."

He leaned his head back against the tree and closed his eyes. "Laura is just one of many things you'll miss over the years because of me. All because I couldn't keep my hands off you."

"I didn't want you to," she reminded, moving to stand beside him. "I fell in love with you the moment I saw you."

"But you were so damned young, so impressionable. God, I should have known what it would be like for you if I took you away." He raised his hand in a gesture that encompassed the area. "This is what you have to look forward to for the rest of your life. Swamps, alligators, and mosquitoes."

"And you," she added.

He shoved away from the tree and presented her with his back. "Yes. And that's probably the worst of the lot."

She touched him. "I love you, Beau. What do I have to do to prove that to you?"

A tremor ran through him, and he spun around, clutching her to him. His body shook as he buried his face in her hair. "Just tell me every waking moment. I need to know your love is as strong as mine. That even this god-awful life I've imposed on you won't destroy what we've found."

She brushed her mouth over his. "Nothing could stop my love for you . . . not anger, not loneliness, not even death."

"What do you want?" Connor's voice brought Ashlee back to awareness.

Shivers ran up her spine as she shook off the strange vision. Hesitantly she met his eyes—but wasn't relieved in the least by the slivers of ice behind those thick lashes. "I-I want to apologize."

"Accepted." He turned away from her.

Her own irritation rose, and she stepped closer.

He threw the broken pieces of branch down. "I'm busy. You'll have to excuse me." He started to leave.

"Connor, I was jealous."

He stopped. After a long pause, he spoke, his voice no more than a whisper. "What?"

Feeling more vulnerable than she'd ever felt before, yet knowing if there was any hope for the growing feelings between them, she had to reach him. She took a breath. "I questioned your honor because I was angry to think you preferred Louise over me."

"That would never happen."

A fluttering in her stomach forced her to swallow. "It wouldn't?"

"No." He faced her, his eyes dark with an emotion that came straight from the heart. Love. "You and Louise aren't even the same species." He brought a hand to her cheek. "She's cold and manipulative, where you're warm and sensitive." He smiled, tracing her lower lip with his thumb. "Why else would you come after me and make sure I wasn't hurt by your remark?"

"Were you?" Her heart was beating so loud, she feared he could hear it.

"Yes." His gaze fixed on her lips. "Trust is important to me."

The heat of his breath sent a wave of tingles rushing over her flesh. "I do trust you. I swear, I do."

"Do you?" he challenged, lightly brushing his mouth over hers. He encircled her waist and pulled her to him. The hand on her cheek drifted down her neck. "How much, I wonder?" He lowered his mouth to hers in slow, deliberate seduction.

"Connor, I . . ."

He pressed his tongue between her parted lips.

She forgot what she wanted to say.

The hand at her throat slipped lower, testing the rise

of bare flesh above her gown, her scar, then farther, to slide his fingers beneath the bodice and ease it down. Damp air touched her bare breast an instant before his warm palm covered her.

Fleeting thoughts of how he'd react to her scars rose, but she suppressed them. *Trust him. He won't be repulsed.* An unidentified emotion fluttered through her, a strong one, and she was suddenly willing to risk everything. She softened against him and slid her arms around his neck.

As if sensing her surrender, Connor sighed, then deepened the kiss. His hand trembled as he caressed her, drew his fingers over the hard tip of her breast, then explored the nub with erotic thoroughness.

He nibbled her jaw, her neck, the sensitive skin of her ear. "I want you, Ashlee. I want to make slow, sinful love to you."

Heat seeped into her and she squeezed her legs together. What if someone saw them? "Y-You mustn't."

He smiled against her ear. "But I will." His fingers trailed beneath her breast, then back up to caress her nipple.

"Oh, Connor . . ."

Stroking her spine with slow, provocative fingers, he kissed a path down the side of her neck, then back to her ear, while his wandering hand found the shape of her bottom.

She was lost in a maelstrom of emotions she wasn't equipped to handle. She dissolved under the narcotic power of his kiss, and was helpless to resist when his mouth moved lower, tracing her scar with loving tenderness, before inching lower still to draw her nipple between his lips. Fire shot to her core, and she arched back, burning in sensations as he suckled.

Her limbs turned to liquid as he continued the sensual torture, urging her lower body against his own, very male one. She instinctively moved against him.

"Jesus," he groaned, drawing her nipple deeper into his mouth, devouring her flesh with an intensity that left her breathless. He eased his fingers between her thighs, pressing the material of her skirt against her most intimate place. The warmth of his hand, and the slow, sensual movement of his fingers, nearly set fire to her flesh. "Connor, no! Oh, God. What are you doing to mmm—"

He captured her mouth with a hunger that staggered her, while his hands worked to remove their clothing. Bare flesh met bare flesh, and she drew in a stunned breath. He was so solid, so hard . . . so hot, she burned where their skin merged.

He eased her down onto their clothing, never taking his mouth from hers. His hand explored her shape, her contours, and her secrets.

She was fast losing control. "Connor . . . please . . ."

He slid his fingers into the curls between her thighs, then parted her to caress the part of her that begged for his touch.

A cry escaped her, and he drew her tongue into his mouth as his finger moved in tiny little circles. Desperately she pushed against his hand, needing . . . needing . . . what?

He knew, oh yes, he did. He quickened the pace, pressed into her, then withdrew to stroke her again.

His mouth mated with hers in a wild frenzy as he took her heavenward, thrusting, withdrawing, over and over until she knew she'd explode.

She arched, twisted against his hand, then erupted in an explosion of sweet, hot pain. Violent shivers racked her body, but he didn't stop. He kept up the erotic torture, driving her beyond satisfaction—into pure, breath-stealing ecstacy.

When her world at long last righted again, he was watching her, his eyes bright, the cords in his neck taut from self-control.

"It gets even better," he whispered as he slid down her body, then bent his head to press lazy kisses to her stomach, her side. He paused at the jagged scar that followed the curve of her waist.

For the barest instant, she tensed, then gasped when he caressed the imperfection with his tongue. "You're beautiful, Ashlee. Every inch of you."

Tears came to her eyes, and she closed them.

He moved lower yet, and her lashes flew up. He nuzzled the curls that shielded her woman's core. "Connor, you can't—"

He stabbed gently with his tongue.

Her breath shuddered to a stop, and she held it as he trailed kissed down her right leg. Unerringly his mouth found the last scar, the one that curved across her inner thigh, and with a tenderness that bordered on reverence, he soothed it with his tongue. His jaw lightly rubbed her woman's curls.

Flames raced through her blood, and she trembled.

He covered her with his mouth, slid his tongue over her anxious flesh.

A moan tore from her throat, and she gripped his hair, meaning to pull him away. Instead, her traitorous hands held him in place. He lifted her hips, made tiny jabs with his tongue, then slowed the pace to maddening strokes.

It was more than she could stand. Fire spread from her core to inflame her entire body, as wave after wave of white-hot pleasure consumed her.

Before the shudders passed, he was moving over her, his mouth taking hers captive. He nudged her legs apart with his thighs, then slipped a hand beneath her bottom to lift her. "Hold on, sweetheart," he whispered against her lips. "This one's going to shatter your soul."

He reclaimed her mouth the same instant he thrust deeply inside her.

She cried out at the flash of pain, but the sound was absorbed by his fevered kiss. For several breathless moments, he remained still. He just held her, soothed her with kisses, and gave her time to become accustomed to the fullness inside her.

At last, he began to move, thrusting, then withdrawing, then easing into her again. The smoldering embers from moments ago flared to life, and her hips rose to join his rhythm.

Her uncontrollable offering was his undoing. Wildly, he plunged into her, twisting, thrusting.

The breath left her. She again arched to meet him. Dug her nails into his back. Tried to get closer . . . closer.

His mouth captured her nipple and drew hard as he forged into her again and again. Tingles shot from her breast and slammed into her core. She cried out as a waterfall of liquid fire cascaded over her, submerging her in a whirlpool of searing pleasure.

She couldn't breathe. Liquid flames licked every inch of her body. The spasms went on and on. Even when he tensed and arched back, they didn't stop, they just kept coming. . . . *Oh, God. She wouldn't live through this.* Still he impaled her, forced her deeper and deeper into the inferno. Her senses spun crazily until, at last, sweet, sweet satisfaction released her. . . .

Breathing hard, she lay there, enjoying the aftermath of Connor's magical touch. No one had ever made her feel so wonderful. So beautiful.

A soft morning breeze drifted across her flesh, leaves rustled overhead, and a chorus of birds offered a sweet serenade. She smiled sleepily. It was as if the whole world rejoiced their union.

"I hope that smile is caused by thoughts of me," Connor teased, outlining the curve of her lips with his finger.

She opened her eyes and nipped him playfully. "Without a doubt . . ." Her words trailed off.

The Silver Witch stood right behind him.

CHAPTER
21

The look on Ashlee's face spurred Connor into action. He whipped around, shielding her with his body, expecting to confront one of the others.

No one was there.

"What's wrong?" he asked, turning back.

Ashlee sat up, clutching his shirt to her chest. "I saw her."

"Who?"

"The Silver Witch. She was standing right behind you, watching us." Ashlee gripped his hand. "The first time I saw her, she was in your room; I thought I was tired and seeing things. Now I know I wasn't. Oh, Connor, I'm scared."

"My room?"

"When you were burned. I didn't believe it then. But this was real."

Having experienced the occurrence himself, he didn't know what to say. And it unnerved him to think the ghost had been in his bedchamber while he was unconscious—not to mention watching them make love.

"I couldn't see her face," Ashlee continued. "But I saw her long hair and silvery gown." She clutched his arm. "I know it was her."

Connor didn't argue. He couldn't. "Ashlee, whatever it is, I'm sure it doesn't intend to harm anyone."

"You believe me?"

He stood and pulled on his breeches. "I have to. I've seen her, too."

Ashlee came to her feet, wrapping his shirt around her.

With her hair tumbled around her face, and leaves and damp grass clinging to the silky strands, she looked so adorable, he wanted to take her again. Slowly this time.

"Why didn't you tell me before?" she demanded.

"Because you wouldn't have believed me. Hell, even I didn't. I kept telling myself it was my imagination."

Her anxious gaze swept the trees. "What should we do?"

Connor knew what he'd like to do. He slipped an arm around her waist and drew her against him. "I can think of a few things."

She shoved at his shoulder. "I mean, what should we do about *her?*"

"There's nothing we can do." His hand slid up Ashlee's bare leg to cup her rear.

She drew in a sharp breath. "Stop that. You can't possibly want to— Not here. Not now—with that thing still lurking around out there."

"She didn't bother us a few minutes ago."

"Well, she does now." Snatching up her gown, Ashlee wiggled into it and pulled the laces together. She tossed him his shirt, then blushed when she saw a

crimson stain against its whiteness. "I-I've got to go."
She whirled around and raced toward the house.

Connor smiled and carefully folded the fabric before sauntering toward the study.

Ashlee was a mass of nerves by the time she started supper. She hadn't seen Connor since that morning, since their encounter by the lake. She could just imagine what he thought of her. The things she'd allowed him to do were unspeakable.

She stopped at the kitchen door, trying to gather her wits and cool the embarrassment rushing through her body. She didn't know which upended her most, the apparition she'd seen . . . or her own wanton behavior.

Determined to put both thoughts out of her head, she twisted the latch and stepped into the cookhouse.

The delicious aroma of roasting meat and fresh bread assailed her. Startled, she sent a searching glance over the room. Dirty cooking pots were piled in the washbasin, flour coated the counters and floor, but on the center worktable sat a steaming, golden brown roast, and bowls filled with potatoes, carrots, and turnips. A loaf of bread was cooling on a wooden platter.

Someone had prepared their supper. Ashlee smiled. Vivian, no doubt.

Warm arms came around Ashlee's waist from behind. A firm male body pressed against her back. "I missed you," Connor whispered, nibbling her ear.

Tingles skittered over her flesh, but she was still too distraught over her earlier, wanton behavior to respond as she wanted. Her actions were appalling. They weren't even engaged, for heaven's sake. She stepped away from him. "Look, Connor," she babbled. "Someone fixed supper. I know it wasn't Louise.

She hasn't touched a pot since we started this journey. It must have been—"

"Me."

"What?"

He again slid his arm around her waist and pulled her against him. "I thought you could use a little rest." He nuzzled her neck. "And I needed to work off some excess energy."

He'd done this for her?

He cupped her breast and massaged with gentle insistence.

She felt her knees go weak, and she leaned into him. "You should be slapped for your forwardness."

"I know." He planted a quick kiss on her lips, then released her. He gave her an endearing grin, forming little creases on either side of his mouth. "Come on. Since I did all the work, the least you can do is help me get this stuff to the dining room."

A tender emotion overflowed the bounds of her heart. She loved him. "You get the roast."

They had just placed the last of the fare on the table when the others strolled in.

Jovial conversation filled the room over the evening meal, but Ashlee added little. Her eyes kept straying to Connor, and the warm looks he sent her way roused heated memories of their lovemaking. It was all she could do to finish her food, then hastily excuse herself.

By the time she reached her room, she was trembly and damp in various places on her body. She had to stop thinking of Connor. That was all there was to it.

After a reviving bath, she slipped into her chemise and climbed into bed, but the memories wouldn't subside. Again and again, she relived the way her body came to life beneath Connor's touch.

"Oh, Beau. I can't stand any more. Please, please take me."

*His husky laugh rippled through the bedchamber.
"Anything you say, duchess." He rolled onto his back
and pulled her over him. "But I'd rather you take me."
He lifted her astride him, then eased her down onto his
rigid shaft.*

*He filled her completely. Her body erupted into
flames. "Ooooh . . . sweet heavens."*

*"Ride me, duchess. Take us both to a place we've
never been." He thrust deeply, urging her on.*

She entwined her fingers in his . . . and held on.

Ashlee gasped and jerked upright in bed. Her heart
beat so fast, it hurt. Unsettled by the visions that kept
plaguing her, she walked out onto the veranda.

Sultry air moved over her flesh like a lover's caress.
"Please stop," she whispered into the night. "Please."

A floorboard creaked outside her door.

Startled, she whirled around. Listened.

The sound came again.

Suspicion flared. Was someone sneaking out to her
father's laboratory? Silently she eased the door open
—just in time to see Louise slip downstairs toward
the study where Connor slept.

Stunned, Ashlee could barely breathe for the band
of hurt squeezing her chest. Numb with disbelief, she
followed, cautiously approaching the closed door.

"I thought you'd never get here." Connor's muffled
voice drifted from the parlor.

Every instinct Ashlee possessed cried out in denial
as she moved down to that door. *He wouldn't do this.*

Louise laughed. "I had to make sure the little puss
was asleep. Wouldn't want her to catch on to our game
at this late date."

"She won't. I've made sure of that. Now, come here.
Show me what I've been missing."

Louise squealed, then there was a moment of silence. "Oh, that feels wonderful. But we need to talk,"

she said. "Wh-When have you arranged the 'accident'? Oh! Don't. I can't concentrate when you touch me like that."

"I'm going to do a lot more than touch you," he growled.

"There isn't time. Branden might rouse. Now, stop that and answer me."

"Oh, hell. Tomorrow."

Ashlee clamped a hand to her mouth to stop a cry of protest.

"And you'll arrange to have Branden in the laboratory when it blows?"

"Mmm, I don't know. Come here, see if you can coerce me into murdering your husband and making you Mrs. Connor Westfield."

"Wait. What about Ashlee?"

"What about her?"

"I want her dead."

Ashlee went cold.

He laughed. "Don't worry. Putting an end to her life will be my pleasure."

Tears streamed down Ashlee's face. She couldn't listen to any more. Feeling as if her insides were shredded, she bolted up the stairs to her room.

Branden stepped out of his chamber—directly in her path.

Only half-awake, he didn't see her in time to brace himself, and she didn't have time to stop. They collided. The impact sent them both sprawling. Branden landed on his back with her spread out on top of him. His head struck a nearby table.

A crystal vase crashed to the floor and shattered.

Branden tucked her head into the crook of his neck and rolled to his side to protect her. The action brought them up against a pair of bare male legs.

Ashlee glanced up to see Connor towering over them, his expression thunderous. Three things struck her at once. He was wearing a dressing robe. He looked ready to murder her—*and he'd come from the opposite end of the hall.*

Shoving out of Branden's hold, she scrambled to her feet. "Where were you?"

"On the terrace outside my aunt's room," he said tightly, glaring at Branden.

Overwhelming joy consumed her. The man with Louise hadn't been Connor.

Branden rose to his feet. "This isn't what you think—"

"Stealing my excuses, friend?"

Ashlee wanted to kick them both. But she remembered Louise, and took off at a dead run down the stairs. She had to know the identity of the man with Louise.

She burst through the door, then skidded to a halt.

The room was empty.

"Where the hell do you think you're going?" Connor demanded from right behind her.

She spun around to see him and Branden standing in the doorway. "Get in here, both of you."

A look of incredulity darkened Connor's eyes, then he crossed his arms and glared down at her. He didn't move.

"What you witnessed was a result of my eavesdropping. I was listening at the parlor door and heard some things that upset me. I was racing back to my own room when Branden stepped out of his. We collided —and you saw the rest."

Connor glanced around his room. "What are you talking about? There's no one here."

"Not now." She flicked a glance at Branden, then back to Connor. "But there was. Louise and a man that I thought was you."

Branden's eyes turned to emerald slits. "What are you saying?"

"I'm saying, I saw your wife sneak into this room, and I overheard a conversation between her and a man. The man intends to cause an explosion in Father's laboratory tomorrow, and he's going to try to get you, and possibly me, to be inside when it blows."

Connor inhaled sharply.

"Why would my own wife want to kill me?" Branden demanded.

Ashlee swallowed, not liking the rage she could sense simmering just below the surface. "So she can marry Connor."

"But I never—" Connor clamped his mouth shut.

"I know you didn't," she said, then turned her gaze on his friend. "And if Branden really thinks about it, he'll know you didn't, either."

"What makes her even think I'd marry her?" Connor grated.

She placed a hand on his arm. "I think, once Branden was out of the way, Louise planned to set you up to compromise her. Your own honor would force you to do the proper thing."

Branden, who'd been staring at the floor, raised his head, his features a mask of pain and regret as he faced Connor. "She showed me a bracelet and said it was from you. It was inscribed . . . 'To my darling, Louise. All my love, Connor.'"

"I never gave her a bracelet, or anything else for that matter."

Sympathy for Branden rushed Ashlee. "She could have purchased it herself."

Branden nodded and pulled in a strained breath. "Connor, I—"

Connor raised his hand. "Don't. I understand."

"I should have known better, damn it." Branden jammed his fingers into his hair. "I should have trusted you—instead of that bitch."

"Will you trust me now?"

"Without question."

"Then, I want you to return to your bedchamber—where I'm sure you'll find your wife—and pretend that nothing happened. Can you do that?"

Looking as if he preferred to strangle her, Branden lowered his hand. "Why?"

"I don't want Louise and her mysterious friend to know we're on to them. I want to see who invites you and Ashlee to the laboratory tomorrow."

"I think it's Santos," Branden declared.

Connor shrugged. "You could be right, but I doubt it. Somehow, he doesn't strike me as someone who'd use subterfuge. But we'll see." He turned to Ashlee, and his tone grew warm. "And you, Miss Walker, need to be in bed."

"Alone? With a potential murderer about?"

Branden made a sound somewhere between a choke and a cough. "If you'll excuse me, I think I'll go back to bed and see how well I can perform." He twisted his mouth in wry humor. "I mean that in a theatrical sense, of course."

When the door closed behind him, Connor turned back to her, his eyes hot with desire. "Come here."

Excited shivers raced through her middle. "Connor, what happened by the lake was—"

"Breathtaking," he concluded, drawing her against him. "Magnificently breathtaking." He lowered his mouth over hers.

All her resistance faded beneath the sweet pressure of that drugging kiss. "Make love to me," she whispered against his mouth. "Take me to a place beyond the stars."

"That's not far enough." He swept her up into his arms and carried her to her bed, telling her exactly where he planned to take her . . . and how they were going to get there.

Much, much later, Connor returned to the study,

and Ashlee stretched in complete satisfaction. Every inch of her body had been thoroughly, deliciously, sated. And the love she felt for Connor went so deep, it touched her soul. She wanted to spend the rest of her life with him.

But there wouldn't be much of one left if they didn't find the potential killer who was waiting to lead her to her grave.

Glimpsing the first light of dawn, and knowing she'd never be able to sleep, she washed, then brushed the tangles out of her hair.

She'd just set the brush aside when she heard a noise beyond the terrace doors. Curious, she opened them and looked out.

A piece of folded paper fluttered on the wood flooring.

Wondering if this might be the means of getting her to the laboratory, she reached for it.

A cloth-covered hand clamped over her mouth. The odor of chloroform stole her breath. She twisted and struck out with her fist, but the man who held her was too strong. Her chest labored, burned. Swirling lights flashed . . . dimmed . . . then everything went black.

CHAPTER
22

Connor came in from the stables just after noon, not surprised to find that Ashlee hadn't roused yet. He smiled to himself. The pleasure they'd shared had been indescribable, and each time had gotten better and better. The little witch was remarkable—as generous in passion as she was in everything else.

Just the thought of their volatile lovemaking sent a tremor of warmth through him. Again. Sighing, he poured a cup of hot tea and leaned back, recalling their memorable night.

He glanced up to see Branden stroll into the room, and smiled. "Good afternoon."

Branden didn't return the greeting. He looked like a man who'd been on the rack as he poured his tea and flopped down in the opposite chair.

"Do I take it the performance didn't go well?"

"I never got the chance. The slut never came back to bed."

"Where did she g—"

A loud explosion shook the windows.

"Son of a bitch!" Connor bellowed, then he broke into a dead run.

Branden was on his heels.

Flames and smoke billowed from the burning laboratory. Santos and Joe scrambled for buckets of water.

"Where's Nathaniel?" Connor yelled over the roar of the fire.

"Inside!"

Instantly Connor charged for the tent. He grabbed a blanket and shoved it into one of the full buckets, then flung it over his head and ran into the flames.

He found Nathaniel and grabbed him under the arms. Using every bit of strength he possessed, he dragged the man out, praying he was still alive.

Nathaniel's groan and strangled cough was the most beautiful sound Connor had ever heard. He sagged down beside him and gave thanks to the Almighty.

"Where's Ashlee?" Branden shouted as he tossed a bucket of water.

Connor glanced around. Vivian and Louise stood back away from the flames, looking stricken. Santos, Branden, and Joe were frantically trying to douse the flames, Joe in his undergarments. But there was no sign of Ashlee.

A jolt of concern shot through him, then he remembered how exhausted she'd been when she'd left his room. She probably hadn't heard the explosion. Relieved that she wouldn't be subjected to this until it was over, Connor helped Nathaniel up and guided him toward the manor.

Vivian rushed to join them, supporting Nathaniel's other side.

Connor saw Branden stalk over to Louise. He gripped her arm and shoved her at Joe. "Tie the bitch up before I break her traitorous neck." Tormented, he returned to help put out the fire.

Once Nathaniel was settled, cleaned up, and bandaged, Connor made for Ashlee's room. He was glad she hadn't seen her father when they first brought him in; his burns looked worse than they were.

He smiled as he opened her door. "Okay, sleepyhead, it's time—" The words froze in his throat.

Ashlee was gone.

He fought down a surge of panic and started to turn, but a white glow across the room caught his attention.

Spellbound, he stared at the Silver Witch.

She stood by the balcony doors, her hand raised, pointing at something beyond the opening.

Wary, he turned in that direction.

A piece of crumpled paper lay on the plank flooring. Keeping an eye on the spectral figure, he edged toward the parchment and snatched it up. The smell of chloroform wafted from the wrinkled sheet, and he grew uneasy as he straightened the page and read the contents. *South. One mile. Beside the lake.*

Puzzled, he glanced up in question.

The apparition was gone.

The sickening odor assailed him again. His blood iced over. Ashlee. Oh, Jesus. *Ashlee.* Dropping the note, he ran for the stairs.

Ashlee came awake to find herself tied to a tree in the swamps. Mosquitoes buzzed close to her ears. The smells of lingering chloroform, stagnant water, and algae made her nauseous. She lifted her head to see a bearded man standing by a bog, tossing sticks into the murky water. "You bastard," she hissed.

He spun around. "Well, I see you've finally come to." He tossed the handful of twigs down and strode toward her. "Now all we have to do is wait for your lover." His mouth twisted into a smirk. "He'll come, you know. I left him a note."

George Acres! "Why are you doing this? What did we ever do to you?" She shifted against her bindings. "For God's sake, I saved you from being set adrift!"

He sent her a damning glare. "I would rather have been set adrift than suffer in that black hellhole. I can still feel the rats crawling on me, hear their shrill squeaks and constant gnawing. And the smell . . ." He clutched his head. "I thought after I done in my pa, I'd never have to go through that again. Not ever. But because of you and that bastard Westfield, I suffered worse than any time with him. At least Pa'd let me out the next morning after he sobered up. But not Westfield. Oh, no. That bloody whoreson left me for three days." Demented eyes stared into hers. "And for that, he's going to die."

Acres walked toward her, then knelt. "After I make him suffer." He trailed a finger down her bare neck. "I wonder how he'd feel watching me slit that pretty throat."

Ashlee jerked her head to the side. "Get away from me."

He laughed, then grabbed the front of her chemise and ripped it open.

She kicked out with her bound feet. Twisted against the rough bark at her back. "You sniveling bastard!"

Her words didn't penetrate his brain. His eyes were glued to her naked breasts. Her scars. "Looks like I ain't the only one who wanted to cut that white flesh."

The hot look in his eyes made her skin crawl. Her stomach tightened with fear. She had to keep him talking, take his mind off . . . her. "Why are you going to kill Connor if Louise wants to marry him? And why Branden? He never did anything to you."

He dragged his eyes from her chest. "What?"

Relieved to have his attention on her face, she spoke quickly. "I overheard you last night with Louise. I heard your plans to blow up my father's laboratory and kill Branden and myself."

He threw his head back and laughed. "Oh, that's rich. The sultry slut and some lackey are after the lot of you, eh?"

"You mean that wasn't you?"

"Bloody hell, I wouldn't go within a yard of that treacherous bitch. No. I was waiting on the terrace for you half the bloody night, listenin' to you and Westfield."

Ashlee's cheeks burned, but her heart began to hammer. He wasn't the one.

"And now that I've got you"—his eyes lowered to her breasts—"I'm anxious to find out what had the blighter moanin' so loud." He cupped her breast and squeezed roughly. "I ain't never felt nothing so soft."

Pain shot through her, and she tried to jerk away. "No! Leave me alone!"

His only response was to bring his other hand up to cover her opposite breast . . . and lick his lips.

Revulsion and fear curled through her, and she tried to shrink back.

He slid his hand under one breast and encircled it, then squeezed, forcing her nipple outward between his thumb and fingers.

"Don't!" The cruel grip hurt, and she squirmed, trying to get free. She couldn't move. He had her pressed fully against the tree.

With a feral gleam in his eyes, he bent his head and covered her with his wet mouth, sucking hard to pull the tip between his lips. He bit the tender flesh, licked, then sank his teeth into her again.

The sickening, slurping sound pushed bile up her throat, and she squeezed her eyes shut. *Connor. Oh, God, Connor, I need you.*

Suddenly George's head shot up, and he lunged to

his feet. He glanced around, then took a rag from his pocket and tied the gag around her mouth. With jerky movements he withdrew a pistol from his waist and slipped behind a tree. Waiting.

Ashlee pushed with her tongue, trying to shove the rag out of her mouth. If Acres had left a note, Connor was coming. She had to warn him! It was no use, the cloth was tied too tight. Helpless, she watched the trees . . . and prayed.

A twig snapped, and she searched the foliage.

Connor stepped into view. He stared at her, assessed the situation, then his gaze lowered to her naked chest. A look of blinding fury crossed his face, and he started forward.

She kicked out and shook her head, but he kept coming.

"That's far enough, Westfield," George Acres ordered, stepping from behind a tree, the pistol pointed at Connor's heart.

"I'll kill you for this," Connor said, his voice soft, dangerous, his eyes on Ashlee. "Depend on it."

Acres cackled, then withdrew a large knife from the scabbard at his side. Keeping the gun trained on Connor, he edged toward her. "I was going to kill your little lady here, and let you watch. But after havin' a taste of her, I've decided to keep her awhile. Gonna sample the rest of those sweet charms." He pressed the knife to the hollow of her throat. " 'Less, of course, you make a stupid move and make me kill her now."

Connor stood deathly still. "It's me you want, Acres. Come get me."

"Don't need to." He smiled. "I can kill you from here." He raised the pistol higher. "I'm a damned good shot, you know."

Connor's eyes narrowed. "You'd better pray you are."

George Acres smirked. "Well, guess we'll have to see, then, won't we?" He squeezed the trigger.

Gunfire exploded.

Ashlee screamed against the gag.

Connor's big body flew backward into the brush. He landed with a heavy thud, then lay motionless.

A sickening silence filled the swamp as Acres waited for several long minutes for him to stir.

Struggling, Ashlee fought the ropes, her eyes on the spot where Connor had fallen.

An eternity passed, but no sound came from Connor. No movement.

Acres edged toward the body until he got a good look. Smiling with triumph, he holstered the pistol, then bent and dragged Connor's lifeless form out into the open. Blood soaked one whole side of his shirt.

Ashlee began to shake. *Help him. God, please help him.*

Stepping closer, Acres eyed Connor warily, then gave him a vicious kick in the side.

Connor didn't move. Didn't flinch.

"No!" Ashlee screamed against the rag. She fought her restraints. "Connor! Get up!" She willed her voice to penetrate the muffling cloth. When he still didn't stir, cold reality settled over her. It was too much to bear. Her mind cried out in denial . . . then shut down. Something inside her died. She couldn't think, couldn't rouse her numb limbs.

Connor was dead.

CHAPTER
23

Through a thick haze, Ashlee heard George Acres chuckle. Connor's body lay at his feet.

Ashlee remained motionless. It was as if her nerves had been severed. She felt nothing at all. Not pain, not grief, not even concern for herself.

Acres untied her. "Come on, beauty, let's see what you got for ol' George beneath that skimpy night-shirt." He tore the rest of the chemise from her body.

The man pulled her up against him, kneading her bottom, sliding his wet mouth over her lips and cheek, biting her neck. She didn't even flinch. Didn't lift a hand in protest. Connor was dead.

She felt herself being shoved to the ground, felt cruel hands on her breasts, her stomach . . . between her legs, but she felt only emptiness.

She was aware of him fumbling with the front of his breeches, then something pushed against her thigh. The veil of numbness deepened.

Suddenly he was gone.

Through a fog, she saw two men fighting. She didn't

recognize either of them. The taller one hit the other one again and again. The beaten man pulled a knife. They fought over it, rolled. The blade flashed between them, then sank into the chest of the bearded man.

She felt nothing.

She watched the handsome victor stagger toward her, holding a hand to his bloody shoulder. Then he dropped to his knees in front of her. For a long time he stared into her eyes, then tears sparkled in his. "Forgive me," he whispered. "Forgive me for letting him hurt you." He lifted a shaky hand and touched her cheek, his features twisted with self-loathing . . . and so much pain.

Still there was only the void inside her.

A tear slid down the man's cheek as he wrapped the torn chemise around her, then lifted her into his arms.

She wondered if she was dead.

The trip through the trees passed in a blur, then they were entering a big house.

Another tall man, with hair the color of onyx, met them in the foyer. "What the hell happened? Is she all right?" He glanced at the man's bloody shirt. "Good God!" He put his arm around the bleeding man's shoulder. "Vivian!" he bellowed toward the stairs. "Get Nathaniel!"

"I've got to get her to bed," the man holding her rasped.

A white-haired man scrambled down the stairs. "Ashlee? Branden, what's happened?"

"Put her to bed, Nathaniel. I'll help Connor. He's lost a lot of blood." The white-haired man tried to take her from the other's arms.

"No!" the man growled. "Don't touch her!" Then, with staggering steps, he climbed the stairs, his arms shaking, his breathing harsh. Gently he laid her on a bed, and brushed the hair out of her eyes. "Forgive me, sweetheart. Please forgive me."

He straightened, stared at the others who'd followed, then slowly buckled to the floor.

Everyone burst into a whir of activity.

Not able to grasp what was happening, Ashlee closed her eyes.

A parade of people came through the room, disturbing her. A thin man with a mustache, and a small, gray-haired woman who kept telling her everything would be all right, and a kind white-haired man who made her drink a foul-tasting liquid.

Then, at last, she was left alone. Peacefully alone. The darkness felt safe.

The sun came up, and the gentle old lady tried to make her eat something. But she couldn't. She felt no hunger.

Again and again throughout the day, the older man kept making her drink the foul potion. By nightfall, lines of worry creased his face. "Oh, Ashlee, love, please come back to us. We need you. Connor needs you."

She wondered why he was saying Connor needed her. Didn't he know Connor was dead?

She saw the thin man talking to the old lady, shaking his head. "Her mind is gone."

The woman started to cry and ran out of the room.

When the sun set again, they left her alone. She stared into the comforting darkness, praying the sunlight wouldn't return, and the people would stay away. The night was serene and warm. It kept the hurt away.

More sunrises and sunsets came, but she lost track of how many. She noticed the kind old man looked worn and haggard. Worried. So hopeless.

He stayed in her thoughts, even into the night. She wished she could help him, but the darkness soothed her, and she soon forgot him.

Out of nowhere, a strange white glow moved

through the blackness, and a woman dressed in silver stood by the bed, looking down at her.

"He is not dead," the woman said in a haunting voice. "But without you, he will die." An iridescent hand touched her limp one lying on the quilt. "He needs your strength to live." A tear slid down her cheek. "Don't leave him."

The light faded.

For the briefest moment Ashlee stared into the shadowy room, then, haltingly, her memory slipped into place. Vivian's illness. The trip to the swamps to find a cure for malaria. Harry's death. The manor by the lake. The stories of the Silver Witch. Someone trying to sabotage her father's experiments. Making love with Connor. *Connor.*

She tried to sit up, to shove the covers back, but she was too weak. Her limbs wouldn't respond. The effort made her struggle for air. Oh, Connor. She started to cry.

"Ashlee?" Her father's concerned voice drifted across the room. He was beside her in an instant, gathering her into his arms. "Thank the Lord. You are all right." He searched her eyes. "Do you recognize me?"

She clutched the shirt beneath her fingers. "Where's Connor? Is he . . . dead?" She held her breath, awaiting her father's answer.

"No. But he is very ill."

Relief eased the knot in her chest. "I have to see him."

"Not yet. You are not strong enough." He pressed her back onto the pillow. "Gather your strength, then you can go to him."

"No. I have to see him now." Her voice shook with emotion. "Please. I must."

In an obvious effort to calm her, he smoothed her

brow. "After you have eaten, I will have Branden carry you to Connor, but only if you eat . . . and only for a moment."

Vivian came bustling into the room with a tray a few minutes later, joy crinkling the corners of her tired eyes. Ashlee didn't feel the least bit hungry, but if that's what it took to see Connor, then she'd eat.

She forced down as much as she could swallow. It seemed to be enough, because her father and Vivian both smiled.

"I'll get Branden," Vivian said, patting Ashlee's hand before she took the tray.

Ashlee turned her head so she could see her father. "Where is Connor?"

"In my room, next door. He'd lost so much blood, and was so weak, we were afraid to move him any farther. I've been sleeping in the parlor with Joe, since Louise is locked in the study.

She felt a flicker of satisfaction, but Connor's form again wavered. She closed her eyes as visions of him lying on the ground, bleeding to death, wavered in her mind.

"Your transportation has arrived, Miss Walker." Branden's teasing voice broke into her thoughts.

She opened her eyes to see him grinning as he walked toward her.

"Remember, only a moment," her father warned as Branden carefully lifted her into his arms.

She would have agreed to one second if it meant seeing Connor.

But when she did see him lying in bed, his skin so pale, her heart almost broke. Tears stung her eyes. He barely resembled the vibrant man she knew. "Set me down beside him. Please, Branden?"

"Ashlee, maybe you shouldn't—"

"Please," she whispered.

Sighing, Branden eased her onto the mattress.

With a trembling hand, she brushed her fingers over Connor's brow. It felt clammy. "Connor? Can you hear me?"

He didn't respond.

She rubbed her palm over the back of his hand. "Please hear me."

Still nothing.

Without regard to Branden's presence, she laced her fingers through Connor's and pressed her lips to them. "I love you."

Connor's eyes fluttered open. He stared groggily, then gave her a lazy smile. "My beautiful Ashlee . . ." His voice faded, and his lashes drifted closed.

"Come on, Ashlee," Branden insisted. "You need to be in bed. Connor's going to be just fine."

Ashlee prayed he was right.

Connor sluggishly came awake to the sound of a door closing. He'd been dreaming of Ashlee. Pain rolled through him when he thought of what she'd had to endure because he'd failed to protect her.

Visions of George Acres rutting over Ashlee's small body wouldn't leave his mind. Bile clawed its way up his throat, and he felt moisture dampen his eyes. He closed them to blot out the painful memory. She'd never forgive him. Never be able to forget . . .

The next weeks passed with agonizing slowness for Connor, but with each new day, his former strength returned, and by the end of the fourth week, he was on his feet again.

But he was concerned about Ashlee. Though she'd recovered long before him, during her daily visits, he noticed she was still losing weight. Her eyes had lost their sparkle, and she avoided mentioning George Acres.

And he knew the reason.

She was torturing herself over the deed Connor hadn't prevented. If only he could turn back the clock. If only he'd stayed with her that night . . .

But he hadn't.

Santos was the first person Connor saw when he stepped out into the sunlight.

The Indian set down the crate he was carrying as Connor approached.

"It's a surprise to see you up and around," Santos greeted.

Distracted, Connor nodded. He was staring at a spot by the lake. "You built *another* laboratory?"

"Ashlee's idea. She wanted her father to continue his work while you were recuperating. We've been watching the place around the clock."

"Why? George Acres is dead."

"According to Ashlee, he wasn't the one who sabotaged the experiments. Nor was he the man she overheard with Louise. Acres wanted revenge on you, but he knew he wasn't strong enough to overtake you, so he took Ashlee and left a note, knowing you'd follow immediately. Nathaniel figures that Acres intended to kill you—then her—and escape back to Charleston without anyone knowing he'd even been in the area. The plan was nearly foolproof. None of us, or my people, had seen him."

Connor's gut clenched. Acres's revenge had been accomplished much better than he'd ever hoped for.

But there was still someone out there. Waiting.

Connor glanced toward the house. There was only one person who could stop this madness.

"Where's Louise?"

Santos shrugged. "In the study. Branden's had her locked up in there since the last explosion."

That suited Connor just fine. Louise deserved worse than that. Angered over how she'd coldly plotted

Branden and Ashlee's deaths, Connor decided it was time to put an end to her vicious game. Past time. "Would you tell Branden to meet me down by the lake—in about an hour?" When Santos nodded, Connor headed for the house.

Louise was going to start talking . . . right now.

CHAPTER

Connor found Joe stationed outside the study door. With a small nod, Connor swept past him, anxious to confront Louise.

She was standing by the window, her arms crossed over her middle. Having never seen Louise ungroomed, Connor was taken aback by her appearance. Her hair was tangled and matted, her face smudged and streaked by tears. She still wore the gown she'd been in the morning of the explosion.

Louise glanced up when he came into the room. Her eyes widened with happiness. "Connor!" She burrowed into his arms, her body shaking with sobs. "Branden's had me locked in this awful room for weeks, and I've been so worried about you. He wouldn't let me see you. Joe told me what happened with George Acres, but no one would tell me if you were all right." She buried her face in his shoulder. "When you didn't come to me after a couple weeks, I feared you were dead."

Connor peeled the woman's arms from around him and stepped back. "You expected me to come to you?"

"Of course I did. I knew you wouldn't allow Branden to treat me this way." She tugged on his hand. "Come on, let's get out of here."

Connor couldn't believe she still harbored the misconception that he was in love with her. And it was time to set her straight. "Louise, I didn't come in here to let you go. In fact, after what you and your friend did, if your incarceration had been left up to me, I would have seen you tied to a chair."

Her head whipped around. "What?"

The surprised look on her face only strengthened his determination. "I don't know why you assume I have feelings other than friendship for you, nor do I care to. But you must understand this association you think is between us is a product of your imagination. I am not, nor have I ever been, in love with you."

"Connor, there's no need to pretend with me."

His patience was wearing thin. He gripped her by the arms. "Will you listen to me? There is no love between us—and there never will be."

Tears came to her eyes. "You're lying to protect Branden."

Connor shook her. "No, I'm not. And you know it."

She stared at him, searching for the truth in his eyes—and found it. Tears rolled down her cheeks, and she wrenched away from him. "I hate you."

"I'm sorry, Louise. It wasn't my intention to hurt you, but things couldn't continue on as they were." Still, he wished he could have made her understand without being cruel. He approached her. "Tell me the name of the man you enlisted to kill Branden and Ashlee in that explosion."

Louise gave a shrill laugh. "Why would I betray the one person who can help me?"

"He's done a poor job so far."

"He's just waiting for the opportunity. My beloved husband has seen to it that this room has been guarded round the clock. But it can't go on forever. My friend will come; don't doubt it for a moment."

The overwhelming assurance in her voice gave Connor pause. Perhaps they should give her friend the opportunity he sought. "Well, I wouldn't hold my breath waiting for rescue, if I were you. And when you're ready to cooperate, just let one of us know." He smiled. "A few missed meals might hasten your decision."

Louise gasped in outrage.

Giving her a mock salute, Connor left the room.

Branden was waiting for him down by the lake as he'd instructed, and he related his conversation with Louise.

"So she's waiting for rescue," Branden remarked on a harsh snort. "I think I'll double the guard."

"Or slacken it," Connor replied, "and give her friend the chance to free her."

"She wouldn't fall for it. My sanctimonious wife is much too smart for that. And I think she's wishing on the moon. If the bastard was going to attempt rescue, he'd have already done so."

Rubbing the back of his neck, Connor stared out across the lake. "You could be right, but I still think it's worth a shot. We've got to do something before someone gets killed . . . or Nathaniel stops his research. And I don't have to tell you what that means for Vivian."

"I don't know what we could do that wouldn't seem suspicious."

Connor thought on that for a moment, considering and discarding several possibilities. "What if we needed everyone to search for someone . . . say, Aunt Vivian."

"I'm not following you."

"What if we stuffed Aunt Vivian away in one of the rooms, then reported her missing. We'd let Ashlee and Nathaniel know, of course, but no one else. We could send everyone off into the swamps to look for her." Connor arched a brow. "Everyone except you and me, that is. We would watch the study."

Branden smiled for the first time in a very long while. "Hell, Connor. You're a genius."

"No. Just desperate. And if we're going to do this, we'd better do it now. Before Louise's friend comes up with a plan of his own."

"Assuming he is going to try," Branden remarked as he headed for Nathaniel's laboratory.

Connor chuckled. "Yes, there is that." Knowing Branden would inform Nathaniel, Connor turned for the house and went in search of the women. He found Vivian and Ashlee in the parlor, sharing a cup of tea, and explained the scheme.

His aunt set down her cup. "Why, Connor. I believe that's a splendid idea. I haven't had an adventure in too many months to count."

He tried very hard not to roll his eyes.

"What about the dining room?" Ashlee offered, her manner distant.

Knowing her coolness stemmed from the ordeal she suffered, Connor wished he could magically erase it from her mind. But he couldn't. "That would work. But Aunt Vivian has to sneak in there without being seen. The drapes would have to be drawn, the door locked, and so on."

Connor glanced at the door that led to the dining room, which separated the parlor from the study, knowing it was impossible to get to it from this side. The door had been bolted from the inside and secured with a stout lock, leaving only the door in the lower hall accessible. And that was right next to the one Joe guarded. "Getting past Joe is the only problem."

Vivian smoothed a wrinkle from her mauve day dress. "Ashlee could divert his attention for a few minutes, couldn't she?"

Ashlee shrugged. "I could try."

"Maybe I should be the one to entertain him," Connor suggested, not wanting to subject Ashlee to yet another man's lust.

"No offense, Connor, dear," Vivian countered. "But I think Ashlee would hold his attention far better than you."

That's what he feared.

"When do you want to do this?" Ashlee asked.

He stared into her beautiful face. "Now is as good a time as any."

She nodded and rose. "Give me a few minutes."

He watched the sway of her hips as she left the room and turned toward the lower hall, desperately missing the spirited woman she'd once been.

"Come along," his aunt urged. "Let's wait in the entry."

When they were in position, Ashlee's soft laughter filtered around the corner of the wall that separated the corridor from where they stood. Connor edged toward the end of the wall and peered around the corner. Joe stood with his back to them, one arm raised and braced on the wall as he stared down into Ashlee's delicate face. She was standing so close, Connor was sure the man could smell her sweet jasmine scent.

Jealousy slithered through him, and he quickly ushered his aunt into the dining room. Once the lock was secured, he hurried back to his former position, then raised one hell of a ruckus. "Ashlee! Damn it, woman, where is my aunt?" He stomped down the hall to where she stood with Joe. "I've searched everywhere. Have you seen her? Did she mention going anywhere?" He kept his voice raised to make certain Louise overheard.

"I haven't seen her." Ashlee turned to Joe. "Have you?"

Light from the hall candle fluttered over his mustache as he shook his head. "She hasn't been this way. I'd have seen her for sure."

Connor tried his best to look worried. "You don't think something's happened to her? That someone abducted her like they did Ashlee?"

"Oh, no," Ashlee cried. Her expression would have done the theater proud.

"Joe, get the others. We've got to find her."

"What about Louise?"

Connor flung a hand. "Just make sure the door's locked. I'm going to check the bedrooms on the off chance I missed seeing her, then I'll meet you and the others out front."

"Have you checked the kitchens?" Ashlee queried, her voice inflicted with distress.

"She wasn't there. But you might look again, just to be certain she isn't now."

Nodding, she hurried toward the rear door, her expression so concerned, she almost had Connor believing the ruse.

After she disappeared from sight, Connor strode to the dining room and jiggled the locked door. "I have a bad feeling, Joe. Get the others. And hurry."

The younger man nodded, then checked the lock on the study door before racing down the hall.

Connor continued to open and close doors, knowing Louise would be able to hear. He swore a few times to give credibility to his futile search, then slammed the last door and headed outside to meet with the others.

Everyone was present; Branden had seen to that.

And Connor could tell by the light in Nathaniel's eyes that Branden had informed him of the scheme.

Within moments, Connor explained the situation and sent Joe and Santos in different directions. When only he, Nathaniel, and Branden remained, he instructed Nathaniel to go into the swamps, then double back and watch the east side of the house.

Connor and Branden would execute a like charade, only they'd sneak into the house to wait.

After a convincing departure, he and Branden met in the dining room. Connor chose to watch the hall door from the entry, while Branden elected to guard the study windows and doors from outside.

Taking up his post, and praying his aunt remained quiet, Connor waited. . . .

Ashlee watched from the concealment of a low, fat palm near the lake that gave her a view of both the front door and the back where the library window faced. She saw Branden race into the trees, then blend into the foliage, and knew Connor had remained indoors.

Thinking of Connor tightened her throat. Ever since the ordeal with George Acres, Connor had been so distant. She'd visited him every single day during his recovery, but he'd talked of only mundane things, and he hadn't kissed her, or even held her hand—not once—since that day. She knew Connor had seen the marks on her breast left by Acres, and she was afraid he now considered her soiled. The thought hurt.

Still, there were times when he looked at her with such desperate hunger in his eyes that she shivered from the impact. No, she refuted. It was her wishful imagination. Connor was distant.

Swallowing against the ache in her chest, she vowed to have this settled soon, hopefully before the other complication she'd just discovered came to light.

Not wanting to dwell on her plight, she fixed her gaze on the house.

Without warning, a wave of nausea gripped her. *Oh, no. Not now.* She had to watch the house. Her stomach churned, pushing its contents upward. Frantically she dashed for the bushes—and became ill.

When the bout passed, she stumbled to the lake's edge and washed her face and hands, then rinsed her mouth. Rather than worry over Connor, she decided, she should throttle him for doing this to her.

Recovered, and feeling better, she hurried to her post and scanned the area. Her gaze stopped on a piece of blue material visible through the undergrowth. It was on the ground. Branden. He hadn't concealed himself well enough. The whole countryside could see him.

Staying within the protection of the trees, she made her way to the spot where he was lying in the weeds. "Branden," she hissed. "You're not hidden well enough. Your shirt's like a beacon. Move back into the ferns."

He didn't respond.

She edged closer. "Branden?"

Nothing.

Concern stole through her, and she scrambled to him. It was then she saw the blood. Someone had clobbered him on the back of the head. Her gaze flew to the study door.

It was open.

Ashlee tried not to groan as she tore off a strip of her chemise hem and placed it to Branden's bleeding wound.

When he moaned and stirred, she breathed a sigh of relief that his injury wasn't serious, then helped him into a sitting position. "Take deep breaths," she ordered. "It'll help restore your senses."

He did as instructed, then clutched his head. "What happened? One minute I was staring at the window, and the next, you were here."

"Someone knocked you unconscious."

Branden's gaze flew to the house, then back to Ashlee. "Louise?"

"Is probably gone."

"Damn it!" Branden roared.

His words expressed her feelings. "Come on," she urged. "We'd better go tell the others."

Connor stared woodenly out across the lake, his fury so alive, it moved. "We've got to find them," he grated. "Our lives may depend on it."

Ashlee eyed Vivian and the men, all of whom were present. Their attention was fixed on Connor.

"I'll search the swamps bordering the lake," Santos offered.

"I'll go north," Joe added.

Connor nodded. "Branden and I will cover the rest."

Standing beside Vivian, Ashlee's father spoke up. "Where do you want me to look?"

"Nowhere," Connor said. "Too much time has already been taken from your work. Time my aunt doesn't have to spare. But stay on the alert and lock the laboratory door, I don't want any more 'accidents.'" Connor didn't even glance at Ashlee, but chose to address Vivian instead. "You and Ashlee are to remain indoors—with the bolts in place until they're caught."

Not wishing for a recurrence of her previous experience, Ashlee didn't protest. She followed Vivian inside and locked the door.

"Who do you think did it? Hit Branden, I mean?" Vivian asked as she filled two cups with fresh-brewed tea and handed one to Ashlee.

Taking it, Ashlee sat down in a chair by the window, her gaze fixed on the men as they departed, Connor in particular. An ache swelled in her throat, and she looked away. "I wish I knew. Unfortunately, I didn't see anything after Branden disappeared into the trees." She wasn't about to tell the shrewd Vivian the reason why. "It was only when I saw his shirt and went to warn him that I learned what happened."

"I don't understand. How could you not have seen Louise and her rescuer? Connor said you were down by the lake, where you could see both sides of the house."

Ashlee shifted uncomfortably. "Maybe they got away while I was darting through the trees to reach Branden."

Vivian studied her. "Young lady, you're keeping something from me."

Trying not to groan at the woman's uncanny perception, Ashlee fingered the fall of silver hair concealing her scar, then gave up and blurted out the truth. "I was ill when the escape took place."

Concern flickered in Vivian's eyes. "Ill?"

"Wretchedly so." Knowing Vivian would figure it out anyway, Ashlee explained. "I'm with child."

Vivian didn't move for several seconds, then she gave a long sigh. "Does Connor know?"

Ashlee stared. "Is our attraction that obvious?"

"About as apparent as mine and Nathaniel's." Vivian smiled. "You haven't told Connor, have you?"

"No."

"Why not?" Vivian asked.

"Because he's been so unapproachable, so cold, since my . . . abduction." Ashlee wished the ache in her chest away. "Connor saw what George Acres did to me. In Connor's eyes, I'm soiled. Stained. Much too dirty to touch."

Vivian drew in a sharp breath. "You can't believe

that. Connor's in love with you. He'd never consider such a thought. And I'm terribly disappointed that you can't recognize the compassion in him. He's a good man, Ashlee. And he'd never shun you over something beyond your control." Her tone softened. "You must know that."

"Then why is he being so distant?" Tears threatened, and Ashlee blinked them back.

Vivian touched her hand. "Knowing my nephew, I imagine he thinks that's what you want. After such an ordeal, he probably thinks a man's advances would upset you."

"Not his," Ashlee cried.

"You know that. But he doesn't." Vivian smiled. "Perhaps when he gets back, you might set him straight, hmm?"

"I most certainly will—"

"Miss Walker!" a man's voice bellowed from outside.

Ashlee whirled around to look out the window.

The guide stood on the grass, motioning to her.

"It's Santos," she told Vivian. "He wants something." Rising, she hurried to the front door and threw it open. "What is it?"

"We've found them," Santos announced. "Connor just wanted me to let you know."

"Oh, thank goodness." Relief washed over Ashlee, followed by excitement. "Who was the man?"

Santos shook his head. "I've never seen him before." He turned to go.

"Wait! Where are they?"

"Couple miles. They should get back before dark. Connor wanted to question them first."

Dark? That long? Ashlee hesitated only an instant. "Could you take me to them?" She was dying to know the identity of Louise's accomplice.

"I don't think that's a good idea," Santos countered.

"Why? There's no danger now." She waited for a response, but he didn't answer. Her irritation rose. "Well? Will you take me? Or do I find my own way?"

He studied her a moment, then shrugged. "It seems I don't have a choice."

Time dragged with agonizing slowness as she followed Santos through the bogs, around stands of shadowy cypress and stagnant water. Mosquitoes tried to make a meal of her flesh, and she waved her hand in an attempt to keep them away. Perspiration slid from her temples. Dampened the valley between her breasts. Maybe this wasn't such a good idea, after all. It seemed like they'd gone five miles instead of two.

"Santos? How much farther?"

He flicked a hand toward a stand of trees. "We're almost there. Just the other side of those elms."

Sighing, she slapped at another mosquito with one hand and lifted the hem of her gown with the other, wishing she'd taken the time to put on a cooler dress.

When they at last rounded the trees, she saw a small village. Thatch huts sat in a clearing.

Awed, she watched Indian men and women perform various everyday tasks, cooking, mending, whittling. They were dressed oddly, she noticed. The men wore little more than loincloths, and the women had on sacklike dresses that appeared to be made of soft leather.

"Where's Connor?" she asked, still staring at the Indians.

"Searching for Louise, no doubt."

A flash of fear streaked through her. She stepped away from him. "What?"

Santos withdrew a pistol and aimed it straight at her heart. "You have a right to be afraid, *Amanda.*"

Terror held her immobile. Amanda? She edged backward. "Santos, what's the matter with you? You know my name is Ashlee." She peered around. "Why did you bring me here?"

As she talked, she saw the others moving toward her. Their eyes were filled with hatred. Fear seized her. She sent a panicked glance at Santos.

He motioned to a group of men, who immediately restrained her. "Tie her. I will return soon with the other—just as the Great Spirit foretold."

"For God's sake, what are you talking about?" Ashlee cried.

He turned those vicious black eyes on her. "Your game is not amusing. We know who you are, and why you have come. The Great Spirit spoke to our shaman. You have returned from the dead to destroy our people. But it is you and your lover who will be destroyed."

"Returned from the dead? Are you insane?"

He glared, then gestured for the men to take her away.

Kicking and fighting, Ashlee was brutally dragged into one of the huts and tied to the center pole. She tried to squelch her fear and understand what the Indians wanted. And what did Santos mean, 'returned from the dead to destroy our people'? Did it have something to do with the legend?

"We haven't done anything to make the Indians angry with us. For heaven's sake, we're practically hermits."

Ashlee's hands began to shake as the haunting words continued.

"Perhaps it's not something we did as much as who we are and what we represent.

The thoughts frightened her. Were Beau and Amanda killed by the Seminole? Did the Indians think she and Connor were that fated couple—who'd returned from the dead? The idea was so ludicrous, it was laughable.

But the Seminole weren't laughing.

And neither was Ashlee. She pulled against the bindings, her gaze darting from side to side, desperate for some means of escape.

A piece of material in a shadowed corner drew her attention, and she squinted to see what it was.

Her breath stopped. "Oh, dear God."

Louise Delacorte lay on a pallet made of palm leaves. Someone had slit her throat.

CHAPTER
25

Connor paused beneath the shade of an oak and wiped the moisture from his brow. He fanned the front of his loose shirt as he glanced at the dense, muggy swampland. He hadn't found a single sign of Louise or her cohort. Not before he and Branden separated to search farther afield, or since.

Waving a mosquito away from his ear, Connor sighed. There was nothing left to do but hope Branden or one of the others had been more successful. Resigned, he started in the direction he'd last seen Branden.

A prickling sensation skittered across the nape of Connor's neck. There was a stillness to the swamps. A presence he'd felt before. Slowly he turned.

Just beyond a stand of trees, a wavering form appeared. Radiant and glowing, it moved just above the ground. The Silver Witch.

Connor didn't move a muscle. He couldn't.

"Go back," the apparition said in a faint, hollow voice. "We need you."

"We? Who needs me? I don't understand." He stared at the figure, trying to hold feelings of panic at bay while he waited for a response.

But there was none. The Silver Witch dissolved into a mist, then drifted into the trees.

A sense of urgency hit him so hard, he trembled. Then he knew. "Ashlee!" He broke into a run, desperate to reach the manor.

By the time he reached the steps, he was breathing hard, his body covered in perspiration, his heart hammering. He stood staring at the door and gasping for air, but he was afraid to open it . . . afraid of what he might find on the other side. To the depths of his soul, he knew he'd lost something vital.

Taking a calming breath, he grabbed the latch and shoved open the door.

Nathaniel stood in the entry, his expression at first startled, then his face broke into a huge grin. "Connor!" He gripped Connor's upper arms. "I have found it. The cure!"

Connor went numb. "You've *what?*"

"Found the cure. I administered the retardant to Vivian just now. The elixir made her drowsy, and she is resting in the parlor. I was just on my way upstairs to inform Ashlee."

Ashlee was upstairs? A weight, heavy and solid, lifted slowly from Connor's shoulders. She was safe. His aunt was safe. Uncharacteristic tears threatened. *Thank you, God.* He clasped Nathaniel's hand. "I don't know enough words . . ."

A gentle smile touched the older man's lips. "There is no need to say anything." He tugged Connor through the door. "Come. I want to show you."

When they reached the laboratory, Nathaniel pointed to a pair of mice isolated in a separate cage. "See those two? They were both injected with a small portion of the malaria disease extracted from Vivian's blood."

Connor studied the rodents. One was huddled into a ball in a corner, shaking. The other was standing on its hind feet, its paws clinging to the side of the cage. The animal's eyes were bright, its nose a healthy pink.

"The one in the corner," Nathaniel offered, "was not injected with the medicine. The other was. And that is not all." He motioned for Connor to join him by the microscope. "Look at these samples of Vivian's blood. The treated one contains no sign of the malaria organism."

Connor's own excitement couldn't be contained. "What's in the medicine you gave Vivian?"

"Coal tar, liquid oxygen, soluble opium salt, seed plants . . ." He waved a hand. "There are too many ingredients to name. But, thank the good Lord, the combination works." He patted a small bulge in the fob pocket on his waistcoat. "I actually discovered this miracle on paper before we arrived in the swamps, but I was not certain of its success until I took a blood sample from the mice barely an hour ago. The instant I was sure, I gave Vivian an injection, and will continue to do so three times a day for the next eight weeks."

Again tears threatened, and Connor swallowed a lump of emotion. "She's going to come through this."

Nathaniel smiled. "It was as important to me for her to live as it was for you."

"I doubt that, but it's good to hear you say it, anyway." Connor motioned to the door. "Why don't we go inside. I'll fix you a celebration drink." After his futile search for Louise, Connor never imagined he'd have anything to celebrate this day.

"Only a short one," Nathaniel responded. "I want to tell Ashlee the news."

Connor nodded as they walked out and headed

across the lawn. "You know, I get the impression you've known my aunt a very long time."

"Longer than you think. If the fates had not been against us, I would have been your uncle instead of Jonathan, rest his soul."

Somehow, that didn't surprise Connor. "What happened?"

Nathaniel watched a bee circle. "I fell in love with her when I was barely into my twenties, but I was from a poor family. My mother was a scrubwoman, my father a seaman. I hated my life, and I wanted out. I had always liked taking care of injured animals, and decided I wanted to be a veterinarian. But when I began reading books on any subject concerning ailments and cures, I became fascinated with research— and healing people. I had just began my practice when I met your aunt."

His eyes softened at the memory. "She was so beautiful. So gentle. And so damned unreachable. Her family was one of the wealthiest in Charleston."

"How did she feel about you?"

Nathaniel shook his head. "She loved me. Said she would give up her family, the fortune she would inherit, everything, just to be with me. But I could not let her do that. My practice was still uncertain, and for all I knew, might never have amounted to anything. I just could not force my lifestyle on a woman I loved beyond life."

Connor hurt for the tortured young man he'd been. "So you left."

He nodded, suddenly looking older. "Yes. And I did not tell her or anyone where I was going. Vivian was just headstrong enough to come after me, and I knew I would not be able to resist her if she found me. She was just too damned tempting." He winced. "Sorry. I should not speak about your aunt in that way."

"Why not? I feel the same about your daughter."

A white brow lifted in surprise, then he cleared his throat. "Yes, well, be that as it may . . . Anyway, a year later, I got word she married Jonathan Makepeace. I was destroyed. I know I shouldn't have been, especially since I was the one who instigated our separation, but I was. Then I compounded my unhappiness by marrying out of spite. Claudine, Ashlee's mother, was wealthy, worldly, and quite the social butterfly. I knew word would get back to Vivian, and that was what I wanted. To hurt her the way I hurt. In the end, I only hurt myself . . . and my beautiful daughter. Claudine was so wrapped up in her social life, she had little time for me or our child. In fact, I do not think I spoke a dozen words to her in the last year or so before she died."

Nathaniel sidestepped a branch lying on the grass. "But Ashlee suffered the most. She was never given the love and attention she needed. Oh, I tried, but somehow my work managed to get in the way, and I always fell a little short in the fatherhood department."

Connor lowered his gaze, still tormented by the situation between himself and Ashlee. Would she ever let Connor touch her without resurrecting memories of George Acres? Would she ever trust Connor to protect her?

Stepping onto the porch, Nathaniel opened the door. "I am going to check on Vivian, then tell Ashlee the news. I am sure she will be anxious. She has become quite fond of your aunt."

"If you don't mind, I'd like to tell Ashlee after I've seen Vivian."

Nathaniel smiled. "Yes. You do that." He turned in to the parlor.

Aunt Vivian was lying on the settee, her eyes closed, her features serene and childishly winsome.

A tender smile pulled at the corner of Connor's mouth.

"Perhaps we should let her sleep," Nathaniel whispered.

Connor nodded. "I'll go tell Ashlee the news."

Dipping his head, Nathaniel took a seat across from Vivian, his eyes fixed on her slight form, his features alive with adoration.

Knowing exactly how Nathaniel felt, Connor slipped from the room.

After he searched Ashlee's bedchamber, the cookhouse, convenience, and grounds, Connor's earlier anxiety returned. Concerned, he headed for the lake.

He stopped at the spot where they'd first made love and stared at their bed of grass, trying to convince himself she was all right. But he knew she wasn't.

A twig snapped nearby, and he swung around.

Santos stood in the trees, watching.

"Have you seen Ashlee?" Connor asked.

"Yes. I've come to take you to her."

Something in the guide's manner set off warning bells. "Where is she?"

"Not far." Santos's hand went to his waist, and before Connor knew what he was about, he'd drawn his pistol. The barrel was pointed at Connor. The Indian motioned with a jerk of his head. "This way."

"What the hell's going on?" Connor demanded with much more outrage than he felt. He was afraid he already knew. Santos was the one who'd helped Louise, who'd sabotaged Nathaniel's experiments . . . and who now had Ashlee. Connor strove to calm the fear racing through his body. "What's the meaning of this?"

"No more talk, Westfield. Just walk."

The urge to overpower the bastard was so strong, Connor had to clench his hands to keep them at his sides. He didn't want to do anything rash until he found Ashlee and knew she was all right. Keeping his fury in check, he strode in the direction Santos had indicated.

As they walked through the bogs and marshes, Connor noticed the gathering clouds and gusts of wind. But his thoughts remained on Ashlee . . . and what Connor would do to Santos when he got the chance.

Over an hour had passed before they at last came to a thatch-hut village.

A group of Seminole men met them at the edge of the clearing, then Connor was shoved toward one of the huts.

Restraining the urge to retaliate, he stooped to pass under the short door. It took a moment for his eyes to adjust to the dark interior. Then he saw Ashlee, standing in front of a post, with her hands tied behind her back.

Relief that she was safe battled with fury at the men who'd done this to her.

Rage won out. He whirled around.

Several lances whipped into view, their points aimed at Connor's chest.

"Don't try it, Westfield," Santos said. "If lances don't get you, my brother here would kill Ashlee before you could move."

Connor swung his head to see a brave holding a bow with an arrow aimed at Ashlee's heart. Connor's own stopped. "What do you want, Santos? Me? If so, then let the girl go. You've got me."

"I want you both," the guide said calmly. He nodded to one of the braves. "Tie him."

Connor's muscles quivered with rage as his hands were tightly secured behind him.

"Why are you doing this?" Ashlee cried, at last finding her voice.

Santos's dark eyes pinned her. "I'm not entertained by your innocent game. We both know why you're here. The legend has not been forgotten."

"About the Silver Witch? We had nothing to do with that."

"Oh, but you did." Santos moved to the door. "We know of the Silver Witch's plan to return in the flesh and destroy us . . . unless, of course, we destroy her first. The shaman speaks often of her revenge on the one who betrayed her and her lover. The one who led her husband to them."

An eerie sensation moved through Connor. "The Seminole did that?"

"Not the Seminole. One brave. He was the bastard of a trapper who had raped his mother. Though he was raised as an Indian, he was never fully accepted, and he blamed his white blood *and* the white man for it. He wanted the lovers gone. Because his skin was light, he could pass among the white man unnoticed, so he went to St. Augustine and learned of the runaway couple. He sent for the woman's husband, and led him to the big house."

His eyes drifted to Ashlee. "It was a mistake. After the white ones died, the woman's ghost appeared before the shaman. She vowed she would return in the flesh and destroy the Seminole for their treachery." He nodded in Ashlee's direction. "She knows this is true."

"If that's the case, then why did you come after me? Why didn't you just kill her?"

Ashlee gasped, and he wanted to protect her, but he couldn't. Connor needed to know the answer.

"Do you think the Seminole are fools? That we wouldn't recognize both of you? Especially when the witch left that locket for our shaman to find?"

"What locket?"

He pulled a gold necklace from his pocket and snapped it open, then thrust it forward.

Connor stared in bewildered amazement.

Snapping it shut, Santos glared, then his eyes drifted to something in the corner.

Connor followed his gaze, and felt a jolt run through him at the sight of Louise's dead body. "Jesus."

The Indian snorted. "She was an imbecile. She thought by tempting me with her white flesh—and your money—that I'd kill her husband and free her to marry you." He laughed humorlessly. "After I 'rescued' her from the study, she waited for me by the lake while I convinced you to let me help search."

"Why did you rescue her?"

"Because confinement was weakening her tongue. She would have soon talked. When I returned to you after she 'escaped,' you no longer suspected me, just as I'd planned. No one did, or you wouldn't have left the witch alone. The Delacorte bitch served her purpose well."

"Then you killed her."

"After I took what she'd been offering."

Ashlee gasped.

Connor's unwilling gaze lowered to Louise's mangled, bloodstained skirt, and he felt bile climb the back of his throat. She was a vicious woman, but she didn't deserve to dic likc that. "I hope you rot in hell for eternity."

"Your curses are futile."

Knowing he'd need every ounce of composure and information he could find to get them out of this, Connor met the Indian's eyes. "You were the man Ashlee overheard with Louise, weren't you?"

"Yes. Louise approached me before we even arrived at the lake, enticing me to do her bidding, to kill her husband. She amused me, so I played along. Later, I had all of you believing I wouldn't go into the house, so I was never questioned when we were overheard."

"I thought the Seminole were afraid to enter the manor."

"You're a fool, white man, to believe everything you're told."

"So it seems." He narrowed his eyes on the man. "And it was you who sabotaged Nathaniel's work, too, wasn't it?"

"Some. George Acres did most. And Joe. He and Harry blamed Nathaniel for Charlotte's death. They wanted to destroy his life's work and him. It entertained me to watch them, then mislead you with false clues."

"And the explosion—the one Ashlee heard you plan?"

"Joe did it before I could. He'd been planning for sometime."

Wishing he could reach Santos's neck, Connor tried to keep his tone level. "Why did you wait so long to take Ashlee? You could have taken her any time during the last months. Why now?"

"My people felt it was fitting for her to die on the same day she died one hundred years ago." He sent her a smug look. "On this day."

Ashlee paled.

Connor's stomach tightened. "What—"

"Enough talk! It's time to begin the ceremony . . . one in which you two will be the guests of honor," he taunted, then abruptly left the room.

The others followed him out and secured the door.

"This is insane," Ashlee cried. "I'm not a witch— and just what did he show you?"

"Just a picture of a woman who looks a little like you." Connor struggled in vain with his bindings. "That's probably why they think you're the Silver Witch."

"What are they going to do to us?"

Connor edged to the window and peeked out, keeping his gaze from Louise's body. Shades of evening shrouded the village. The wind blew across the encampment, stirring dust and debris. Several Indians stood guard around their hut and in the center of the village. Other braves were laboring in the gusty breeze to pile sticks and brush high around a tall pole.

Connor closed his eyes. "You don't want to know."

"Yes, I do, Connor. Now, what?"

He forced his eyes to hers. "They're planning to burn us at the stake. Just like they did the witches of Salem."

He expected her to cry out, to wail and scream, but she did none of those. Instead, she straightened her shoulders and lifted her chin. "My aunt Hattie, they are!" She kicked the post behind her with her heel. "Get over here and untie me, then I'll do the same for you. We're getting out of this horrible place."

Admiring her spirit, Connor quickly freed her hands.

"How are we going to get by the guards?" Ashlee asked in a hushed voice as she unknotted his bindings.

"Maybe we can force our way through the back wall." After pulling out of the restraints, he crept to the rear of the hut and tested the strength of the palm barrier. "With a little good fortune, we may be able to burrow through."

She placed a hand on the wall. "Too bad you don't have a knife."

He inspected the branches overhead that had been secured with heavy vines. Grasping one, he twisted and pulled, then twisted again. At last a piece of the branch broke off. "This may do in place of a blade," he suggested.

"You're truly amazing, Mr. Westfield."

"So are you, Miss Walker."

The seductive undertone in his voice caused her to shiver. She rubbed her arms. "You might want to hurry."

The wind howled, testing the hut walls as Connor began the task.

Fearing discovery, Ashlee watched the entrance.

The minutes ticked by with stomach-tightening slowness. Only the sound of the wind and the light rasp made by Connor's makeshift tool could be heard in the dim interior of the hut.

"See what they're doing," he prompted.

Inching to the front window, she peeked out and frowned. "They're standing in a circle around a huge pile of branches. It looks like they're praying."

"How many are there?"

"About thirty."

"Damn."

She turned around. "What?"

"If we get through, you'd better hope no one sees us. We'd never escape that many."

"How much longer?" she whispered, her gaze returning to the Indians.

"Not much." The branch scraped louder, faster.

She watched him work, noting how the muscles in his upper arms bunched and knotted beneath the fine linen. Tiny beads of perspiration glistened in the hollow of his neck, visible beyond the open front of his shirt. Studying him, she knew that no man had ever made her feel the way Connor did. Completely whole. Cherished. Loved.

He shoved against the wall with his shoulder.

A cracking, tearing sound filled the hut, and a small portion of the wall gave way.

"We're through! Come on."

She hurried toward him.

Just as he bent to go out the opening, a lance sailed across the gaping hole and imbedded in the side, blocking the way.

"Oh!" she cried, slapping a hand over her mouth.

Connor stood to his full height, listening to the muffled chuckles coming from the other side. "The bloody bastards were waiting for us. Probably have been the whole time I was working." Anger tightened his jaw.

"What are we going to do?"

"I don't know," he sighed. "I just don't know."

The door flew open.

Gasping, Ashlee whirled around to see Santos standing in the entrance. A cruel smile curved his mouth. "I'd have been disappointed, Westfield, if you hadn't tried to escape."

"You must have had a good laugh."

"Actually, we had quite a few bets on how long it would take you to break through." He smiled. "I won."

"You bastard."

Santos's grin vanished, and he jerked his hand toward the opening. "This way. Now."

Connor remained still. "If you want me, Indian, you're going to have to come get me."

In a movement so quick, Ashlee didn't see it coming, Santos pulled his gun and pointed it at her chest. "I said now."

Panic shook every cell in her body.

Connor's face went ashen.

"Outside."

Not taking his eyes from the weapon, Connor hesitated, then moved forward.

The Indian stepped back, allowing him to pass through the door, then motioned for her to follow.

She wanted to refuse, but she didn't dare. One wrong move and he'd kill her.

Wind slapped her hair across her face when she walked into the open. Her skirt billowed outward, and she tried to hold it down. Santos urged her forward, and she saw several Seminole standing on either side of them, forming a path to the pile of branches. The men and women in various degrees of nakedness chanted low as they moved down the line.

Terror skittered up her spine.

When Connor reached the mountain of wood, he stopped, his head bent, his clothes molded to his powerful frame by the wind. But he didn't turn back to look at her, and that only added to her fear.

Two braves stepped from the line, each holding a strip of leather. Their big hands latched on to Connor, and they dragged him up to the pile, then slammed his back against the center post. With rapid movements, they tied his hands around the pole.

Connor still didn't look at her. He just stood there like a rigid soldier, his eyes staring straight ahead, his features taut.

Santos nudged her forward with the gun, straight into the men who'd tied Connor.

She kicked and scratched, called them every vile name she could think of, but either they didn't understand or they didn't care. They dragged her up to the post and tied her back to back with Connor, her hands around the pole below his. "I'm not the Silver Witch," she screamed at them. "You've made a mistake!"

Drums began a slow, heavy beat. The overpowering scent of cypress rose from the pile of dead branches.

"Connor?" she whispered, desperate for reassurance. "They aren't really going to do this, are they?"

He lowered his fingers and wrapped them around her wrist. His thumb gently stroked her pulsing veins. "Yes."

Panic shot through her.

As if he sensed her rising hysteria, his fingers tightened. "Just hold on to me, sweetheart. I won't let you go. Not until . . ." his voice grew rough. "Not until I'm forced to."

Tears rolled down her cheeks, and she lowered her lashes. It wasn't fair. She and Connor had had so little time together. She'd never feel his arms around her again. Never know the joy of watching him smile or hearing his laughter. Never again see his eyes flash with intelligence or darken with passion. But worst of all, she'd never hold their babe in her arms. A knot formed in her throat. "Connor, I'm going to have your child," she said brokenly. "I just wanted you to know." Then she prayed.

The hand on her wrist trembled, and he made a disjointed sound.

Suddenly the smell of smoke filled her nostrils, and her eyes sprang open to see several Indians holding torches to the branches at their feet. "Connor! Oh, God, Connor. Make them stop!" She kicked at the dry wood.

A ring of fire flared from the outer edges, slowly working its way upward and toward the center.

Thick, hot smoke filled her lungs, and she turned her head to avoid the breath-stealing fumes. It didn't do any good. The smoke was everywhere. She coughed again and again, trying to breathe. Her lungs burned. Dizziness stole her ability to think. Heat seared her.

The drums thundered louder. A gust of wind swirled. Flames shot into the air, until she could no longer see the Indians. Higher. Higher. Consuming her.

A horrified scream tore from her throat.

"Ashlee! Damn it, listen to me!"

Through the roar of the inferno and the ringing in her own ears, she heard his command.

"Grab the pole and pull with all your might. Then dive to the left. Do you hear me? It's our only chance."

A wall of black smoke and red-gold flames filled her vision, but she clutched the pole. *Their only chance. Their only chance.*

"Now!" he bellowed over the crackling blaze.

Blindly she obeyed, jerking upward with all her strength.

The pole lifted several inches.

The heavens opened up in a downpour. Smoke and steam surrounded them.

"Dive!" Connor ordered.

She lunged sideways—*straight into the flames*—and right through them.

They hit the ground hard, so hard the pole between them broke and fell away.

"Roll!" he commanded.

She didn't question him. She just did it, and within moments, she felt cool reeds, wet, spongy soil, and blessed rain. Oh, God. It felt wonderful.

"Sit up and put your back against mine. Hurry. Before they realize we've escaped."

Shaking violently, Ashlee made several attempts before she got herself into a sitting position. "Hurry," she whispered. "Please hurry."

Connor's strong fingers worked rapidly, until she felt the bindings loosen. She jerked her hands free and attacked the leather around his wrists.

The instant his hands were released, he grabbed her and pulled her to her feet, running frantically for the swamps. Waist-deep in murky water, they wound their way through dense, branchless tree trunks. Rain pounded their backs as they raced deeper and deeper into the uncharted bayous.

Something scaly brushed Ashlee's leg, and she opened her mouth to scream.

Connor's hand covered her lips. "Don't," he whispered. "If you make a sound, they'll hear you." He stroked her jaw. "It was only a lizard, sweetheart. Only a lizard."

Swallowing, she closed her mouth.

He pulled her into a hug. "That's my girl. Now, come on."

Wind whipped through the trees, plastering her dress to her body. The bottom of the swampy pool sank farther away, until the water nearly reached her breasts. "Connor, it's getting too deep."

"It's all right, there's . . ."

A torrent of rain slammed into them, drowning his words.

She shielded her eyes with her free hand, trying to see through the blinding downpour. But the brutal wind and vicious rain made visibility impossible. Her only hold on reality was Connor's hand wrapped around hers.

He pulled her, forcing her to trudge through the water. But soon the water level receded, and her feet touched solid ground.

"We've got to find shelter!" he roared over the wind and rain. "This way!" He yanked her to the left.

Trying to gather her wet skirts and run, she stumbled after him.

The rain became brutal. It stung her cheeks. Connor picked up the pace. He ran so fast, her feet barely touched the ground, then he was shoving her inside an alcove of twisted branches so thick, the rain couldn't penetrate.

Connor pressed her onto her back on the spongy ground and covered her with his body. He held her so tight, she had to gasp for air. "What's happening?" she cried into his shoulder.

"It's a hurricane."

CHAPTER
26

Ashlee closed her eyes and buried her face in Connor's strong shoulder. Fear shook her, and she began to cry.

"Don't," he groaned, cupping her face with his hands. "You've shown more courage than any woman I've ever known; don't fall apart on me now."

She began to shake. "I can't help it. I can't—"

He sought her lips.

The heavens roared, but the elements couldn't compare to the power in his desperate kiss. His wet, open mouth devoured hers, sliding, grinding, his tongue plunging deeply, drawing the fear from her as he made her aware of only him, of the fierceness of his passion.

She was caught up in a maelstrom of sensation. Heat, cold, wet . . . and scalding desire. With an urgency borne of danger, she clung to him, arched into his hard body, sought the taste of him, the vibrant power.

The ferocious wind screamed through the branches as he tugged at her clothes, baring her body to his strong hands.

"I love you, Ashlee. I love you so much, it scares me," he groaned into her mouth. He kissed her hard and long, then dragged his lips away to kiss the rain from her naked skin.

His hot mouth closed over her breast, and he nursed ravenously, moving his head from side to side, nibbling, suckling.

She cried out from the sheer pleasure.

His fingers found her woman's opening and slid effortlessly inside her. He withdrew, then thrust deeper, again and again.

Need shook her. She lifted her hips, ground against his tormenting hand, seeking more. So much more.

He drew those teasing fingers upward and slid them over the tiny bud that pleaded for notice. His thumb joined the melee, circling, stroking, caressing in sweet torment.

"Connor!" she screamed above the wind. "Oh, God! I can't stand any more."

He pulled his hungry mouth from her throbbing breast to kiss and nibble his way downward. He gripped her bottom and lifted her, plunging his tongue deeply into her. His mouth slid from side to side, taunting her, tormenting her with the erotic movements. He raised her higher, plunged deeper, harder, faster.

The rain, the wind, and wild need slammed together, tossing her into a spiraling whirlpool of flames. A tortured moan ripped from her throat as pleasure scorched every cell in her body. She shook, cried, and exploded into a million tiny pieces.

He drove her on and on, refusing to release her from the heart-stopping spasm that consumed her soul. Then he was inside her, thrusting, taking her beyond sanity, beyond passion, to a pleasure so volatile, she knew she wouldn't survive.

A hoarse, masculine groan penetrated the wind, and he threw his head back. He shook with the frenzy of the storm, taking her with a fierceness that rivaled nature's own feral power. He convulsed again and again, igniting one explosion after another, until she felt the pull of sweet death.

At last he slumped over her, releasing her from the inferno that charred her soul. She burrowed into his shoulder and clung to him, crying, laughing, and trembling.

He held on to her and kissed her over and over, shielding her from the elements with his powerful body, and making her forget the vicious storm that surrounded them.

It seemed like hours before the wind eased and the rain slowed to a light drizzle. Still he didn't release her. Safe and secure in his wondrous embrace, she sighed and closed her eyes, giving in to the pull of sleep.

Connor heard the deep, even sound of her breathing and gave a sigh of his own. She'd finally given up. He closed his eyes and recalled the savagery of their lovemaking. Never had he experienced anything so primitive, so beautiful. And that it should come from such a tiny bit of a woman left him shaken. The power she had over him was more frightening than the hurricane they'd managed to survive.

His body stirred at the wanton images floating through his brain, and he eased away, not wanting to awaken her from her much-needed slumber.

Dragging on his clothes, he sat beside her, watching, until sunlight at last seeped in through the thick, gnarled roots, then, on his hands and knees, he crawled from their haven and looked around.

Devastation surrounded him. Hundreds of trees lay like fallen soldiers, their limbs bent and twisted, their cloaks of green stained by the blood of the red earth. Yet sunlight moved over the mangled corpses, promising new life.

"It's horrible, isn't it?" Ashlee remarked from behind him.

He turned to see her standing close to him, unashamedly naked. "Yes."

"We were so lucky."

He pulled her into his arms. "I think we're charmed."

She nuzzled his chest. "I certainly feel like it."

For several seconds Connor held her, enjoying the pleasure of her naked warmth and trying to find the words he wanted to say. "Ashlee? What you said yesterday, before we escaped the Indians, was it true?"

"I wouldn't lie about something like that." She took his hand and placed it over her flat stomach. "Our babe is tucked safely in here."

His hand shook, and he clutched her to him, burying his face in the crook of her slender neck. "A child. Our child." He blinked against the stinging in his eyes. "I don't deserve such happiness."

"You deserve much more," she whispered.

Running his fingers over her silky hair, he tried to apologize for his rash behavior. "Ashlee, I'm sorry about last night."

Her head came up. "What?"

"I can only say in my defense that I lost control during the storm. Otherwise, I'd have never taken you like that. I had every intention of giving you all the time you needed."

"Time for what?"

"To get over what George Acres did to you . . . over how you must loathe a man's touch."

Her eyes grew tender. "Is that how I reacted last night—like your touch repulsed me?"

"No. But I realize you were too frightened to think clearly."

"I see." She drew little circles through the hairs on his chest. "That's why you've been so distant lately, too, isn't it? So you could give me time to get over my ordeal?"

"Yes."

"Well, I have news for you, Mr. Westfield. I never once associated George Acres's brutal attack with what you and I share—nor have I ever dreaded having your hands on me. Quite the opposite, in fact. I've rather shamelessly been anticipating it."

"Then it doesn't bother you—"

"Nothing about you bothers me . . . well, except for your high-handedness and the way you jump to conclusions without first talking to me, but I'm working on those flaws."

Chuckling, he set her away from him, his eyes growing bright at the sight of her nude body. "I think we'd better start for home before I reveal another of my flaws. My insatiable appetite for you."

"That's a flaw I can live with."

He swatted her bottom. "Get dressed."

"Are my clothes salvageable?"

Recalling how he'd carelessly pulled them off her last night, he wasn't sure at all. "Let's take a look."

Fortunately he'd only broken a couple of ties and created a few new openings. With minor alterations, she was able to preserve her modesty. Now all they had to do was find their way to the manor.

"Do you have any idea which direction we should go?" Ashlee asked as she tied the last of her skirt together.

"I'd say north." Connor scanned the few standing

trees for signs of moss. "That way." He pointed to his right.

Walking wasn't easy with all the tangled reeds and fallen trees blocking the way, and several times they had to wade through bogs to get around the carnage. Not that he minded too much since Ashlee had to lift her skirts nearly to her waist. The sight of her smooth white thighs and nicely curved bottom did wonders for his stamina.

"Here we go again," he muttered, seeing another pile of rubble blocking their way.

She sighed. "I think you're doing this on purpose, just so I'll have to expose my limbs."

He gave her a devilish grin. "The thought had crossed my mind."

Scowling, she hoisted her skirt to her waist and tromped into the murky water.

He watched the jiggle of her naked rear, and had to restrain the urge to reach for her.

Suddenly she slid forward, down into the dirty water. "Connor!"

He lunged for her, but he wasn't quick enough. She disappeared below the muddy surface. "Ashlee!" He dove in after her. Blindly he searched, but he couldn't find her. He swung his arms in wild desperation. His fingers touched something hard. He gripped it and pulled. But it wasn't Ashlee. Releasing the object, he felt it brush his arm as it floated to the surface.

Near hysteria, he dove deeper, his lungs burning for air. He felt her skirt brush his wrist and nearly cried out with relief. He followed the material to her waist, then attempted to pull her up. She wouldn't budge. He tried again.

Nothing.

She twisted and clawed at him.

Terror filled him, and he ran his hands down her

legs. Her feet were tangled in thick, slick vines. Furiously he tore at the limbs, yanking on her legs as he worked. When she was at last free, he caught her to him, then lunged for the surface.

They came up sputtering and coughing, gasping for breath. He pulled her to him and just held her until her shaking—and his own—subsided.

"I was so frightened," she sobbed against his shoulder. "The ground disappeared beneath my feet. My dress pulled me down and I sank into the vines. I couldn't move. Couldn't get away."

"Shh, sweetheart. I know. But it's all over now, and you're safe." He smoothed the wet hair away from her face, and smiled. "Let's get out of here."

He guided her back to solid ground and helped her pluck debris from her clothes. "Come on, I think it's this way." He gestured ahead of them. "And from now on, I'll lead."

She took a step, then froze. "Oh, dear God!"

Anxiously he looked around for the newest threat. And what he saw almost sent him to his knees. A strange unnerving stillness claimed him as he stared at the object.

Kill the bloody whoreson! Slit his throat and dump him in the swamp.

Beau struggled wildly with the duke's men, using every ounce of strength he possessed, but it wasn't enough. They dragged him into the trees, farther and farther away from Amanda.

When they reached the bog, they shoved him to his knees. "You filthy cockswain," one of the men snarled. "Dyin's too good for the likes of you." The man snagged his hair and pulled his head back. "Take this to your grave with ye, bastard: Your ladylove's goin' to meet the same fate as ye this day."

Terror exploded, and he twisted insanely. Then he

felt it, the searing pain that burned across his throat, the sudden, frantic gasp for air that wouldn't come, then the stagnant water that consumed him. . . .

Suppressing a shiver of terror, Connor stared at the decaying skeleton . . . knowing they had just found Beau.

"It's him, isn't it?" Ashlee whispered in a quivering voice.

"Yes."

She wasn't afraid anymore. Not of this long dead man who lay at their feet. Unbearable sadness filled her.

Suddenly a white light moved over the skeleton, and Ashlee glanced up to see the Silver Witch standing across from them.

Connor's arm went around Ashlee, and he drew her back, his eyes on the unearthly apparition.

The woman was crying. Ashlee could hear her sobs as she knelt beside the man who had once been her lover. Gently an iridescent hand touched the jawbone, the outline of the mouth. "Oh, my beautiful Beau," she whispered in haunting tones. "I will never stop loving you."

The spectral figure rose, her head lowered, her sobs still echoing through the trees, then she looked at Connor, her features a hazy blur. She raised an arm and pointed to the west, then turned to walk away.

Out of the trees ahead of her, another ghostly figure appeared. A man.

Ashlee experienced such overwhelming joy, she nearly burst into tears. It was Beau. She knew it as surely as she breathed.

Through blurry eyes, she watched the translucent couple face each other. Touch. Their fingers entwined, then with pure, unblemished love so strong it transcended time, they walked together into the trees and vanished. At last, Beau had been released from his earthly bounds. By uncovering his remains, they had somehow set him free.

Ashlee began to sob.

Connor pulled her into his arms and held her. When he at last spoke, his voice was rough with emotion. "They'll spend eternity together, sweetheart. Don't cry for them."

CHAPTER
27

Ashlee knew Connor was right. The love Beau and Amanda shared was strong enough to endure even beyond eternity. A warmth filled Ashlee and she slid her gaze to Connor, studying him as he lifted a branch out of their way. Sleek muscles played beneath his tight flesh, arousing her female appreciation, but she knew that wasn't all that drew her to him. He was strong and intelligent, yet gentle and compassionate. Sometimes vulnerable. She smiled. Even his high-handed arrogance had its appeal.

Connor tossed the limb aside, then turned to look at her. "What are you smiling at?"

"All your wonderful attributes. And how much I love each of them."

His eyes darkened. "I love you, too, Ashlee. As much as Beau loved his duchess." He pulled her against him and kissed her thoroughly. "Maybe even more."

Ashlee's knees felt weak. "I think we'd better go while I can still walk."

Reluctantly he agreed.

Following the direction the Silver Witch had indicated, they headed out, this time keeping as far away from water as possible, both deep in their own thoughts.

A light, misty breeze blew, and Connor slapped at a mosquito on his neck. What he'd give for a bath about now. The thought spawned a question he'd had in the back of his mind for several weeks. He stopped and faced her. "When I found you in my bath on the ship, I got the impression that someone had tormented you about your scars. Is that true?"

Good heavens. Since she'd been with Connor, she'd almost forgotten her disfigurement altogether. And she'd put thoughts of the incident with Stephen out of her mind. "Listen, I—"

"The truth, Ashlee. The whole truth."

Pulling away from him, she sighed. "There isn't that much to tell. I was engaged to a man before the accident, and I thought he loved me. After I recovered, he accepted an invitation to a dinner party without consulting me. I was angry at first, and still nervous about my appearance, but I agreed. In the beginning, I had a lovely time, and when the orchestra began to play, we danced and danced. Eventually we ended up in the gardens for a cooling stroll."

She stared down at the ground and kicked a pile of soggy leaves with her toe. "The moon was full and bright, and he became amorous—until he removed the lace filler from my bodice and saw the scar on my breast. Oh, he pretended to restrain himself for the sake of my virtue. But later I overheard him complaining to one of his friends how he'd have to bed me in the dark—and with his eyes closed—long enough to gain an heir. And if he wasn't in such dire need of my dowry, he couldn't force himself to even hold my hand." She gave a brittle laugh. "He'd already found a mistress to remove the distaste he would feel after we made love."

"That son of a bitch."

"Yes," she agreed. "But I did retaliate by lacing his punch with some of Father's medicinal opium. When the drug took effect, Stephen made a complete fool of himself, insulted a score of influentials, and when he learned I was to blame—which I took pleasure in telling him when I broke our engagement—he spread word that *he'd* cried off because he found that I'd been so severely damaged by the explosion that I wasn't capable of performing the marital act. All in all, it was quite a notorious scandal."

Connor was silent for so long, she became uneasy. At last he spoke. "Who was your fiancé?"

"Stephen Frankenburg. Why?"

Connor's eyes gleamed menacingly, and he took her hand. "Just curious." Without another comment, he started walking.

Ashlee wasn't sure what to think about his quiet acceptance. It was so unlike the volatile man she knew. She just hoped he wasn't planning anything rash when they returned—which would be very much like him.

She was so engrossed in her thoughts, she didn't see the Indian village until they were beside it.

Nothing remained except tangled debris that was once shelters . . . and mangled corpses.

Leaving her next to the clearing, Connor examined the rubble, then knelt beside one of the bodies. He picked something up and put it in his pocket, then rejoined her.

"What did you find?"

"Just a little keepsake. Come on, let's go." He ushered her toward the lake not far from the site.

They followed the shoreline until they reached the manor just after noon.

Thankfully, the storm hadn't damaged the house.

"Connor! Ashlee!" Vivian cried when they walked into the parlor.

Branden and Ashlee's father surged to their feet.

"What happened?" Branden demanded.

"Are you all right?" her father asked.

Connor held up his hand. "We're both fine. And if you'll hold the questions a moment, and let us catch our breath, we'll tell you everything."

"I'll pour some tea," Vivian offered.

When Connor and Ashlee were seated, cups in hand, Connor related what happened, purposefully omitting Joe's part in the sabotage for the moment, and wondering at the man's absence. Then Connor told Branden about Louise's death.

No expression showed on Branden's face, but Ashlee could see the pain darken his eyes. "Walk with me."

Connor sent Ashlee a reassuring look and gave her a quick kiss. "I'll be back in a few minutes."

"Don't be long," Vivian warned.

Connor followed Branden to the water's edge.

Neither of them said anything for several seconds, then Branden finally spoke up. "I wanted you to know why I believed Louise when she told me you bedded her."

"It's all right, Bran. It doesn't matter."

"The hell it doesn't." He lowered his head, his face taut with grief. "I did love her, once. I truly did. But things changed after our wedding. She avoided my attempts at lovemaking. Talked of you day and night. Then she started asking me for a divorce, which I couldn't have given her if I'd wanted to. When she realized I wasn't going to relent, she showed me the inscription in that bracelet and told me she was pregnant with your child. I went crazy." He shoved his hands into his pockets. "That was the day of

Edenbower's soiree, the day I called you out. It should have never happened, Connor, and I apologize for doubting you. I can only say in my defense that Louise knew just where to hit to hurt me most. She continued to torment me, even after we came here."

Connor wanted to hit something when he thought of all the tortures Branden had been through because of that selfish woman. "If she were still alive, I swear, I'd turn her over my knee."

"My sentiments exactly," Branden agreed. Then he became quiet. "I've got to find her, Connor. She at least deserves to be buried."

"I'll show you the way."

"No. Not this time. I'd rather go alone."

With a deep understanding of Branden's pain, Connor nodded, then gave him directions.

His emotions upended, Connor headed for the house and found that dinner was waiting and everyone was just sitting down at the table. Except Joe.

"Where's your assistant?" Connor directed at Nathaniel as he sat next to Ashlee.

Everyone at the table went silent.

Uneasy, Connor glanced at each of them.

Nathaniel cleared his throat. "Joe's dead, Connor. He was in the laboratory, when the hurricane struck. The structure was destroyed, with him in it."

"I'm sorry," Connor said with sincerity. Joe may have had a hand in the subterfuge, but he was Nathaniel's friend. And Connor was glad there would be no need to tell Nathaniel of Joe's involvement. "Where were you during the storm?"

"In here. Vivian and I were trying to calm Branden. When you and Ashlee disappeared, he became frantic with worry. It was all we could do to keep him from going out into the storm to look for you."

"Thank God you found the cure for Aunt Vivian before the laboratory was destroyed this time."

"Yes," Nathaniel agreed. "Everything was lost, including my notes."

"Are you going to attempt to re-create them?"

"No." He patted his pocket containing the vile of malaria medicine. "I have all I need, and after Vivian and I are married, I am giving up research to tend the ailing again."

"After you what?" Connor asked, surprised.

Aunt Vivian blushed. "Nathaniel and I are going to be married as soon as we return to St. Augustine."

Ashlee smiled. "That's wonderful! Are you going to live there, too?"

Nathaniel shook his head. "No. I want to go back to Charleston. I only left there because of Vivian." He smiled tenderly. "And I am going back for the same reason."

Connor's heart warmed at the adoring looks on the older couple's faces. "Welcome to the family . . . Uncle Nathaniel."

"Thank you," Nathaniel said with obvious sincerity, then his eyes twinkled with mischief as he added, ". . . son-in-law?"

Ashlee drew in a sharp breath.

Connor grinned. "Well, that's something that needs to be discussed yet." Trying not to laugh at the expression on Ashlee's flushed face, Connor speared a fried trout. "After dinner."

Full and content, Connor excused himself from the table and retired to his room for a long, soothing bath. But he had just settled into the tub when someone knocked on the door.

"May I come in?" Ashlee's voice drifted through the panel.

He stretched in the water and leaned back. "By all means."

She stepped inside, and stopped on an indrawn breath. "Oh, I didn't realize—"

"Close the door and come here."

Her gaze fluttered away from his, but she did as instructed. She stopped beside the tub, looking at the curtains on the far wall. "I wanted to talk to you for a minute."

"About what?"

"Marriage."

His gut drew into a knot. "What about it?"

"Do you plan to propose to me?"

"If I'm given the chance."

She fingered the folds of her skirt. "Is it because of the babe?"

Connor relaxed. So that's what had her worried. And, in typical Ashlee fashion, she'd wanted to confront her fears. He reached out and took her hand. "I love you, sweetheart. And want you to marry me . . . whether you're with child or not. Does that answer your question?"

Unbridled joy illuminated her eyes. "One of them."

"There's more?"

She nodded.

"Like what?"

"Where you want to live."

"With you."

She smiled. "Where? Here?"

That gave him pause, and he glanced around the room. "No. Beau and Amanda lived here because it was the only way they could be together. They never enjoyed the freedom to love openly. We have that freedom, and I plan to shamelessly flaunt it. We can live in St. Augustine, Charleston, London, Paris, wherever you choose. I can build ships anywhere there's water."

"Charleston," she said without reservation. "I want to be near my father, and I know you want to stay close to your aunt." She grinned sheepishly. "But I'd like to see all those places."

Love for her overflowed. He stood up, water sheeting down his bare body. "Then I'll take great pleasure in showing them to you. Come here." He drew her against him. He wanted to drown in her beautiful mouth.

Their lips met and fused. She opened for him and welcomed him inside, exploring his tongue with her own. "I love you," she whispered, kissing his jaw, his neck, his shoulder, all the while pulling at the laces on her gown until she was as naked as he was.

With a boldness he'd never imagined, she stepped into the tub with him and wrapped her arms around his neck, pressing against him. "I wonder if Beau and Amanda had doubts at first, too."

"I'm sure they did." He stroked her spine. "And I know something else."

"What?"

He kissed her nose. "Why she roamed the swamps. Why you had the dreams, and why I've had such mixed feelings about this place since I set foot on the beach." He slid a palm over her smooth rear. "And what we have to do with all of this."

She stepped back and sat on the rim of the tub, her hands gripping the sides, her appreciative gaze roaming over his naked form. "Go on."

Connor sank down into the water and leaned his head on the rim, enjoying the view. "She roamed the swamps, as you know from the legend, because Beau's body had never been located. And until it was, their spirits couldn't join."

"I figured that."

"And did you figure we were the key?"

She tilted her head, spilling silvery curls over one shoulder. "I don't understand."

He wasn't really sure he did, either. "I think their love went beyond anything you or I can imagine. They gave up everything just to be together. But they only had one year in a lifetime of years. They wanted more. And through us, they can accomplish that."

"How?"

"I'm not sure, Ashlee. But I believe their spirits somehow took us over. We became them in the flesh. They wanted a life together, children, grandchildren, and through us, they could have it all."

"Are you saying we're the embodiment of deceased lovers?"

"Something like that."

She sent him a disbelieving look. "And just where are your facts, Mr. Westfield?"

"Isn't my summation enough?"

"No."

"Weren't the dreams enough to convince you?"

She hedged. "Perhaps, but, too, I could have heard the legend in my childhood and carried it with me. And the dream just kept it alive . . . or something like that. At least, it's a possibility."

He sighed. "Doubting woman." He reached over the side of the tub for his breeches, and withdrew an object from the pocket. "Is this fact enough for you?"

She took the gold locket. "Isn't this the one Santos showed you?"

"Yes. That's what I stopped at the Indian village to retrieve. Look inside."

Ashlee carefully opened the clasp and read the names engraved in gold on the bottom. "Amanda and Beau." Her gaze moved to the tiny paintings. The blood left her face. "It can't be."

"But it is," he whispered.

The miniatures were the exact likenesses of Connor and Ashlee.

Her hand trembled. "Oh, Connor. . . ."

He took the locket and dropped it on the floor. "Don't try to understand it. Just accept it, then put it out of your mind." He pulled her down on top of him, causing water to slosh over the edge of the tub. "Think only of us, and all the glorious years ahead."

He slid his hands over her firm little rear and nibbled her neck. "Years that Beau and Amanda never had. Years that won't have a single wasted moment . . . because I intend to spend each and every one of them loving you."

Judith McNaught
Jude Deveraux

Jill Barnett
Arnette Lamb

A Holiday Of Love

A collection of romances
available from

POCKET
BOOKS 1007-02